MW01128849

BEING
FOUND

AREND RICHARD

Cover Design: Mihai Costea
Interior Book Design: Abby Skolits

First Paperback Edition

For Ed.

BEING
FOUND

BOOK
ONE

CHAPTER 1

I'VE BEEN HEARING the thoughts of everyone around me since before I can remember. Before I even knew how to speak or understand the English language, I could understand what everyone within a thirty-foot radius was thinking. It might sound crazy, but thoughts don't require interpretation at all. Everyone, no matter what language they speak, country they are from, or religion they practice, all think in the same "language."

Our minds as people are made up of the sum of our experiences. Our lives are a compilation of moments that we remember, and moments that we try to forget. The moments, especially of our adolescent years, shape the person we become over time. To the average person, those moments are based on situations where someone said or did something to them. When you can hear the thoughts of everyone around you though, the most memorable moments in life seem to stem from the *thoughts* of others. And let me tell you, thoughts can have a much stronger effect on your life than the filtered words people choose to speak to you.

For instance, most people will have a memory of a time they made their fathers proud. Of course, I realize that not everyone has a father or a great relationship with the one they have, but the idea of "making a father proud" is something we can all understand. Whether it was the first time they caught the ball with him while playing catch, or maybe it was the moment he taught them how to drive. Their father probably had a smile on his face, gleaming from ear to ear. "That's my boy!" Or, "That's my girl!" he probably said. Well, I had that same moment. Except entirely different.

When I was fourteen years old and a freshman in high school, I joined the school musical. I never mentioned it to my dad, up until the night before the show. My father, a man who can only be described as a classic blue-collar, hard-working, covered in grease type of masculine man, was never quite fond of my desire to sing. He always wanted me to be more like my older male cousins. Wrestlers, football players...you name a sport, they excelled in it. But of course, I was nothing like my somehow genetically related cousin counterparts. Up until puberty hit, I was a short and chubby guy with a soft swerve in my step. After puberty, I sprouted like a tree, quickly reaching over six feet tall. The weight I had previously accumulated had stretched out on my new frame, and I was now a skinny and wispy version of my previous self, with that same signature swerve. Puberty had not changed my desire or ability to hit balls or tackle other boys for "fun." The majority of balls I had interacted with throughout my entire life were more thrown AT me than TO me.

My father didn't react at all when I told him about my upcoming role in the school musical. He had no thoughts about it, negative or positive, which is why I hadn't told him prior. After years of being his son, I knew that not giving him enough time to think about something was usually my best shot at getting a decent reaction. So I didn't have to "*hear*" anything about it.

The next night my dad showed up to the show. At the end of my big song as Seymour from the *Little Shop of Horrors*, I kissed the girl who played Audrey. The crowd went wild. The auditorium filled with sounds of cheers and whistles, as is customary to do when two people kiss on stage. When our lips separated, I remember seeing my father standing in the back row of the auditorium with a video camera, gleaming from ear to ear with an obnoxious smile. For a moment, I felt like he was proud of me. Not for singing in a show of course, but for kissing a girl. As I continued to focus on him I *"heard"* his thoughts: *"Oh Dear God. Please don't let my son be a faggot."* The sincerest prayer I had ever heard my dad make. And that's taking into account fourteen years of going to church every Sunday. I must admit that if I had never heard my father's thoughts, we probably would have had a much better relationship. He always acted like he cared and tried to be supportive, but his mental dialogue was full of disappointment in me as a son.

Needless to say, *"hearing"* things has made my life different in almost every way from any other person. When you *"hear"* things so often, it becomes another form of communication. A one-sided communication mind you because people can't *"hear"* me back, or each other for that matter. This is incredibly interesting when you're listening to two people say things to each other while thinking completely the opposite of what they are saying (which happens a *lot* more than you might think).

That's why I got away from everything and moved to the big city. I visited New York City once in high school for a class trip. Somehow it turned out to be the most peaceful place I had ever been to. Though my classmates complained of construction, rude New Yorkers, and clashing subway cars, all that extra noise seemed to drown out the thoughts of those I was surrounded by. There was this one girl in my 11th grade class named Anna who always thought so loudly about herself and constantly compared how much better she was than everyone else inside her mind. One day while our class was having lunch in downtown Manhattan, I realized I couldn't hear Anna's thoughts even though she was just at the end of the table from me. It was at that moment that I knew that I would one day live in New York City.

I can't say that I "*hear*" everyone, though. There have been three people throughout my life whose thoughts I couldn't hear. The first was my mother. Marsha Lynn Winthrop. The most beautiful woman in all of Erie, Colorado, a thought held by multiple men and women. Whether from a place of appreciation or envy, everyone thought my mother was beautiful. She was the first person to pull me out of the chaos of my mind and into a more "normal" reality.

Everything I did with my mother was real to me. I spent most of every day wondering if this "*experience*" I was having was real. Wondering if my life was real. At times it was so intense that I would start to think everyone was in on some secret about me. When I saw *The Truman Show* at seventeen years old, I had never related to something so much. I almost convinced myself for a while that I was living inside of a TV set, and even lashed out at those around me for pretending to not be able to hear my thoughts, like I could theirs. I quickly rescinded those claims when they began to think I was acting crazy enough to be put in a mental institution.

Spending time with my mother pulled me back into "reality." Her words were spoken from her to me. Her thoughts were all her own. Kept private and secure in her own mind. I felt safe and normal with my mother, as any kid should. On days when I struggled the most, she would take me aside to a place where it was only her and me. She would tell me to focus on my breath. She would say that I was given this "gift" for a reason. "Don't fight it," she would tell me. "Be grateful you've been given something no one else has." When she died on the day before my twelfth birthday, I was forced into going back to deal with the chaos that was my mind.

The next person to be radio silent to me was my college roommate, Daniel. I walked into that dorm room on the first day full of terror. I was happy to be getting out of my father's space, and I know he was happy too. Without my mother as a buffer of understanding between us, our relationship deteriorated rapidly. The fear of dealing with someone else's thoughts about me exclusively for the next year was daunting, to say the least. While I originally wanted to get my own apartment, the school I had chosen to go to had a one year minimum for living in on-campus housing, so I had no choice. Hopefully, we would get along, and there wouldn't be an issue, but I could almost guarantee that wouldn't be the case. Through my experience up to that point, I hadn't been the best friendship companion for a guy. Due to the aforementioned *"Please don't let my son be a faggot."* situation. When I entered my new temporary dwelling, Daniel was already inside unpacking his things onto his desk. He looked up at me immediately with a huge smile on his face.

"You must be Cameron?" he exclaimed. Daniel was a tall and gangly eighteen year old with an acne situation to match his awkward body. His red curly hair matching the hue of his complexion.

"Yes, and you must be Daniel?" We shook hands firmly and his sweaty palms were noticeable. After a few moments, I realized I hadn't heard a thought from Daniel's mind.

Something that never happened. Usually within the first five seconds of being around a person, let alone having a conversation with them, their thoughts were loud in my mind.

But the thoughts never came. Which at the time just made me even more confused. In my many theories about why I could "*hear*" people, I had always assumed my mother and I were somehow biologically connected in a way that I was immune to her thoughts. That theory had always sort of crumbled due to my father. But even still, I believed my mother and I had some bond that surpassed my ability to "*hear*" the rest of the world. Not "*hearing*" Daniel really threw me for a loop.

Though I only made it through one year of college, my relationship with Daniel became one of the strongest bonds I'd ever built. His brain somehow continued to be muted to mine. It allowed me to develop real bonds without all the awkward moments I had encountered with so many others before. Moments where I somehow just knew the right thing to say, or moments when I had a problem with a friend, but couldn't explain to them why I had that problem. Because they had been talking shit about me in their head, but not out loud, which I've come to learn is a pretty normal thing. People will always have issues with each other mentally. Even with their closest friends. It's discerning which of those thoughts mean anything versus the thoughts that come to the surface and are spoken that is important.

But the loop I was thrown from Daniel was so much smaller than the roller coaster I was thrown into with the third person. *Him.* The man on the subway. I felt him as soon as I walked onto the PATH train back home to Jersey City from Manhattan. The day had been long and insanely exhausting. Two jobs, sixteen hours on my feet, and all I wanted was to get back home and shut my brain off. But my brain, and my entire body, were working overtime on this train.

Thoughts differ from physical reality. I can "*hear*" thoughts, but I can "*feel*" physical intention. Most commonly I would "*feel*" people staring at me. Whether it was a girl with a crush, which gave me this light sweet giggly sensation from my tummy to my toes. Or it was someone looking at me with jealousy, (which happens quite a lot more than you'd suspect for the most ridiculous reasons) which felt like deep dark anger that would wash over me out of nowhere. From what I've gathered, this is a pretty normal sensation for most people to pick up on. Only for me, it's amplified x100. But the sensation the man on the subway was giving me was neither light and giggly nor evil and dark. From the moment I stepped on the train, I was overwhelmed with intensity. Someone was staring me down, that much was for sure. As I searched the faces of the train trying to find the source of the intensity that I was sure was being directed towards me, I also felt a tinge of focus. As though whoever was staring at me was trying to get me to notice them.

The doors to the train rolled shut. "This is the train to Journal Square." the female computerized voice said over the speakers. "The next stop is Grove Street." I continued to pan the train for the source of the intensity as the doors shut and the train jerked away towards the next stop.

It was the evening commute time and the train was packed. An elderly woman sat in front of me staring at me. I listened to her thoughts to see if she was the source of the intensity. Her thoughts were concerned with why I was looking around so frantically, making me realize I was acting in a way that was bringing attention to myself. I calmed down, closed my eyes, and took a few deep breaths. Finally, when I opened my eyes, they settled on the back of the train car. He stood there, next to the trains locked box of controls, standing with his arms crossed, left hand over right. Staring directly at me. Intensely.

Who is he? I wondered to myself.

There were easily thirty bodies between the intense man and me, so it was difficult to get a good look at him. The one thing that bore through the crowd of people were his eyes. Locked dead on me. A deep color that I hadn't seen in an eye before. They were…purple?

As we approached the stop before mine he finally moved. He took a few steps forward as the train came to a stop. Never wavering with the heavy braking of the train. His eyes never left my face, even if I would look away and back. If my life were a movie, at this moment I would be an Anna Farris-like character desperately trying to redirect attention away from myself while stumbling all around. He would be a calm strong Colin Farrell type (he looks nothing like Colin FYI) moving gracefully towards me. His eyes were still focused on me. His intention was stronger than his stare. I knew he was coming towards me. I knew he wanted to say something to me. And in some weird way…I felt he was THERE for me.

The train came to a stop. The voice of the train exclaimed "This stop is…Grove Street." The doors slid open noisily and people began to filter out. Amongst the commotion, I was absolutely sure that not a single person was aware of what was going on between myself and the purple-eyed man. No one even seemed to notice him. Which is crazy because the intensity was so apparent that it felt like you could barely walk forward without it blowing your hair back. Heck, I could barely remain standing, clinging to the train pole for dear life as a wave of intensity washed over me constantly.

In what seemed like only the blink of an eye, he cleared the twenty-foot gap between us. Smoothly walking past, brushing my shoulder with his. As he became parallel with me his head turned, and what happened next sent a spine curdling chill down my back. *"Hi, Cameron…"* he thought. His eyes locked dead into mine. An expression of dumbfoundedness on my face. Except what I heard wasn't a thought. Thoughts seem to roam freely in the air, like radio frequencies that I can pick up on when I'm near and focused enough. This was less of a radio frequency and more of an Instagram DM that bypassed the "Requests" folder and sent a notification directly to my brain that couldn't be ignored. The next message was even crazier.

"Pay attention."

By the time the shock had worn off from what had just happened, he was gone. Vanished. The doors had once again closed, and the train was moving. Every bit of intensity that had filled the air for the past ten minutes had left with him, and suddenly I felt as though I was in an alternate universe. No actually, I felt as though I had come back to this universe. Finally able to breathe again, the thoughts of the people around me once again flowing into my head. The almost gentle crashing of the wheels of the train against the tracks…I was back on Earth. And the place I just was…I had never been to before.

I looked around me and noticed a few passengers giving me eyes of concern. *"What's wrong with him?" "Is he about to throw up?" "Fuckin' druggies,"* were all thoughts being loudly expressed. I must have turned green. I felt like I was going to be sick. I took my phone out of my pocket and turned on the front-facing camera. I hadn't turned green at all. I was suddenly the palest white I had ever been.

I quickly took a deep breath and steadied myself, reaching for my bottle of water from my bag. I took a couple slow, smooth sips and refocused my mind as the train pulled out of the underground section of tunnels out into the warm open darkness of the June night. My hands shook slightly, and I hoped no one around noticed how many attempts it took to screw the lid back on tight.

What had just happened? I asked myself.

I had never felt a feeling like that before. The intensity was blinding and I was almost sure that it had to be coming from him. I couldn't remember a single thing that had happened in the last fifteen minutes aside from the interaction with the man on the train, and I was having a hard time bringing myself back to reality now. My memory of the event was nothing more than his face and his words or thoughts. Everything outside of him was a rush of black moving light that filled the train. As other thoughts continued rushing to my brain, I realized that during that entire twenty-minute train ride, I didn't hear a single person's thoughts. Was it the intensity blocking it out?

Let's go over the facts, I thought to myself. *A guy stares at me on the train. That stare projected energy I hadn't felt before. I call it energy because I don't know what else to call it. He was handsome…Was he handsome? Why does it matter if he was handsome? Okay, he definitely was handsome…So maybe that does matter. Was it lust? I've felt lust before. Was it mutual lust? Had I never experienced a real mutual attraction before and just not realized it? But wait! His thoughts! I couldn't hear anything from him! Never in my life has someone looked at me and not had a thought in their head. That's not how people work in my experience. Whether they even realize it or not their minds are always on. Always projecting. And he noticed me first...I felt the intensity before I even saw his face, so that rules out mutual lust...* The train came to a stop.

"This stop is Journal Square." said the voice over the intercom.

Or maybe it was MY body reacting to him? Stranger things have happened...

Doors opened.

But even if that's the case, that still doesn't give me a single clue as to what is going on!

I stepped off the train and made my way towards the escalators.

Then I suddenly stopped dead in my tracks as I hit the fifth stair on my way outside. One small detail threw a wrench into any idea I could put together.

He knew my name.

CHAPTER 2

THE ONLY SUNLIGHT that my tiny garden level apartment in Jersey City ever received just so happened to come steaming onto my face at 7am every day. A sensation which is about as pleasant as having a very large man sit directly on top of you while you're trying to sleep. Some people might be into that, but it's not my cup of tea.

As my mind pulled from the dream world back to "reality," I covered my face with my comforter and tried to get another quick fifteen minutes of sleep before throwing myself back out into the world. But the sun had different plans. It was summer now, and the heat was finally starting to take over again. The rays seared through the comforter heating my entire bed like an oven. I moved around irritated and fitfully, moaning my frustration out loud to no one. When I felt my whole body begin to sweat under the heavy covers I finally pushed myself to wake up. With one swift jerk upwards I was out of bed and irritated with the window. I gave it a dirty look like I did every morning before heading to start my morning pot of coffee.

The first thoughts to hit my mind as I poured a cup of coffee were of the man on the train. Already my mind was racing to search for new explanations and looking for things to *pay attention* to. I had barely been able to fall asleep last night as my mind raced with replays of the encounter. I couldn't have gotten more than three hours of sleep in total, and I knew that would weigh on me as the day went by. I decided to click on the TV to distract myself.

I flipped the channels until I came to the national news coverage. They were covering a story about Prince Amjad, the beloved Arabian Prince, and the AWSS or: "Antarctic Water Storage System," which had just become fully functional this morning. A massive undertaking, no doubt. With the threat of climate change looming over our planet, it was nice to see someone powerful doing something about it. *It sure helps that he's handsome too*, I thought to myself. I wasn't the only one either. He was rated "Most Eligible Bachelor on the Planet" by *GQ Magazine* last year, and several other media outlets had given him similar accolades in the past few years. You couldn't open a magazine or turn on a TV without hearing about him. Women and gay men everywhere wanted him, and straight men wanted to be him. Outside of his constant philanthropy, Amjad lived a life of regal abundance. His home was filled with exotic animals that he had rescued and cars that numbered in the hundreds. I didn't have social media on my phone because I had no desire to connect with anyone that I knew, but from time to time, I would check out his Instagram page to see his newest toys and projects. And of course, his gorgeous smile.

The AWSS system that he had pioneered was created to capture the freshwater that melted off the ice in Antarctica, with a second system being set up in Greenland as well. The water would be put through an advanced filtration system that would not only clean the freshwater but test it for new bacteria and disease that may be hidden within the ice. This was an important task as many scientists believed that prehistoric bacteria and disease were stored within the ice that could wipe out humanity. The plan was to then save the water and return it to Antarctica once we had climate change under control where it could be frozen again and balance could be restored to the poles. Or, if we were unable to turn the tide, the water would be used as a drinking water supply if humanity ever needed it. With more than half of the world's politicians still denying the ever-increasing devastation of climate change, it appeared that we would be needing it in the future. Skeptics of his system said that he was trying to harvest all the freshwater for his country in the Arabian Peninsula. Some extreme conspiracy theorists said he was trying to discover a new disease to kill off a large number of people for population control. In my personal opinion, Prince Amjad meant to do exactly what he said he would do.

"If we store the freshwater from the ice that is already rapidly melting, we will at the very least obtain enough water for our species to consume for thousands of years," he told an American reporter, his voice strong, his middle Eastern accent thick. I found it quite attractive. "Best case scenario, we will be able to replace the ice on our lowest continent when we've halted the effects of the Climate Emergency."

"How soon do you plan to have people drinking this stored water?" she asked.

"That decision is not in our plan at this time. For now, we only plan to save the water."

He's Jesus, I thought to myself. Though many people shared my opinion, even more thought quite the opposite of him. Some thought and also said, verbally and on social media, that Amjad was the antichrist. The first sign of the apocalypse. Due to my virtuous religious upbringing, I was too familiar with the concepts of the end of the world, the book of Revelation, and the antichrist. I could understand the argument seeing as Prince Amjad was so well loved by the majority of people, that he could be the great deceiver, Satan himself. Of course, he wasn't the first good Samaritan to make a difference in society, and I didn't think he would be the last. Just an honest good guy.

It wasn't just that he saved the largest storage of freshwater on the planet either. He had taken the United Arab Emirates to the moon, the first nation to do so since America in the 1960s. He launched thousands of satellites that formed a grid which provided fast internet to everyone on Earth for free. Connecting more people to the greatest source of knowledge than ever before, which uplifted new nations onto the world stage. He also co-founded the largest decentralized finance platform for cryptocurrency in the world. Taking a great amount of financial power away from the world's governments and giving it back to the people. And he was so handsome. Prince Amjad had single-handedly changed the world more than any human since…Jesus? *What I would do to hear the thoughts buzzing around in his head*, I thought to myself as I took my first sip of coffee. The reporter then sent the coverage back to the anchors at the desk. With that, I turned my TV off.

I looked around my apartment, taking stock of my life now at twenty years old. The space was far from being warm and cozy, or even nice for that matter. That being said, of all of the places I've ever lived, it was my favorite. When you have 400 square feet, you make do with the available placement for furniture. Aside from my bed, the remainder of my studio apartment was filled with the cabinets of my kitchen along one wall, the desk of my office which doubled as a dining table crammed into the corner next to the bathroom door, and a fridge placed randomly opposite from the kitchen and next to my bed. It was lacking in feng shui to say the least. It wasn't as if anyone was ever inside my apartment for it to make any difference how it looked though. For me, it was perfect.

The walls were decorated sparsely with the few things I had brought with me through every move I ever made. I have never much cared for physical possessions. At the time I might have enjoyed them, but as I move through life I tend to have no problem throwing something away. A beautiful tapestry of an elephant hung from the wall above my bed. It's bright violets and deep indigos danced together in a rainbow effect. A picture of my mother, father, and me hung just to the right side of my bed. And my 32-inch HDTV, which sat atop my dining room desk. I love TV and couldn't live without it. I can only hear what the actors are saying, not what they're thinking. So it's quite an escape from my usual view of the world.

The final item that hung on the wall above my bed every night was a necklace that my mother wore. A clear stone that I still had yet to identify sat inside a beautifully wrapped gold setting. The stone was in the shape of a teardrop. The gold wrapped around in a figure-eight style over top of it. She had worn it every day. The only time I ever saw her take it off was when she would caress my forehead with it when I was having a bad day of being deafened by the thoughts of everyone around me. When she died, my father kept the necklace for himself. I used to go into his room, almost every day, and touch the stone. Sometimes for hours at a time while my dad was at work and I was home alone. I never told my dad that I wanted the necklace.

He had loved my mother so much, and my mother loved

him. There wasn't a day that went by after she died that my father didn't think about her. His thoughts about her broke my heart every time I would hear them. I think it's one of the things that drove a wedge between us as I grew older. Because even with our differences of opinion, it was impossible for me to listen to his sadness every single day. But on the night I left home forever, I couldn't stop thinking about the necklace. If I hadn't taken it, my heart would be full of regret daily. I had never worn it, just kept it near. For some strange reason, I felt a desire to put it on and wear it today. So I did. As I put the necklace on, I wondered if I was *paying attention* to some gut feeling more than usual. The memory of the man on the train flashed in my mind which sent a chill of anxiety down my spine. I thought about putting the necklace back, just to be stubborn to whatever mental war was going on inside my head. But I kept it on.

After taking a quick shower and getting dressed, I grabbed my portable coffee mug out of the cabinet and filled it to the top. Today would be a long day. *Every day is a long day*, I thought. First, an eight-hour shift at the bistro, followed by an eight-hour shift of running the evening coat check at the Modern Art Museum. All while being on high alert and *paying attention* to everything around me. Whether I wanted to or not.

* * *

On my way out the door, I made sure there was still some cat food on the steps that lead up from my semi-underground home. Jersey City was filled with strays of every shape and size. I don't mind cats, even though I'm severely allergic to them, but moving here made me have a small distaste for them. Luckily, I had discovered that putting out food for them stops the *"I'm so hungry please feed me!"* thoughts that were occurring outside my unit on a nightly basis. The meowing was pretty terrible too. Oh yeah, I can *hear* animals too. Sort of. I can relate through broken pictures and some very very small words. As I said, thoughts are a language that requires no interpretation, however, it can be harder to understand someone who doesn't use any language at all.

I headed down the mile-long hill that separated my neighborhood which was called "The Heights" (not to be confused with "The Heights" where Lin Manuel Miranda set his musical) with the downtown area of Jersey City. On my way, I passed an area full of shops that had stood as long as this city, but had changed names and owners countless times. Mom-and-pop shops usually run by Indian immigrant families. The Indian culture was strong in my neighborhood and it was quite a lovely experience for me. The thoughts of Indian families were generally quite wholesome and usually related to family. However, that wasn't always the case.

Once, an old Indian woman ran off of her stoop to spit and screech at me. I couldn't understand a word she was saying, but she kept thinking repeatedly, *"You don't belong here. You don't belong here. You don't belong here."* I almost wished I hadn't been able to *hear* her at all. Being able to chalk it up to some crazy old lady yelling crazy old lady things at me would have been much easier than dealing with the fact that your presence somewhere is so NOT WANTED by everyone there. It didn't matter where I went, I would never find a place that I could fit in. So far, this little neighborhood of Jersey City had been the most like home for me in my adult life.

It never mattered the person or their thoughts. I would always do my best to smile at every person I made eye contact with. I had found that smiling at someone is the best shot at getting a positive thought response back. Especially in Jersey. People really didn't want to interact with each other at all, but they especially didn't want you to disrespect them or give them a look that could be deemed as dirty. I learned that lesson very quickly. People who would never dare to say it out loud would think constantly *"What the fuck are you looking at?"* a lot more than you'd think. One of those people was the man I picked up my daily breakfast sandwich from.

I never knew his real name, and I don't think he bothered to tell me. But I always thought of him as a Ron. Because everything about him reminded me of my dad's brother, my uncle Ron, aside from his entirely different cultural background. I swear you could switch my uncle Ron's skin color and they'd be the same person. *Ron* was not flashy; everything about him was simple and clean save one giant Gotti gold ring that he proudly displayed on the pinky finger of his right hand. I smiled at Ron every day, and Ron smiled back. Though he smiled, there was always a tinge of *"Fuck you,"* or *"You don't belong here."* Which I'm sure as you have gathered is not all that fun to deal with, but his bacon egg and cheese sandwich was the bomb, and it only cost $2. Starbucks could never.

After giving Ron his money and throwing one last smile his way, I turned and headed for the door. Stepping out into the fresh morning light was fantastic. I was glad to be living somewhere that I was forced to walk outside once and awhile. Or every day. Children ran across busy streets to get to school. It always baffled me that any kids lived here. This city seemed rougher than anything I had ever seen before. But these kids also brought a certain innocence to it, and maybe they were the last thing standing between this comfortable balance of light and fun while still being busy but not entirely unsafe.

As I approached the final walk sign between myself and the train station, I was overwhelmed with a stressful feeling. I suddenly felt like my left leg was completely asleep and immobile. I had gotten used to the *feeling* of someone else's issue being projected onto me, and I knew that I wasn't the one having the problem. I looked around. Very few people were even near me. One man was running a jackhammer into the sidewalk down the street, singing loudly in his head to a classic Selena song. An old lady stood across from me waiting to cross to where I was, but she didn't seem distressed, and her thoughts were extremely racist about the black man walking up behind her on the crosswalk. His thoughts were entirely focused on his anxiety around a job interview he just finished. He really hoped we would get the job. To my left there was a woman, sitting out front of a coffee shop with her baby in a stroller. She thought about her high school friend who was leading a much more promiscuous life than her. She wasn't jealous, she told herself. Since I hadn't sensed any words being yelled in distress, I assumed the baby must be the source. Babies are full of thoughts, but they are also without language. The baby must have been sitting very uncomfortably in the car seat and was beginning to feel a little panicked.

The mother sat calmly sipping her coffee looking at her cell phone as her baby cried softly. I walked over slowly and as I did I saw that the baby was under two heavy blankets. Which seemed a little extreme for the temperature. At this point, I was sure that the stress signal was coming from the baby. As I stood next to her, I could sense it. Her mind seemed to lock onto mine. She needed my help, and mom wasn't paying attention.

What to do in a situation like this? I wondered. I knew that telling the mother her baby was uncomfortable would make me seem crazy. And reaching into the stroller to grab her baby would seem even worse. I thought again about just telling her, but I knew she wasn't the type of woman who would listen.

"Excuse me," I said to the mother. "I'm an aspiring photographer, and I was wondering if I could take a picture of you and your baby? I really love taking pictures of people in this area of the city. I can send you the digital copy right away."

She turned to me with a face of excitement. Clearly the type of person to want to have her picture taken at every opportunity. "Of course!" she yelped. She reached into the stroller and pulled the baby out. The pain in my leg subsided as she raised the baby onto her lap.

I took a camera out of my bag, snapped a picture, and asked the woman for her email address. I told her I would send the picture over as soon as I had it edited and thanked her for the opportunity. She thanked me as well. My plan worked perfectly. The baby had stopped crying, and I felt an extreme sense of calm wash me over. The baby felt comfortable again.

I looked down at my phone to check the time. I was going to be late for work. As I hustled through the side entrance of the Journal Square PATH station, I felt a strong sense of frustration. I couldn't tell where it was coming from, but it was more than just one person. It felt as if I was suddenly extremely frustrated, which is a drastic change from the feeling of concern I had just had from the interaction with the baby. This change meant it wasn't coming from me directly. This had happened before, and it meant the same thing almost every time. I pushed open the glass doors after flying off the escalator. Jogging towards the next set of escalators, I slowed slightly so the cop standing by the MetroCard machine wouldn't yell at me. I fumbled with my pockets to get the cash I needed to throw $20 more on my card. *Why didn't I ever take it out before I got to the damn thing?* I asked myself. I thought I might be okay; I hadn't heard any door opening or closing sounds yet from the train below. I was cutting it close, but the train shouldn't leave for another minute or so. I pressed the screen buttons faster than the machine could keep up with me. Just as the machine spit my card back out, a voice came over the intercom.

"Attention passengers, all trains from Journal Square to Manhattan are on a delayed schedule due to track issues." She then repeated herself, just as muffled as the first time.

I walked around the corner and saw the source of my earlier frustrated feeling. Hordes of people standing on the platform, waiting to go to work. It must have been a while because there were far more than just one train cycle worth of people there. Some of them broke away rushing upstairs to get an Uber or a Lyft. Others just looked back at their phones, not caring. This was the main reason it was so difficult to get work in Manhattan when you live in Jersey City. Because employers know that the reliability of this train doesn't exactly score an A+.

I was now in a predicament. Without the train, my commute time to work was over an hour, and it would cost more than I'd make in a day to get across the river using the alternative options. I dragged my unwilling body back above ground to call my boss and give him the news.

CHAPTER 3

I ASCENDED THE filth-ridden stairs of the PATH station slowly to call my boss and let him know the news of my late arrival. My first job every day was waiting tables at a fancy French bistro in Midtown Manhattan. The call to my boss went extremely well. Because I was always such a diligent employee who was willing to come in and wait tables whenever someone else called in, my boss told me to take the day off. "You deserve it," he said.

Interestingly enough, as soon as I got off the phone with him I received an email from the manager of the Modern Art Museum where I worked coat check. A sudden booking for a private event had come in this morning and the coat check staff wouldn't be needed. Quite an odd set of circumstances for me to get a day off from both jobs. I couldn't remember the last time that had actually happened, or if it ever did. On any other day, this might have been great news. But today, it sent a chill down my spine. *Is this something I should be paying attention to?* I wondered.

"*Pay attention.*" Those two words were all that I could focus on, and I was, in fact, paying attention. Every street sign looked brand new, every person who passed me had a motive for something. But *why* was I paying such close attention? Because some man that I had never seen before had "thought" a comment to me? Sure, I couldn't *hear* any of his thoughts prior to that comment…which is an event rarer than a solar eclipse. And yes, he may have been incredibly handsome. Wait, was he handsome? Why do I keep saying that? Why would I think that?

I had come up with two possible explanations as to what in the hell was going on.

Option 1:
None of it happened, and I just imagined it all. Maybe I dreamt it. Sure I had no memory aside from that of getting home last night, and the memories of entering the train and after leaving were all intact. But maybe I had fallen asleep on the train while standing up and had myself a bad nightmare.

Option 2:
There is no denying that I have a "gift" that not everyone else has. If you believe (as I do around 76% of the time) that there is more going on in this world than meets the eye, then my ability to *hear* things has to come from some higher power or something. Right? So, it's entirely possible that other people have the same (or similar) ability I do. Perhaps this guy *did* actually know who I was, or something about me, and his message to "pay attention" may have been a warning.

Either way, the man on the subway had gotten to me. And now I had a whole day to think about it. *Awesome*, I thought to myself sarcastically.

My eyes focused straight down JFK Blvd as my severely uncomfortable dress shoes hit the pavement with determination. When I finally crossed the upper section of the 1 and 9 Highway, the sidewalks were free of any other human traffic. The occasional car passed by, to which I slowly turned my head to make sure they weren't trying to ram me off the road. Something I had certainly done before, but not with the severity of attention I was giving it today. I was only two blocks away from home now. I was almost in the safe zone.

That brought another question: if nothing happened, how long would I be constantly on alert? That was an answer I didn't have, along with the rest of the answers.

Turning onto Hopkins Avenue, the street where I lived, the sun shined on the stoop leading down to my apartment. Something there glistened in the light and caught my attention. As I came closer I realized that it was a small, shiny piece of paper. A ticket of some sort that bounced its reflection of light into my eyes as it moved with the breeze. I picked it up off the top step and studied it closely.

It was a free pass for the ferry from Jersey City to Manhattan. As I looked at the back, I noticed it expired tomorrow. *Well that's coincidental*, I told myself. It had been quite a long time since I went into Manhattan for anything other than work. I told myself I deserved to enjoy my day off in the city, suppressing the idea that I was somehow *"paying attention"* to this random ticket showing up on my doorstep the day before it expired. I headed into my apartment, changed into a more comfortable outfit of jean shorts, sneakers, and a blue t-shirt. A last-minute thought crossed my mind to make sure I still had my mother's necklace on, which I did.

You really are paying attention to everything, I thought to myself with frustration. And with that, I headed out the door to catch the ferry into the city.

* * *

The ferry ride was beautiful. I had somehow lucked out on getting the entire top deck to myself. A slow day for ferry

travel perhaps? The wind drowned out the sounds of anyone's thoughts on the decks below. Leaving me to a peaceful
trip across the Hudson River. Manhattan looked gorgeous
as we approached, the One World Trade building directly in
front of me glimmering in the sunlight. I had always wanted
to see the view from the top, but could never find the time or
the money to do so. While I was lacking in money right now,
especially after having an unplanned day off from both jobs,
I figured I'd still make a go of it. It was my day in the city and
the One World Trade Center called me to it.

As the view of the city became cropped smaller with our
approach, the enhancement of the tighter view magnified.
The city was so inspiring to me. It reminded me of what I
envisioned for my life here when I first took that Greyhound
bus from Denver. Yes, I moved here for the "peace and quiet" of my mind, but there was something else that pulled
me here. I actually moved here to sing. I had big dreams of
starring in a musical on Broadway since I was a teenager.
Though those dreams hadn't seen much success in the nearly
two years I'd lived here.

The reason I had gotten the lead in my high school's
musical was purely based on my singing ability. I definitely
couldn't act. If I had been able to, maybe my dad wouldn't
have thought I was gay immediately after kissing a girl. Looking back at the old video of me in that show, it's so apparent
to me that I have no idea what I'm doing when it comes to
reciting my lines. But you better believe that the moment my
big solo comes, I steal the show.

I got my voice from my mother. When I was growing
up she would always be the lead soloist in the church choir.
I adored listening to my mother sing. Her voice wasn't just
a standard voice either. If she wanted to, my mother could

have left everything and toured as a singer or starred in a number of shows on Broadway. Everyone told her that she could, even people in the church. Mom would always be so grateful for the compliment, but she'd say, "My life is here with these two boys," gesturing towards my father and me. I always admired her for that. Because even though I couldn't hear my mother's thoughts, I could tell that she longed for that life.

I will never forget when my mother starred in the local production of *Chicago*. She played Roxy, the lead in the show. It was one of the only times I heard my mother sing outside of the church. My dad and I were both wowed by her performance, and those memories of her are some of my fondest. She inspired me quite a bit in my future endeavors and dreams.

I leaped from the ferry onto the dock with ease behind the rest of the passengers. On my way out, I asked the ferry attendant if my ticket was good for a return trip. Unfortunately not, he informed me.

"You only get to go one way," he said in a Jamaican accent.

The ferry dropped me off in Midtown Manhattan. Just north of the One World Trade Center. I decided to follow the river as far down as I could before heading directly into the city. The parks and paths that lined the Hudson River on the Manhattan side were filled with people rollerblading, running, and enjoying hand in hand walks. Something about today caused people's thoughts to be oddly pleasant. Odd only because a walk through Manhattan would normally reveal thoughts filled with curse words and sexually deviant thoughts. On the outskirts of the city today though, everyone was grateful to be enjoying the sun outside.

"It's such a beautiful day," thought a somber elderly woman as she walked by. I wished my thoughts to be as sweet as hers one day.

"I want ice cream!" thought a little girl with her dad before expressing the sentiment out loud.

"I'm going to have the best tan in all of Hell's Kitchen," thought a gay man in a speedo laying out in the grass.

Cutting into the city from the banks of the Hudson River, I veered to the right upon my final approach to the building. I wanted to check out the 9/11 memorials. It was one of the first destinations I went to see after moving here, and likely every tourist who visited the city made a point to go. I hadn't been since that last time, and I wanted to pay my respects.

The massive memorials carried such huge energy around them. Feelings of sadness and honor overwhelmed me as I looked over the edge into the cascading waterfalls that slid down the black granite. These feelings could be felt by everyone who came here, that I was sure of. Each memorial was carved out in the shape of the original World Trade Center Buildings. Both were quite deep holes in the ground that had a shallow pool of water in the base. The pool recycled the water back up to the edges of each pit and released water back down the sides infinitely. The edges of the memorials were lined with the names of the victims who were lost on that terrible day in history. I traced a few of the names carved along the edges with my finger. Visions of the day started to flood into my mind. I was only one when the two towers went down, so I had no memory of the incident directly. I had seen old news footage from that day. But the visions that filled my mind now seemed to be from the people that were there that day. This happened the last time I stood here too. I found myself getting lost in the mental imagery when suddenly—

"Sir!" a man with baggy trousers and suspenders said to me loudly. The visions stopped. I was here in the present moment again. He had…interrupted them? "Would you like to see a free show this afternoon?" The man in front of me had to be in his late sixties. He reminded me of Popeye the Sailor Man in real life, with a little extra hair. Bulky strong arms on a lean body that was quite short.

"Um, I'm not sure," I said. Guys like this were everywhere in New York. Always trying to get you to go see their one-man show or rap concert.

"Do you like *Chicago*?" he asked. The way he said it sent an equal amount of chills down my spine as it did excitement to my brain.

"What?!" I said grabbing the pamphlet from him. "No one's doing Chicago right now!" I examined the pamphlet. I knew every show that was currently happening in this city. I had auditioned for most of them.

"They're doing it at the Ambassador. It's a dress rehearsal for the new traveling tour. This afternoon ONLY."

The pamphlet agreed with what he said. *Pay attention*, I thought. Or my subconscious thought. Or someone thought to me, "The tickets are free?" I asked with confusion.

"Totally free. You just gotta rent one of these bike's for 30 minu—"

"Oh okay. I see." I cut him off. Suddenly feeling stupid for my earlier enthusiasm. There was always a catch.

"No, you didn't listen," he said stepping back in front of me. "You have to rent one of these bikes for 30 minutes and leave us a review on Zucker." Zucker was the app for NYC tourists to find the hottest things to do. It must have been a trade with the theater to help the bike rental company get sales.

"All right, I'll do it," I said. "But do I have to ride the bike? Can I just leave a five-star review and take the ticket."

The man looked at me a little sideways. It was then that I realized I wasn't hearing his thoughts. Gears were definitely working inside that skull of his, but there was no radio frequency for me to pick up on. I started to panic.

"Sure!" he yelled exuberantly. Snapping me back into reality again. "Here's your ticket."

I took the ticket in my hand. Sure enough. Today's date. 4:30 PM at the Ambassador. I looked at my watch. It was already 3 PM. The day had gone zooming by, which I thought would be quite the opposite as I expected it to drag on. I shook my head and looked back up. "Thank y—" He was gone. I looked around to get my bearings. Thinking maybe he had gone back to the bicycle rental shop. I approached it swiftly looking around for him. There was no sign.

A young woman inside the small rental shack was all that could be seen. "Excuse me!" I yelled gently to get her attention.

"*What NOW?*" she thought loudly. "Yes?" she said with sass.

"I was wondering where the guy handing out the tickets went?"

"A cop?" she asked.

"No…the tickets to *Chicago*?" I clarified.

"I don't know what you're talking about," she said matter-of-factly.

Another spine shiver. *What the fuck is going on*, I asked myself.

"Go away...Freak," the girl thought. I smiled and kept moving towards the street. The show started soon.

I guess the One World Trade Center will have to wait for another day, I thought to myself. I headed underground to take the subway up to the Ambassador theater. As I descended down the staircase to the subway station that was just starting to get that lovely urine smell that seemed to encapsulate New York during the summer, I wondered if I should download the Zucker app and give the bicycle rental shop a review. I pulled out my phone and saw that there was no service.

The 1 train pulled into the station as I walked down the final set of stairs at the perfect time. I loaded into the subway car with a mild rush of people all around me and stood holding onto the pole as the doors closed. The thoughts from everyone in my immediate vicinity started to rush into my mind. This was the exact reason I moved here. To the average person who can't read minds, this train car would be relatively quiet, save the music coming loudly from the headphones draped around a rider's neck. To my mind, the subway was like being in a crowded bar where everyone is talking. That might not sound very appealing to be constantly surrounded with, but constant noise is better than a distinct conversation that you can't help but listen to. I could look at one person and focus on them to pull out their thoughts from the cloud of chatter if I chose to, otherwise, the noise would all melt together into a background noise that was tolerable.

As I became aware of the thoughts all around me, I realized that the abrupt disappearance of the man who had given me the ticket had distracted me from the fact that I hadn't been hearing his thoughts. It seemed now that everything was back to normal as I was bombarded with the inner dialogue of everyone on the train, but I had definitely not been able to hear anything the old man was thinking. With this realization, the earlier 76% of me that believed my gift was from some higher power became quickly bumped up to 80%. Something weird was definitely going on, and whether I liked it or not, I needed to *pay attention*.

⁎ ⁎ ⁎

Up until the moment I rounded the corner of W 49th street from Broadway, I didn't believe that the Ambassador Theater was showing a dress rehearsal of *Chicago*. On the long subway ride uptown, I had gone from believing in some higher power orchestrating my day, to feeling like there was some big joke everyone was playing on me. I hadn't truly felt this way since I was a teenager, and it wasn't fun. This would be the last and final leg of the joke journey that everyone must have been in on about me. I thought today would finally be the day it was all revealed to me. But as the Ambassador came into view, a small sign out front stated "Dress Rehearsal Showing of Chicago" and "One Afternoon Only" below. Somehow, The Ambassador Theater was really showing *Chicago* for one afternoon only, and somehow, I had a ticket.

I walked through the doors of the theater into a small group of people. Not the usual overcrowding the lobby of a major theater producing a major show would usually have. Only about thirty people muddled around the room, conversing amongst themselves. The amount of people made sense for a dress rehearsal showing. This would be the casts last opportunity to perfect their show before heading out on tour. They needed an audience, but not a packed crowd.

"May I have your ticket please?" the female usher asked. She smiled at me when my eyes came up to meet hers.

"Oh, yeah." I rummaged through my pockets, trying to remember which one I had put it in. Finally retrieving it from my back right pocket of my shorts. "Here it is."

She ripped the stub, handed it back, and said, "Your seat will be through the center doors, four aisles down. Enjoy the show."

I moved forward further into the lobby. I hadn't eaten a single thing yet today and was feeling pretty hungry. I looked for the concession area to grab a snack before heading to my seat. I made my way up the center staircase which was adorned with a bright red carpet. The concession area came into view on the far left side of the theater lobby. As I approached, I saw a woman standing in line that looked strikingly familiar. *Kaylee?* I asked myself. It couldn't be. The woman at the concession stand looked exactly like my best friend from high school. The only person I had ever told my secret to outside of my family. I tried to make my way closer and—

"Excuse ME!" said an overdressed woman I had accidentally just bumped into while walking forward and not paying attention to where I was going. She was wearing a full-length red gown, as if attending an opera of the olden days. It didn't make any sense at this matinee show. Her outfit would have made me feel underdressed if anyone else had been dressed like her. Which they weren't.

"I'm so sorry!" I said, urgently trying to look past her to the concession stand. The woman with blonde hair who had grabbed my attention was now at the counter, conversing with the concession attendant. I could only see the side of her face and the olive green sweater she was wearing.

"Sorry isn't GOOD enough!" the woman thought. I looked away from the girl who I thought was Kaylee and

back to the woman's face. "YOU ARE STILL STANDING ON MY DRESS!" Suddenly everyone was looking at us. I looked down at my feet. The very tip of my left shoe was just barely touching her dress. I jumped away quickly. Embarrassed.

"Really I am so sorry. It was a total accident." I backed away slowly from her. She puffed and pouted. Upon closer inspection the woman was gorgeous. She looked like a blonde Salma Hayek. Despite her beauty, I couldn't believe she was behaving like this in public. But then again, I'd seen worse in New York before.

Everyone else's thoughts turned towards the situation at hand as well. Some rather concerned thoughts for the woman in distress, but even more thoughts of embarrassment for her and compassion for the situation she was putting *me* in. But I didn't care. Once I was a few feet safely away from damaging anyone else's garments, I focused my attention back onto the concession area. The woman who resembled Kaylee was gone.

The lights of the lobby flashed a few times, indicating the show was about to begin. *Ten minutes early?* I thought about checking my watch to confirm.

"Pay attention," Creeped into my mind. At this point, it was starting to feel like a default. I couldn't tell if the thought was coming from somewhere else entirely, or if my brain had automatically defaulted to having it come up whenever possible. Either way, it was really annoying.

There's no way that was Kaylee, I thought to myself. But for some reason, I couldn't shake the inexplicable feeling that the woman who I had just seen was my childhood best friend who had also become a missing person four years ago.

* * *

I couldn't enjoy the show at all. Not even when Roxy and Velma sang my favorite song: "My Own Best Friend." Though the cast was doing a great job with minimal mistakes, I spent the first half of the show looking around like an idiot trying to find the girl who looked like Kaylee. The second half of the show I sat with my eyes closed, listening to everyone's thoughts to see if I could recognize any of them. Which you might think would be hard, but typically people who are engaged in watching something are pretty thoughtless. Unless it's relating to what they are watching. Still, I couldn't hear anything that reminded me of Kaylee.

As the show neared its end, with about ten minutes remaining, I had a strange desire to get up and leave. *Ten minutes early*, I kept thinking to myself. It was rare that a show would start on time, let alone early, and I felt as though it was a sign. I was really getting tired of the whole *pay attention* scenario now. But something told me if I didn't go now, I would miss my chance to see the girl who looked like Kaylee again. That was a risk I wasn't willing to take. I got up from my seat and made my way quietly towards the exit, only opening the theater doors as far as I needed to avoid letting light in and disturbing anyone.

At first, I stood next to the doors where I had come in. I told the usher who had taken my ticket originally that I just needed some fresh air. Which didn't make any sense to her. *"You're still inside though,"* she thought to herself. She saved her judgment for me in her mind only, which I appreciated.

But then I figured that Kaylee could come out of any of the doors. She clearly wasn't sitting near me. *If that even was Kaylee*, I told myself, *which it probably wasn't*. I knew I didn't have a good enough vantage point to see every person who would leave the venue. And I didn't want to miss being sure about what I thought I had seen.

Should I go outside? I wondered. *Would she still be able to get by me?* I started to panic a bit. It seemed as though my day of paying attention had led on an interesting journey that was now culminating in being reunited with my best friend who I thought had been dead for years. The pressure of it all was too intense, and I didn't want to miss my opportunity to see her. *I might be paying too much attention*, I told myself as I tried to calm my anxiety.

The theater had three exits out of the front. From a certain vantage point across the street, I was able to see all three doors. The night sky was falling quickly. Bright lights of the theaters and billboards now outshone the daylight below the buildings in the city streets. I leaned against the brick of the building facing the theater getting ready for the show to let out in the next few minutes. Then the door furthest to the left on the building cracked open. I jumped back up. *It IS her?*

The woman who exited the theater was either Kaylee or her identical long lost twin sister. Sure I hadn't seen her in nearly five years but I knew her face. I knew her. It was her. I was nearly sure of it. I was a bit taken aback, and Kaylee was able to gain a bit of distance from me down 49th street by the time I composed myself. I followed from across the street. My mind buzzed with ways to greet her. I thought of just shouting her name across the street! But something felt wrong about that.

"*Pay attention.*" The thought crept in again. *SHUT UP!* I screamed to myself mentally.

By the time I had Kaylee in my view again, she was a healthy distance in front of me but still manageable to follow. After a few blocks though, I realized there was another man that seemed to be following her in front of me. At first I thought it was purely coincidental; there were people out walking the streets all around us. But it was the way he intentionally strode towards her rapidly that made me concerned. Half of me fought to call out her name and get her attention there in the street. The other half of me demanded to stay cool and *pay attention.*

After following for about ten minutes, the man had reached Kaylee, and he must have said something to get her attention. The way Kaylee first looked at him seemed to be a look of concern, however, she immediately continued walking. I couldn't hear either of their thoughts. I think because they were too far away. The man then joined her stride. A few times they looked back and forth at each other while conversing, indicating they must have known each other. The man was quite a bit taller than her, just over six foot. He dressed in all black clothing, including a coat that was horribly out of place for the summer.

Kaylee and the mystery man entered Central Park through the southernmost entrance. I followed quickly, trying to tighten the gap between us. Their pace became more casual throughout the park which allowed me to get right up behind them. They were having a conversation about something I couldn't quite make out. Oddly enough, at this distance I definitely should have been able to hear their thoughts, but I still couldn't. I decided to pass in front of them in the hopes that Kaylee would catch a glimpse of me and say something. I approached Kaylee's right side and turned sideways a little, pretending to look at the view of the park. Kaylee didn't seem to notice me, or if she did, she didn't say anything. I didn't want to seem any weirder than I already had so I pressed on in front of them until I came over a small hill. Pulling off to the side to "catch my breath," I waited for them to catch up with me.

After more than enough time passed that they should have caught up with me, they didn't appear. *They should be here by now*, I thought to myself. As soon as that thought crossed my mind, I heard a woman scream behind me. I ran back to the top of the hill where they should have been, and there was no sight of either of them.

CHAPTER 4

THE ONLY PERSON I ever told about my secret "gift" besides my mom was my best friend in high school, Kaylee. Some said that we could have been twins, and we loved to tell people that we were. Our birthdays were only two days apart and we truly looked a lot alike. It was easy for me to be best friends with Kaylee because she was a *real* good person. Not like those people out there who say that they're good people, but an actual good person. I can recall the number of times I "*heard*" Kaylee have negative thoughts in her head on one hand. Three of those times were solely towards her boyfriend that she had Sophomore year who had cheated on her frequently. Even though she wanted to boil his skull a few times, and yes, that's literally what she thought, she was still an incredible person with the most optimistic outlook on the world.

When I first told Kaylee about my "gift," she believed me completely. I thought she would test me, but she never did. Eventually, I would share things I was *hearing* with her from other people. Like the time our school's head cheerleader, Anna, walked by us in the hall and was thinking about how jealous she was of Kaylee's hair. When I told Kaylee, she smiled, and she ended up making it a point to show Anna some new tricks for getting more volume in her hair later that day.

That was Kaylee for you. If I was someone so overexposed to the truth of the world, jaded and corrupt, Kaylee was the exact opposite. Not sheltered from the truth of the world though. Just willing to do her part to make a difference.

A week before my sixteenth birthday, and nine days before hers, Kaylee went missing. It was the talk of the entire town of Erie. Our normally safe and quiet town where everyone knew each other by name, or at least what family you were from, was suddenly not as safe as everyone assumed. A beautiful girl who everyone knew and loved had gone missing. It was a Wednesday when her father filed a missing person report. She hadn't been seen since the Monday before at school.

I remember that Monday clearly. Because Kaylee had made a big to-do with me about running for Homecoming Princess. Not that she wanted to win, but that she had somehow received the most nominations in our small student body. The junior class had spoken, and they wanted Kaylee to represent them as royalty for our school dance.

"I just don't get it," she said to me as we ate our slices of pizza from the school cafeteria. "Why wouldn't they nominate Anna? She's the one who wants it." Her thoughts matched her words exactly. Kaylee did not identify as a Princess by any means. Homecoming or not.

It didn't surprise me at all that she had been nominated though. If Kaylee had ever competed in a beauty pageant, which she wouldn't, she would most assuredly win Miss Congeniality. "I think everyone voted for you because they actually like you, and they don't like her," I said.

"Well, I don't want it," she said as she handed me the crust of her slice. I loved the crust, and she always gave hers to me.

"You know I'd love to be Homecoming Princess," I joked. Kaylee was the only person I was out of the closet to in high school.

"You don't want to be Princess," she laughed. "You just want to dance with Justin."

She was right. Justin was the typical jock type guy in our school. A shoo-in for Homecoming Prince. "Can you imagine?" I asked dreamily, scarfing down the crust of her pizza.

"Maybe someday," she said knowingly.

"Can I borrow some of that?" I asked.

"Borrow what?"

"Some of that hope you have in the future." I wiped my mouth of pizza grease. "Or should I say, willful ignorance."

"Do I think there is a world where a sweet guy like yourself will be able to dance with a handsome guy?" she asked. "Sure. Do I think that it's going to happen to you when you're too afraid to even come out of the closet? No."

"I'll come out of the closet if it means a hot date with Justin for the rest of the school to see," I joked.

"I hate to tell you, friend, but there's no hope of that happening," she said, holding my shoulder. "The Justin and you thing. Not the 'you coming out' part. That can still happen!"

That was Kaylee. Always an advocate for me to live my truth. We both knew that I wouldn't come out in high school. It would make me the only openly gay person in the whole school. I was too scared for that, and we both knew it.

"I do still think it's okay for you to wait until you've gone to college though," she said reassuringly.

"Glad to know I have your approval," I joked.

"Whatever. Either way, I know I'm not going to be Homecoming Princess, so dreading it now really doesn't matter."

"I feel like the only way you can accomplish that at this point, is to boycott the dance."

"Bingo," she said as she stood up from the round cafeteria table.

And that was the last conversation I ever had with my best friend whom I had known since pre-school. I didn't think much of her saying she would boycott the dance, because I knew that I ultimately would boycott it with her. I imagined we'd probably go steal some beer or wine from one of our parents and have ourselves a great night of underage drinking at the lake, you know? Like you do. But then Kaylee didn't show up at school the next day. Or the day after.

I wasn't immensely concerned. I figured Kaylee had gotten sick. Until that Wednesday afternoon when two police officers showed up at my door. Before they asked my father to speak with me, I could already hear jumbled thoughts about someone who was missing. I also heard Kaylee's name mentioned.

"Cameron?" the chubby officer with a classic handlebar mustache asked me as I came around the corner. My dad stood between them and me. His mind filled with thoughts of concern that I had done something wrong.

"Yes," I said. My head hung low.

"Do you know Kaylee Crankowski?" he asked.

"Yes," I said again. My fear of authority showing in my one-word answers.

"Don't worry, you're not in trouble," the other officer said. He was shorter but better built than Officer Mustache.

"We just want to ask you some questions. When was the last time you saw her?"

"Yesterday," I said. "No wait, Monday. She wasn't at school yesterday." An honest slip-up.

"Do you mind if we come in for a minute?" Mustache asked my father.

"Not at all officer." My dad moved to the side to let them in.

I told the officers everything I knew. They told me Kaylee had been missing since Monday. She never came home from school. Or at least her dad never saw her come home from school. I told them about the conversation surrounding homecoming. And of Kaylee's lack of desire to participate.

"Would Kaylee have run away because she was embarrassed about being nominated?" the more handsome cop asked. Detective Williams was his name. Even he knew this reasoning lacked motive.

"No," I said. "We weren't going to go to the dance anyway."

"Why not?" Mustache Officer Hanley asked.

"We just never do…" I said shyly.

Weeks after the police had interviewed me there were still no real answers. Plenty of people floated rumors and ideas around our small town. The gas station attendant at the local quick mart said he saw a suspicious man with a young blonde woman in his passenger seat fill up for gas in a dodgy-looking car. The kids at school thought that Kaylee had run away to escape her dad's high expectations. Their understanding of who Kaylee was surrounded around how she had always pushed herself to be the best at whatever she did. Academics, sports, or otherwise. So everyone at school assumed her parents had to be pressuring her to do it.

The police, however, thought that her dad was responsible. That he had killed her in a fit of rage. They even thought that when they had first interviewed me. Of course, they didn't tell me, but they had asked me plenty of questions about her father. My answers would either confirm or deny the theories they were floating in their mind.

But I knew better than that. Kaylee's dad wasn't a high-pressure man. He wasn't a man prone to rage-induced outbursts. In fact, I don't think I saw him angry even once. He was a quiet and simple man named Dale. He worked as a mailman for USPS and was well on his way towards retiring. Kaylee's mother had died in childbirth and her father always treated her like the most special thing on earth. I knew her father wasn't capable of harming her. Not for one second.

I went to his house just a week after she had gone missing. He and I had several interactions over the years. I had spent half the days after school at his house, and Kaylee spent the other half at mine. It wasn't weird in any way for me to stop by and see him. But going over there to listen to his thoughts to investigate for myself what had happened felt strange. I had never used my gifts for anything like this before.

I knocked gently on the door.

"*Who could this be?*" I heard Dale think before he opened the door. His thoughts were ones that I was very familiar with. They had always been sporadic and minorly chaotic. I could pick his thoughts, or anyone I knew well, out of any crowd with my eyes closed.

The poor man looked terrible. His eyes were heavy and surrounded by black circles. He wore a bathrobe that loosely covered a grey wife beater and his boxer shorts. I had never seen him in a state like this. Normally he was the classic polo shirt and shorts kind of dad. He sighed some relief.

"Cameron," he said calmly. "What are you doing here?" I studied his face and listened to his mind before responding. "*Do you know where Kaylee is? Are you coming to tell me?*" He wondered hopefully.

"Hi, Mr. Crankowski," I said with a slight smile, hoping to ease his tension. "I just wanted to stop by and see how you're doing." I held up the plate I carried over from my house just a couple blocks away. "I made you these cookies." I had made them the night before. It seemed impolite to just drop in on the man, and movies and TV had taught me to always bring food to people who are grieving.

"Thank you," he said, taking the cookies. "These look great. Would you like to come inside?" Though his thoughts said, "*Please just leave me alone.*"

"Sure," I said, ignoring his actual desires at a chance to get a little closer to figuring out where my friend had gone.

I entered the home of my longest friend and was greeted with a totally new aroma than I was used to here. Cigarette smoke. I was accustomed to this smell near my own home because my dad had smoked my entire life, although he never did it inside, thank goodness. But Mr. Crankowski was never a smoker before. This whole situation had really been taking a toll on him.

"Please excuse the mess," he said. It truly was a mess. I could see that dishes lined the kitchen counter through the hallway. The living room was in disarray. Not surprising because Kaylee had been the primary keeper of the house, always taking care of her dad just as much as he took care of her. I always thought he was a bit on the edge of losing it, but seeing this now, he clearly had fallen off that edge.

"Have you heard any updates?" I asked, avoiding the use

of his daughter's name to avoid triggering an emotional response for either of us.

He made his way to the recliner he always sat in when he got home from work and motioned for me to take a seat on the couch next to him, which I did. The coffee table in front of me where Kaylee and I had put together puzzles on the weekend when we were little was now strewn with empty beer cans and cigarette ash that couldn't be bothered to land in the ashtray.

"Nothing," he said. "Have you?" "*Please tell me you've heard something. You must know something. Why has it taken this long for you to come and speak to me?*" His mind rushed.

I took a deep breath, reminding myself to answer the question he had actually said out loud and to not react to the questions I heard racing through his mind. "Nothing."

His chin began to quiver. A tear rolled down his right cheek. "*She really is gone,*" he thought. Of course, he had sent the police officers over to question me the day he filed the report. If her best friend didn't know where she was then who would?

"I'm sorry," he said. "Forgive me, but can I get you something to drink?"

"Oh please, Mr. Crankowski," I said, assuring him. "I've been here so many times, I can get myself a drink." I stood up and headed for the kitchen to get myself some water. Not because I was thirsty. I had hardly had any sort of appetite since she went missing. I just wanted to escape the solemn air of the living room for a second. The intensity was so heavy I thought I might get stuck on that couch forever.

I pulled down a glass in the kitchen from the cabinet to the top right of the sink. I turned on the faucet and waited for the water to run as cold as possible before sticking my glass underneath. As I turned off the spout, I heard, *"Please tell my dad that I'm okay."*

I paused. My hand froze on the faucet. *"Huh?"* I thought to myself.

"Please tell my dad I'm okay." The voice in my head belonged to Kaylee. That much was for sure. But where was it coming from?

"Kaylee?" I thought louder.

"Cameron. Please tell my dad that I'm okay," The thought came in again.

"Where are you?" I asked hurriedly in my mind.

"Cameron. Please tell my dad I'm okay."

I got that already. *"Kaylee! WHERE ARE YOU?"* I all but screamed in my mind.

Nothing.

"Hello?" I mentally pleaded.

Nothing.

I waited a few more seconds.

Nothing.

I was now frozen with one hand on the faucet and the other holding a full glass of water. *"What is he doing in there?"* I could hear Kaylee's dad wondering.

Whoever that was wasn't talking anymore. It was odd too; normally when I would hear Kaylee's thoughts they weren't directed at me. And they also came with a slew of random thoughts before, after, and during. Just like with anyone else. These thoughts were too clear. Until that day on the train with the mysterious and handsome man, I had never experienced such a thought before. Another direct message to my brain. I could tell that she wasn't anywhere near me. But her thoughts were coming directly to my mind. *Were they her thoughts?* I asked myself.

Then suddenly, "*Cameron. PLEASE TELL MY DAD I'M OKAY!*" This time the thought was a yell.

I turned around to leave the kitchen.

"What's the matter?" Mr. Crankowski asked as I entered the living room. "You look like you've seen a ghost!"

I looked in the mirror that hung above the couch. Indeed my face had gone pale white. My body was shaking. Replaying his words in my head, "*a ghost.*" I began to wonder if I had just heard a ghost. A ghost wouldn't say they were okay though. Right?

"I think I'm supposed to tell you," I started slowly, "that Kaylee is okay."

His face too went white. His mind blank. After a moment he asked, "What do you mean?"

I began to worry. "It's just a feeling I have." I regretted saying that the second it left my lips.

"*He DOES know something!*" he thought. "You know something!' he shouted, standing from his recliner pointing at me. "*This little liar knows where she is!*"

"I don't," I said back, frightened. The intensity he met me with shook me up. "I swear."

"What do you mean you have a feeling?" he asked pleadingly

"I don't know…I just." I stammered. "I—I —I'm sorry."

I headed directly for the door, setting down my glass of water on the entry table. "WAIT!" he yelled. "If you know something, Cameron, you HAVE to tell me. I haven't slept right in a week. I can't eat. I can't go on without her. PLEASE tell me!"

He grabbed onto my arm as he fell to his knees in the entryway and his thoughts melded with his pleas. For a moment I thought about explaining everything to him. My gift, the thoughts popping in my head in the kitchen, and that I knew they were from Kaylee. But then I also thought of how he might not believe me. He might think I was lying to protect her. Or if he did believe me, he might tell everyone about my secret. There was no right answer.

"I'm sorry," I said again. This time more forcefully as I broke away from his grip on my arm and headed out the front door.

"WHAT DID YOU DO TO HER?!" he screamed after me as I headed down the lawn, quickening my pace into a jog away from his house. "Cameron! COME BACK HERE!!! I AM GOING TO TELL THE COPS ABOUT THIS!"

And tell the cops he did. That evening they were back at my house. Asking me all the same questions again. He had told the cops everything I said about my feelings. I told them it was just that. A feeling. Nothing more. My dad even backed me up and said I had feelings about things a lot since I was little. He even told them I was usually right about my feelings.

"Not saying he's right in this case," my dad said to the cops while sitting next to me. "But he has feelings about things that he shares a lot. Always has. His mother would encourage it." He sounded ashamed.

"We will be back to ask your son some more questions," Officer Hanley said, standing up from our couch and heading for the door.

But they never did come back. The rumors and stories around Kaylee's disappearance quieted over time, and life in Erie got back to normal after several months. I never heard Kaylee's thoughts again. But I knew in my heart that she wasn't dead. I knew she was still there somewhere with us.

Her dad eventually moved away from Erie. Most people

in town thought he murdered her. I don't think he could take that pressure anymore. After visiting him that day, I knew for sure he hadn't done anything to her. His heart and mind were crushed after she disappeared. I don't know whatever happened to him in the long run, but I hope he's okay.

CHAPTER 5

I DOUBLED BACK quickly on the Central Park trail and headed for the sound of the scream. There was a small dirt path about fifteen feet behind me that led into the woods of a now dark, forested area.

"WHERE IS HE?!" I heard a man scream just ahead of me to the left off the dirt path. I moved closer towards the sound and there, in a small clearing shrouded in trees, was Kaylee. The man who had been walking with her now had her pinned against a tree with a knife pointed at her throat. His full weight pressed against her with his arm into her chest.

What do I do?! I wondered fiercely. *Go get help? It might be too late. There are hardly any people in the park as it is.* The man pulled the knife down across Kaylee's throat. I was almost sure it was her. Then—

"*Cameron, DO SOMETHING!*" a thought screamed into my mind. It was Kaylee.

I closed my eyes and gritted my teeth. My best friend in the world was alive, and she was about to not be. I had to do something. As I jumped out from the cover of the bush, the man who had Kaylee pinned *exploded?* That was the only explanation. Where the man was, he was no longer there. In his place, and scattered throughout the area, a million small chunks of flesh steamed in puddles of blood. The knife that had been at Kaylee's throat fell to the ground with a thud. After only a few moments, Kaylee turned her head directly toward me.

The blast of the man's body had sent me directly onto my ass, falling into the bush I was hiding in. I stood up and looked directly at her with a face that I am sure would say shock. Half my body still was hidden by the bush.

"Well, are you going to come and help me?" Kaylee asked, almost sarcastically.

I stepped out from the bush and approached her. She stood there next to the tree with half her face and green sweater covered in blood. Her blonde hair was somehow untouched. "I'm so sorry," I said with the same sarcastic tone, only mine had a little more panic in it, "not only do I feel like I'm seeing a literal ghost but I also just saw a man explode into a million pieces."

"Boo!" she said, approaching me with a smile. I wasn't laughing. Her trademark sense of humor was still intact, apparently.

As I met her in the middle of the clearing, I studied her face even closer. Yep. My eyes can confirm that face, slim with blue eyes and a button nose and a small smattering of freckles. Her hair, the same blonde as mine was before it darkened with puberty. Her essence, somehow pink. This was my friend Kaylee.

"Where have you been?" I asked, unsure how else to phrase a million questions I had in my mind.

Kaylee dusted off her jeans and just as she was about to speak, someone else did.

"We don't have time for that." The voice came from behind me. I was so spooked that I jumped around as fast as I could to face my attacker. "We have to go."

It was *him*. From the train. He looked me dead in my eyes and then…cracked a smile? It was dark and hard to make out his distinct features. But I knew it was him the minute I saw the glimmer of those purple eyes.

"So glad you could make it, Nick," Kaylee said as she walked past us both quickly. Her sarcasm continued to him as well.

"Where are you going?!" I asked Kaylee. She continued walking. I looked at Nick, and he nodded after her, motioning for me to follow. I held his eye contact for a second, thinking maybe I didn't want to turn my back on him. Also thinking his smile was nice. *No, it's not. It's just a smile*, I thought. As Kaylee was about ten steps away now, I hopped into a jog after her. Nick followed in a stroll, looking all around us with reason.

"Kaylee, I'm just saying, some context would be amazing right now," I pleaded. Her pace had quickened now just beyond a brisk walk. "Who was that? Why were you being attacked? Are you okay?!" The tone of my voice rose with each question.

"We need to get somewhere safe," Kaylee said, completely ignoring my line of questions.

"They don't know who he is yet. We can go to his place," Nick said from behind. My head whipped back and forth to their conversation that I was clearly not a part of.

"He who?" I said, somehow knowing I was the 'he' in question.

We were approaching the outskirts of Central Park on the east side now. Other people were walking around enjoying a normal evening in the city. I knew because I could hear thoughts starting to pour into my brain. Which is when I realized I hadn't been hearing Kaylee's thoughts. I knew that I could when we were younger, even when I didn't want to. But now, at this moment, when I'm sure her mind had to be racing because mine was, I couldn't hear a thing.

"Where do you live?" Kaylee turned sharply to ask me, looking me directly in the eyes.

"Jersey City?" I answer-asked.

"The train will take too long. You've gotta be out of the city within the hour. Someone probably saw what happened and took a video. They will know who and where he is in no time."

"Right," Nick said, walking briskly ahead of us towards the exit of the park onto the street. Kaylee put her arm out to stop me. I slammed against it with the same thud I felt when my dad used to throw his arm out to stop me every time a stoplight would quickly turn red. I turned to her and she was watching Nick. I too focused my attention on him as he approached a man exiting his car. They shared a few words, and in just a few seconds, Nick was waving us over to the car. Kaylee relaxed her arm and started to move towards him. I followed blindly like a sad little puppy dog.

"Hop in the back," Nick said to me as we approached the car.

I opened the back door and sat down. Still in a state of confusion, I looked back at Kaylee. I scooted over on the seat to make room for her and she closed the door still outside the car. I jumped as fast as I could for the door causing it to fly open and hit the curb. "Wait what? Where are you going?!"

Kaylee, who had already started to walk away from the car, turned to me with a face of concern. "Cameron,

You remember that thing you told me about you when we were kids?"

"Obviously!" I yelled with frustration. She was obviously talking about my ability to hear thoughts.

"That thing is a gift, and you're about to find out where it came from," she said seriously. I took a breath. "You have two choices. You can get in that car and find out, or you can walk away now and forget any of this ever happened. But you only have moments to decide."

"Where would I be going?" I asked, still hoping for some bit of sanity in all this.

Kaylee took a step back towards the car, placing her hand on top of mine where it rested on the door frame. "You'll be going to the place where I went four years ago."

With that, she turned around and started running north on 5th Avenue. The sound of her shoes on the pavement quickly fading. The sound of my heartbeat pounding in my ear. I couldn't process everything that was happening quickly enough, and a deeper sense of panic was beginning to set in. The adrenaline that coursed through my veins since seeing Kaylee held at knife point was not slowing down for a second.

"Tick tock…" Nick said from the driver's seat.

I stood with one leg in the car and the other leg in the city. I knew time was short. But I needed to think about this decision. I'm not sure why, though. If someone you cared about that you thought was dead showed up and told you they have the answer to the question you've been asking your entire life and all you have to do is get in this car, why would you not do it? And with that conclusion made, I sat down and closed the door. *What am I doing??* I thought to myself.

Nick turned the car on and accelerated away very quickly. I looked off into the direction where Kaylee had run off, wondering if she was okay. Hoping she was okay. Praying that wasn't the last time I would see her.

"She will be fine," Nick said. His eyes watching me in the rearview mirror. Those deep, purple eyes. Highlighted by a strong brow bone and seemingly perfect eyebrows. Not too thick, not too thin, but no sign of being groomed to look that way.

Oh yeah and I'm just supposed to take your word for it, Mr. Crazy Handsome guy. And not crazy handsome just crazy not handsome, I reiterated in my head.

"Not crazy," Nick said. My eyes bolted to the rearview mirror to meet his, "but I'll take the handsome compliment."

"You can hear my thoughts?!" I asked aggressively, already knowing the answer. *Because I never thought you were handsome*, I thought childishly.

"It's kinda hard not to hear your thoughts when you're screaming them so loudly back there," he said, sounding like a condescending uncle. Still playful, but I took it as condescending. "And yes, you did think I was handsome."

"No, I didn't," I said. *Yes, I did*, I thought. Not only could I not hear this guy's thoughts like everyone else, but he could hear mine?!

"You can lie to me all you want. Your mind doesn't lie, and you've got that shit turned up to eleven." Did I hear him chuckle while he said that? Then his tone changed. "Is there anything you need to get from your place before leaving the city for a while?" I only saw the profile of his face as he spoke to me over his shoulder from the front seat of the car.

"Need for what? I still don't understand why we have to go anywhere," I said, sounding like a five year old as I played back my own voice in my head.

"Let's put it this way. We have to go somewhere because there are things you need to know. However, the current need for rush stems from the fact that you exploded a man in Central Park," Nick said nonchalantly.

"WHAT?! I didn't do that! What are you talking about?!" I screamed from the back seat, grabbing hold of the seat in front of me.

"You and I both know that you did," he said. No humor, no play, no judgment. Matter-of-factly.

The thing is…he was right. I knew that I did.

* * *

Seeing as we are all up to speed on the whole "mind-reading" situation, there's something I haven't quite revealed yet. But the thing is, I'm not really comfortable talking about it, because up until the point that a man's body projectile vomited itself all over Central Park, I wasn't comfortable knowing it myself. So instead of just saying it, I'm going to tell you a couple of stories.

Story #1:

When I was seven, my parents took me to an air show. Planes are cool to any little kid, regardless of gender or sexuality, and my dad was sort of a fanatic for the aerial industry. I always loved the air shows and used to tell my dad I would be a pilot one day. That dream never really went away, to be honest. As an adult, I still daydream about flying my own little plane. A nice Cessna that I would take up to Canada or down to Mexico for the weekend. Anyway, I digress.

During the actual air show portion of the air show, there was supposed to be a big fancy reveal of a new design of the 747 from Boeing. The plane was absolutely beautiful. Not a full two-story like the later Airbus A380, but a semi two-story with a private lounge on the second floor. I didn't actually get to see the inside, because you had to buy tickets. Buying extra anything wasn't really my dad's style. I was able to experience it through the mental images of other show attendees though. It was amazing. I remember hoping that one day I would be able to fly on that plane. It's funny, because even now at nearly twenty-one years old, I've still never flown. Yet I dream of it regularly.

My mom and dad found a nice little spot on the grass strip lining the runway where we were able to put down a blanket to watch the show. The excitement of children filled the air all around. I recall the sky being clearer than I had ever seen it, or had noticed to. Not a cloud in sight. The engines of several planes getting ready for takeoff could be heard just down the runway. Old planes, new jets. Planes of every size and sound. Mom made us peanut butter and jelly sandwiches for lunch that day, and she unpacked them for us to eat before the show started. I loved PB&Js, but I remember the way they compressed in my mom's bag made them taste a little soggy.

The 747 was the show opener, and the crowd was thrilled. It was painted white with a long blue stripe that ran the length of the beast. The Boeing logo was prominent on the tail wing. The takeoff of the jumbo jet went swimmingly. The crowd actually cheered just for the wheels leaving the ground as it rushed down the runway. It then did a couple of low passes overhead that were pretty daring. I had never seen a plane fly that low before, and it was majestic to my seven-year-old self. My dad said, "With half-empty tanks and no passengers they can do some crazy stuff!" Crazy was right. Entertaining for sure, but I couldn't get rid of the feeling that it was too dangerous.

On the fourth pass, the plane pulled straight up into the sky at a nearly 90-degree angle. A maneuver a plane like that really shouldn't make. Suddenly the right side engine of the plane burst into flames, followed by the left shortly after. The members of the crowd gasped. The plane began freefalling from the sky just over the airfield. After a moment, the nose of the plane became pointed at the ground. I remember hearing panic amongst the crowd, in their thoughts as well as their screams. The jet was headed straight for the stands of people who came to watch the air show. It was all happening so quickly. My father screamed for us to run. My mother grabbed my hand and pulled me but I couldn't look away from the nose of the plane. A half-eaten sandwich hanging from my left hand. I could hear the pilot's thoughts screaming with concern that something had gone wrong.

In the moments that a crowd of people expected there to be a large scale explosion, nothing happened. I lost consciousness just after what should have been the moment of impact. I was awoken by my mother's screams, and as I came to, I thought I had surely died and was now in heaven. She held me in her arms sobbing. I regained my composure quickly, and once I sat up I saw the 747 that should have been in a fiery mound where I laid, sitting perfectly unharmed on the runway next to us. No one made a sound except my mother's screams and a few other children crying in the field. Every person stood in shock, staring at the plane.

"*Did anyone else see that?*" Someone questioned their sanity.

"*Did we die?*" someone closer thought.

There is one video out there on YouTube you can see.

I've watched it many times. It's pretty grainy and terrible, being it happened during a time that predated everyone carrying around a camera in their pocket. The speed of the plane was also hard for the cameraman to follow. What you can see is the 747 makes the loop in the sky and begins catapulting itself towards the ground. It drops in and out of frame as the cameraman rushes to keep his eye on it. The video was taken from a bit further down on the runway, so when you see the camera continue down and finally land on a crowd of panicking people, you really get the whole perspective. Then the camera pans back up slightly, as the operator realizes he's gone too far down. But now the 747 just hovers there. Nose pointed at the ground. Engines ablaze. It slowly starts to tilt back to its proper angle with the tail coming level with the nose. Then, it hovers directly on the runway, sets down less than gently with a bit of a hop. The camera then pans back to the crowd of people, some of them still running, but most of them in awe.

How the plane landed was never explained. It is regarded as a strange phenomenon across the internet with some alien conspiracy theory behind it. Some people say it didn't even happen. That the video is just an animation or trick of the light. The hundreds of people who were there that day gave testament. But eventually, their stories faded. Some of them didn't even believe it themselves. What do I say? Well, I was there that day, and I didn't see any aliens.

Story #2:

I'll make this one brief.

On a walk home from school in Colorado at fourteen years old, I saw a neighbor's Border Collie being attacked by a German Shepherd I had never seen before. The owners of the German Shepherd were nowhere in sight. The owner of the Border Collie was screaming for someone to help. The Border Collie was getting messed up pretty bad, and by the time I came into the picture, the thoughts of the Border Collie were around its own death. A dog contemplating the fact that it is about to die is tragic. Thoughts of his owner streamed through his mind, overwhelmed with sadness. Almost as soon as my anger washed over me, the German Shepard was gone. Exploded into a thousand tiny pieces. Just like the guy in the park. The Border Collie's owner made eye contact with me, questioning what we had both just witnessed. Only a moment later, she picked up her dog to rush it to the vet in the hopes of saving its life.

I later saw that Border Collie and its owner again. The dog was able to make a full recovery. The owner and I always shared knowing looks, but we never spoke of what happened that day.

In Conclusion:

Those are two of the more significant things that happened. There are a lot of little stories too. A school bully getting whacked in the face by opening locker doors in high school. The time my dad slipped on the edge of our roof that he was fixing, and miraculously landed safely and softly on his butt on the ground below, appearing to literally float down.

Every time something like this would happen, in the back of my mind I knew that I had something to do with it. It was more than just thinking to myself *Did I do that?* There was some level of me that always knew, and the minute Nick said it, I knew it for sure.

* * *

I clutched my mother's necklace with my right hand grateful that I paid attention today for many reasons. "No," I said to Nick. "I don't need anything." I felt a deep wave of sadness wash over me as I worried about my apartment, my things, and my job. I had gotten up and left everything in life once before, but I wasn't sure that it was something I wanted to do again.

"You want answers," Nick said, seemingly listening to my thoughts of concern. "It will be worth it."

He was right. I did want answers. But this situation had brought up more questions than answers so far. Who was he? Where was he taking me? How did he know Kaylee? Nick's response had taken my mind off the worries of leaving everything behind and brought up worries of everything that was happening.

Nick was heading into the Holland Tunnel now towards New Jersey. "This is all going to be a lot easier for you once you understand one thing." His single pointer finger raised in front of the windshield as he said this.

"Okay..." I said, focused on Nick now.

"You came here for a reason," he said nonchalantly.

"Came where?" I asked.

"To Earth."

CHAPTER 6

I WOKE UP in the back seat with the sun once again boiling my face. The sun never ceased to surprise me with its ability to wake me up in frustration. It was only a few moments before I realized I wasn't waking up in my bed at home, though. As I opened my eyes, the first thing I saw was a car door with my feet pressed against it. Suddenly the entire night before came flooding back to me. I shot up in the back seat realizing the nightmare had been all too real.

Where is that guy? I wondered. He wasn't in the front seat. I looked through the windows coming to another realization that we were parked at a highway fuel stop. I knew about these from the several stops the bus had taken when I came to New York from Colorado. On the East Coast, these stops are a little larger. More like a fast-food mall every fifty miles. *He could be anywhere,* I thought.

I fell asleep shortly after Nick's comment about *Lesson Number 1.* My mind was racing, trying to decipher what he could have meant by saying I had come to Earth for a reason. Somewhere along that perplexing mental journey, I must have dozed off. Heavily too, I might add. Normally I'm the lightest sleeper you've ever met. I can wake up at the sound of my upstairs neighbor's thoughts being too loud. Apparently, I slept hard enough that Nick was able to park the car and get out without stirring me.

One thing was for sure, I had to pee. I opened the back door and slowly stepped outside, reaching my arms all the way up in the warm summer air to stretch.

As I walked into the fast-food mall gas station, I still hadn't seen Nick. There were a few people in the parking lot getting their gas. Some lovely thoughts floated around in the air:

"*Camping! Camping fun, CAMPING,*" thought a small child.

"*Yes! Nineteen MPG! You've done it again Normster!*" someone's father thought to himself.

"*Is there a taco bell here?*" wondered someone else's mom.

Someone else had an Eagles song stuck in their head. Which would most likely get lodged in mine now too.

And: "*I can't believe I'm moving to the big city…*" thought a young woman in a beat-up Subaru. That one got to me a bit.

While I looked for Nick, all these thoughts and more filled my mind. I had actually gotten pretty used to ignoring people's generic thoughts. Someone reading the instructions at the gas pump normally wouldn't make it all the way to my mind, unless I was looking right at them. All in all, the vibe this morning for my surrounding area was pretty chill. But no sign of Nick.

I figured I would see him inside. On my way to the bathroom, I didn't catch a glimpse of him in any of the lines for food. *Maybe he left?* The thought briefly crossed my mind. *Maybe the whole ploy was to get me out in the middle of… where am I?* I wasn't sure. *That doesn't make sense though. They wouldn't do all of this just to leave me in the middle of nowhere at a fast-food mall gas station.* I zipped up my pants and headed to the sink. Splashing some cold water on my face and wiping it dry with a paper towel, I realized that I looked different. Hard to put a finger on how, but somehow the person looking back at me in the mirror today didn't feel like the same person as yesterday.

The smell of coffee filled the area as I exited the building. I wanted some, but I didn't have any cash on me. Hopefully Nick would, wherever he was. Rounding the corner to go back to the parking lot where the car was parked I saw Nick. His back was turned to me and he was talking with another man. I jumped quickly behind a pillar so he wouldn't see me. *Who is that guy?* I thought. Then I realized Nick could probably hear me thinking so I decided to focus on them instead of thinking my own thoughts.

I could just barely hear their conversation: "All I can say, is that you won't regret it," Nick said to the man.

"I do not believe that I will, sir," the man replied. He was older. Maybe in his sixties. He spoke with a thick Russian accent. "But can you please tell me one last time…"

"All will be well with you," Nick said, smiling at the man.

With that, the man bowed slightly with his hands in prayer. He then handed something over to Nick and walked away.

"You can come out now. We're late." Nick yelled loudly enough for me to hear. Clearly, he knew I had been standing there.

I came around from the pillar to see Nick hopping into the driver's seat of a different car. "Who was that?" I asked opening the passenger door to get in.

"The owner of this car." Again, matter-of-factly. I sat down in the passenger as Nick put the key into the ignition, started the car, put it in reverse, and then looked up at me and smiled.

"Are we taking his car somewhere for him?" I knew this was a stupid question to ask. Based on everything I had seen in the last twenty-four hours, there was no way we were running this car down the street for this guy as a favor.

"Not in so many words." Nick pulled the new car onto the freeway.

"How many words then?" His "beat around the bush" tendency was really starting to irritate me.

"He will get his car back in the future. Or, he will get an even better car. Or, something better than a car."

"Okay, I'm gonna go ahead and move past that insanity and just ask, why did he let you take his car? Do you know him?"

"No," he responded flatly.

"Did you give him something in exchange for it?"

"No."

That was it. "Pull over," I demanded.

Nick looked at me through his sunglasses. This was my first time getting a real good look at him from the front seat. Since the first time I had seen him on that train, I could only remember the outline of his face and the piercing purple of his eyes. I took him all in now sitting next to me in the daylight. His face, strong and round, displayed confusion and frustration. Aside from his eyes, everything else about him was classically handsome. His lips, while ample and full, were not as wide as one might expect. His jawline was strong with a five o'clock shadow. He wore a black t-shirt and dark blue Levi's. His right bicep was hard to look past as his sleeves strained to keep a grip on it. I'm sure the left one was great too. It was just blocked by his torso. A good torso, mind you.

"We don't have time to pull over," Nick said firmly.

"I don't care what *you* have time for. PULL. OVER," I said firmer.

Nick pulled the car onto the shoulder slowly. Once we came to a complete stop, he put the car in park and crossed his arms over his chest. "Now what?" he asked

"I'm leaving!" I yelled, knowing half the observations about him that I had just made were floating around in the space between us and he had definitely heard them.

Nick turned towards me ever so slightly and took off his sunglasses. He folded them nicely and tucked them into the collar of his shirt. When he looked back up at me, a chill went down my spine. Those eyes…From a distance, anyone could mistake them for any other color. You might not notice the difference right away. But being less than two feet away, I was lost swimming in the deep, royal purple ocean that his eyes created. "Are you?" he asked confidently. I had just been staring at him instead of leaving the car like I meant to.

"If you don't start giving me more than two word answers and riddles, I will exit this car." I placed my hand on the door handle.

"And where are you gonna go?" he asked with a small smile creeping up.

He was right. We were somewhere in Pennsylvania now according to the road signs. I had no idea where I would go or how I would get there. Nonetheless, I didn't appreciate his tone that I had nowhere else to go. I have always had this problem with men telling me what to do. I blame my relationship with my dad. "To be completely honest with you," I started seriously, "I don't give an exploding fuck where I go, as long as it's not here with you in this car."

"That's not what your thoughts say," he quipped.

"You know what?! Shame on you for that!" I asserted, opening the door. "I've been hearing people's thoughts for twenty years and even I know there's a fair time and place for that." By now I was standing outside leaning into the doorway to yell at him.

"By your society's standards, sure." He turned his head forward again. The arrogance of this man was really starting to infuriate me. "But it's not *my* fault that I can hear *your* thoughts."

I stood up straight, slammed the door as hard as I could, and started walking against the traffic. I had taken twenty steps and wouldn't look back. I didn't care whether he was still sitting there or if he had driven away.

"Cameron." Another direct message from Nick to my mind.

I stopped.

"Please get back in the car."

I started walking again.

"I promise to answer your questions."

LIKE AN ASSHOLE?! I scream-thought back.

"Not like an asshole," he thought.

It still wasn't good enough for me. I kicked my foot against the road so hard my shoe went flying into the ditch next to the highway. I then threw my body onto the ground in frustration. Sitting comfortably in a small cropping of grass, anyone driving by would be able to see me. I thought of this and how much of a child it all made me feel like. But I couldn't muster the spirit to walk further away from the road right that second. I just wanted to cry. I couldn't, but I wanted to. So I just sat there.

"I'm not from here," Nick thought to me.

I mocked his thoughts in my own mind. Not directly to him, but he could probably still hear it. *I'm not from here. Wah wah wah blah blah blah fuckin psycho ass drives me to PA for nothing.* My thought process was still full of frustration.

"*I'm not from Earth.*" This time his thought was louder. Not volume-wise, but louder than the thoughts in my own head. It interrupted my immaturity and stopped my thoughts dead in their tracks.

I looked back towards the car. *Not from Earth?* I wondered. *So you're an alien?* I thought a little louder. Now I was sure he was crazy.

"*Alien is an extreme word developed by your species,*" Nick thought from the car. "*An appropriate term for your current evolutionary placement, but an extreme word nonetheless. The universal language for what I am compared to you is more akin to your word for 'neighbor.' Or perhaps, a cousin.*"

No sarcasm. No arrogance. Just a straight-up answer. An absolutely insane one, but hey, when you can read minds and no one else can, you are a little more perceptible to crazy stuff.

"*I will tell you more,*" Nick thought. "*If you just get in the car.*"

I sat for a moment contemplating the last twenty-four hours, unbothered with the idea that Nick was listening to my entire thought process. Which went something like this:

How is it possible that the last forty-eight hours makes more sense to me than my entire twenty years of life on Earth? Oh and Earth, speaking of which, is a place I apparently chose to be. But that doesn't make any sense to me. I don't remember being born here, but there are pictures of me as a baby with my parents. Unless I came in a swapped lives with whatever baby that was in the picture, I'm pretty sure I'm from Earth.

My mom used to talk about Angels all the time. She told me that Angels weren't what the Bible said they were exactly, but that they did exist. That they came from other places in the Universe to help people. When we would stare up at the stars together some nights before bed, she would ask me if I could see the Angels. Sometimes I said that I could, even though I couldn't. The idea of angels always stuck with me.

Was the homeboy in the Cadillac an Angel? Well, if he is, Angels sure have an attitude. Mom was right; they are NOTH-ING like the Bible says. But then again, I don't think he's an Angel. I'm not sure I even believe that he's an Alien—whoops sorry neighbor? As if I actually care about the proper word— like he says he is. But I also don't understand how he can hear my thoughts. I've heard people's thoughts all my life but no one could ever hear mine.

Is that what it's like for people whose thoughts I hear? Is this what it was like for Kaylee growing up? Was she always concerned about me actually hearing her thoughts? I don't think so. I think I would have heard that. Speaking of Kaylee, WHAT THE LITERAL FUCK?!

Suddenly the driver's side door of the car closed with a thud. Nick had stepped out. I could hear all of this happening but I refused to look. *Oh God* I thought. He took a few steps to approach me. When he pulled up next to me he sat down directly to my left. Using his hand to catch himself on the ground and lower down slowly. Did his knee touch mine accidentally? Or was that on purpose? *WHY AM I THINK-ING ABOUT THAT?! Oh my God, he can hear all of this. FUUUUUUUUCK!*

CLAP.

Nick clapped his hands together loudly. I looked at

him. "There," he said. "Now maybe I can get a word in." My thoughts had stopped. "Now watch."

Nick's eyes left mine and he looked ahead across the patch of green between us and a section of Pennsylvania forest. He held out his right hand, palm side up. I looked at his face and saw a look of concentration. A very *gentle* concentration. I tried to follow his line of vision to determine what he was looking at. I couldn't see anything remarkable aside from a mass of trees and moss.

Then suddenly, something came flying out of the forest directly in front of where Nick's hand was raised. Was it a bird? No, too small. A butterfly? No, it seemed to be moving pretty direct and not bouncy like a butterfly would. As the small object came closer I realized that it was a hummingbird. A beautiful hummingbird at that. Its colors were a bright fuchsia and teal that glistened in the sunlight.

The hummingbird came so close, so directly to Nick's hand that I thought it might land on top of it. THEN IT DID! The tiny bird landed and then nuzzled its head against the area where Nick's thumb met his palm. IT FULL ON NUZZLED HIS HAND.

I looked at Nick with a look that could only spell shock.

"You want to touch her?" he asked

I shook my head no quickly.

Nick brought the bird close to his face and whispered, "Thank you." Then he gently pushed her (assuming it was a "her") back to the sky, and she dove into the forest. Nick pushed himself off the ground and brushed his hands together. "If you want answers, I will give you answers. But I need you to get back in the car."

I slowly placed my hands underneath myself to push off the ground when Nick offered his hand to help me up. Everything inside of me wanted to take that hand. But I looked away and got myself up instead. Thinking that he must have heard me want to grab his hand, I said, "If there's one thing I know," I began, "it's that willpower is different than thought."

With that, I walked past him towards the car.

* * *

The ride of the Cadillac we had acquired along I-80 West was smooth. Nick made a great choice in which car to coerce out of someone. The light hum of the tires coupled with the way the trees would ripple was soothing for me. I've loved car rides ever since I was a little kid. One of the best ways for my mom to get me to fall asleep was to drive me around in the neighborhood late at night. Here now in this car with Nick, it reminded me of those moments. Just a little though. Not being able to hear his thoughts or anyone else's. Not having to focus on driving the car. Only needing to focus on my own mind, which was loud as hell.

Of course, I was having this entire thought process while sitting there, and I know Nick heard all of it. "You know, I didn't coerce that guy or anything."

"Huh?" We hadn't said anything to each other since we got back in the car. It had been nearly an hour. My mind needed a lot of room to process the situation I had witnessed with the hummingbird. It was beautiful. Magical. I swear the bird looked directly into his eyes.

"I asked him very politely if I could borrow the car, and that if anything happened to it I would be sure to replace it," Nick said calmly and matter-of-factly.

Coming back to my senses, I said, "People don't just give strangers their cars though..."

"Do they not?" he asked. I thought it was sarcasm but remembered he's an alien.

"No. Not here."

"I think the closest word for it in your language would be sincerity. I used sincerity." He looked over to me to check my reaction. Which was confused but intrigued. "One of the things that my people are gifted with," he went on, "and bear in mind your planet is not my first planet so the language is rough. We have the ability to push ideas through a being's mind, directly to their 'soul,'" he said with air quotes.

"So you hypnotized him?" That was the first sense my mind could make of all this.

"No. Hypnotization happens in the mind. People use it to convey a false truth. You can lie to a person's mind. You cannot lie to their soul. Or a soul cannot lie to another soul."

I let that toss around in my head for a second before asking, "What's the difference between a mind and a soul?"

"A mind is where a being's physical reality is processed. It's part of your body. A soul is something entirely separate from the physical reality of any being. It is with your body, but it's not part of you."

"So like basic Buddhism then?"

"I'm not familiar, I'm sorry," he said, almost sincerely apologizing so I didn't make him pull over again. His tone had really changed.

Noted, I thought. "Everyone has a soul," I explained. "That soul lives tons of lives. You get done with this one and then you get another one. If you're bad you come back as a shit flea and if you're good you come back as Kim Kardashian."

"I think that's Hinduism," he said, smiling slightly.

"Oh so you know everything there is to know about Hinduism but you've never heard of Buddhism."

"I've heard of it I just wanted to hear you explain it."

I smiled. Then I stopped smiling. *Noted that his tone has in fact, NOT changed,* I told myself.

"The soul is the infinite being that drives all of us. Everybody's got one. I've got one, you've got one," he said pointing to me. "I just spoke directly to that man's soul with my own. I asked if I could borrow his physical possession for a very important task in this reality. Speaking directly to the soul of a being usually results in a much more enlightened reaction. The mind of any being can be corrupted by physical reality. It is likely that humans are not inclined to loan each other objects of value, because of the lack of trust you have for each other as a species."

"But his soul isn't corrupted?" I asked, trying to grasp.

"No soul can be corrupt. Our souls choose these physical existences to attain spiritual enlightenment on a physical plane. The hardest of all planes to attain it." He was smiling at his explanation. "When he dies, or anyone dies for that matter, their soul awakens immediately. Most people realize they have forgotten their entire purpose of why they chose to live in the first place, and they try again."

I digested what he just told me. Honestly, nothing about it was all that strange. The idea of humans having souls isn't a brand new one. My mom had also always talked about her soul and my soul growing up. So the idea isn't foreign to me. Except that AN ALIEN WHO CAN CONTROL HUMMINGBIRDS TOLD ME, SO I'M PRETTY SURE THAT MAKES IT REAL.

"So, I have a soul?" I asked.

"Yes," he said flatly. I was a bit taken aback by the way

he said it. Almost, I don't know…Can't put my finger on it. Nick seems to pick up on my thought pattern and continues, "That man's soul was very trusting of mine. My soul has no reason to lie to him, and my soul is very trustworthy. Any other soul can see that."

"Is that how you got me into this car?" I asked aggressively. Had he coerced me into this whole thing? And if so, was that a bad thing if he had spoken to my soul directly?

"I promise that I've never spoken directly to your soul," he said calmly, again listening to my thoughts. "In this lifetime at least."

"Ok, let's skip over that very weird 'in this lifetime' comment for now. Let's say I take all this at face value for what you're saying. What is the important task you told him you needed to complete?" I asked.

"At this moment," Nick said patiently, "it is to deliver you safely to your destination."

"Vague," I said sarcastically. Nick rolled his eyes, and somehow I felt it. I knew he wasn't going to give me any more information. "Can we stop for coffee?"

"It's vague because it needs to be vague. Too much information too quickly is not going to help you calm your mind. Which should be your number one goal right now." He paused. "And no."

Nick exited I-80 onto PA-36 towards Hickory Township. "Are we there?" I asked.

"Almost."

"We really can't stop for coffee?" I asked.

He handed me a bottle of water from the back seat. "Calm your mind."

"Before I do," I say, "who was that man who was attacking Kaylee last night? And where did she go?"

"That *man* was looking for you," he began. "I'm not sure who he was, to be honest. We didn't think anyone else knew you were here. And don't worry about Kaylee. She'll be fine."

"Why was he looking for *me*?" I pressed. I let the 'we' comment go and the non-answer about Kaylee. Knowing that he wouldn't give in to too many questions.

"Power."

"Power?" I repeated as a question.

"The greatest power Earth has ever seen," he said too flatly.

"I'm sorry...WHAT?"

"This is not for me to tell you," he said. "What I can say is you brought with you a great power when you came to Earth."

The greatest power Earth has ever seen? YIKES, I thought. *Now I know this can't be real. I'm definitely dreaming. Confirmed nightmare.*

"What do you mean brought with me? You said last night that I 'came here for a reason.' What does that mean? Am I an alien too?" I pressed.

"I've already told you too much. You need to do breathing exercises and attempt to calm your mind. You hold all the keys, and the answers are a lot faster for you to get yourself than to be explained."

I gave up. I don't know if it was a force of energy from him, or if I was just tired of trying to pull information out of him. But I leaned back in my seat and started to watch the warping of the trees as they flew by. A beautiful alien man driving me through Pennsylvania. *Wait what? Not beautiful OH and...* my thoughts switched to words. "What planet are you from?!" I suddenly jumped back with a caffeinated amount of energy.

"My home is called Valnor," he said. "Do you know how to meditate?"

Valnor, I thought, spinning off into a totally new train of thought, completely ignoring anything Nick had to say about meditating or breathing.

CHAPTER 7

THE CAR CAME to a stop which woke me up. I had fallen asleep again. My inability to stay awake in a moving vehicle was honestly irritating at this point. "Where are we?" I say as I sit up straight in the seat and let my eyes adjust. We're surrounded by forest on all sides except the dirt path we drove in on behind us. The path seemed to dead-end here in a little dirt lot. The forest dense, the air humid.

As I started to panic slightly, visions of myself being butchered in the forest streaming through my mind, Nick said, "We're here." His voice was calm and perhaps even reassuring, once again, hearing my thought patterns. "Well, we're almost here. Just a thirty minute, maybe hour-long walk. Depending on how quickly you move." He opened his door and steps out of the car.

"I don't know. Without any coffee, you're probably going to want to bet an hour," I replied, opening my own door to step out into the sunlight.

"Here, take this." He tossed me something over the roof of the car. Then a second thing. To my gay surprise, I caught them both. A granola bar and banana. "There's clean drinking water just up ahead." He started walking away from me. I followed behind, fumbling with my granola bar to get the wrapper open. I was famished.

Then, not carrying anything but the clothes on his body, Nick dove into the forest. I did my best to keep up and follow behind. There appeared to be no path or set route that Nick followed. At the same time though, I noticed we never really ran into any branches, bushes, or other obstructions. Maybe a small pivot one way and then another to avoid them. Nick somehow seemed to know each perfect step to take for an easy trip. Anyone else trying to make this trek that didn't know the way would likely get pricked and poked a million times. I was able to manage eating half of my food while moving. I didn't bother to ask where we were going, because I was sure there wouldn't be a full answer. Something I was very tired of. Not to mention, I wondered that exact question in my mind which Nick definitely heard. He didn't care to answer then either.

After a few minutes, I heard the sound of moving water up ahead. Nick turned to me to say, "We are going to cross this river. You'll need to take off your shoes so that you can cleanse yourself before we enter the higher dimension."

A higher dimension? I wondered. "Cleanse myself of what?" I asked.

"Life," he replied simply.

I took the last bite of my banana. *At this point that… that makes a lot of sense.* Nick smiled at that. Aliens, higher dimensions, and cleansing myself? *Am I sure I'm not dreaming?*

The river was absolutely gorgeous, flowing through a lush Pennsylvania forest with a warm blue hue. I love nature, always have, but water especially. I tucked the granola wrapper into my pocket and tossed the banana peel on the dirt next to the river. I sat on a low lying rock near the edge of the water to remove my shoes. It was then that I realized that Nick's shoes were already off. He wasn't holding them or anything.

"Are you leaving your shoes here?" I asked.

"I took them off in the car," he said. I didn't remember that at all. I was still a little groggy from my nap. Had he walked all this way through the forest barefoot?

Standing up, I waited behind him as he took his first steps into the river. The golden light of the early morning bounced off the skin of his neck that poked out of his black t-shirt. His carefulness of where he put each foot caused his upper body to dance for balance with his arms stretched like a scarecrow. His shoulders were so strong, with that nice little raise of muscle between his neck and his deltoids. *What is that muscle called?*

"Trapezius." He turned around when he was halfway through to see me *not* getting in the river. Thinking about neck muscles. Admiring him. He smirked at me.

As soon as I realized, I put my foot down into the water to set off. "OWWWWWWW!!!!" I screamed, jumping up to bring my foot out of the water. I then lost my balance and dropped my left foot into the water as well. "WHAT THE FUUUUUUUUCK!" The rocks in this river felt like blunt-ended razors everywhere. The pain was excruciating. I knew for sure I wasn't dreaming now.

I looked at Nick and saw him lightly chuckling at me. By this point, I had fallen backward and put my butt back on the shore, the weight of my feet off the rocks. "You can't just walk into a higher dimension without a little pain," Nick said. He walked through the water back to me so casually that my mind couldn't understand it. "Come on. It's good for your feet. Reflexology." He reached out his hand to me. And this time, I took it. "*Mind over matter*," he thought to me as he hoisted me back up to my feet.

The pain was immense, but it was lessened incredibly by the distraction Nick's hand was currently offering. It was soft but thick. As though it had been calloused before and restored to extreme newness after. At first, he had his hand palm up towards me in the casual "let me help you there" kind of way. Once I was on my feet, he readjusted to hold my hand in a cup formation. You know, like couples do. And then he didn't let go. He started walking forward. My jaw must have been on the riverbed. My mind tried to wander off to places that I preferred it didn't. So I took some deep breaths and tried to stay in the moment.

I continued stepping. With each new step, my body felt lighter and lighter. The rocks pressed in just a little less. My hand was still on Nick's. We were about three-quarters of the way across when I started to notice the forest in front of us. It was completely and utterly different from the one on the other side. The same flora, but enhanced. Everything had a glow, an edge, a vibrance. There was something of a haze or filter that made everything glossy. The smells were fresh and intense. Like the way the forest in Colorado smelled on the first day of summer camp. More than just a smell though. It brought with it a feeling: joy. Before I knew it, we had taken our last step out of the river.

The rocks that lined the shore of the far side were soft and round. Deep and dark river rocks, unlike the sharp edges on the other side. The dirt underneath the rocks and leading up to the forest seemed to have a glitter in it. Gold splashes of light shone on the forest floor. The plants that sat just in front of us marking the start to the forest, seemed to breathe with me. Rising with my inhale, and relaxing with my exhale. Birds chirped from within the trees in harmony. My body began to perspire slightly all over. I felt incredibly warm. The closest I had ever felt to this before was the one time I took mushrooms with my roommate Daniel in college. But even that trip couldn't compare to the beauty I was witnessing now.

This is amazing," I said, turning back towards him, only then realizing we were still holding hands. Then realizing that it was me who had a death grip on his hand. "Oh. Sorry," I said, shaking it off and brushing my hands on my pants. *AM I FIFTEEN?!* I screamed internally.

* * *

Twenty minutes of hiking through the magic forest later, I'm drenched in sweat. It felt good though if I'm honest. Normally to have my clothes soaked in sweat, especially when I'm not working out, would irritate me. Now though, the sweat felt good and natural. I was also sweating profusely in ways I normally wouldn't. If I were to go out for an hour-long run, my armpits might have a bit of a tinge to them, and the hair on my head would be a mop, and honestly my butt crack But right now I was sweating from every pore in my body. When I looked at Nick to see if he was experiencing the same thing, a small bubble dripped right off the tip of his nose. *His perfect nose.*

"You're sweating to cleanse your body as naturally as you possibly can to perceive this space," Nick said. I still hadn't gotten used to the idea that he could hear my thoughts. No personal processing. No personal ideas. Nothing. If I thought about it, Nick heard it. My oh my how the tables had turned. "It feels good doesn't it?"

"Yeah," I said, walking at the same pace he was. It really did feel good in a way that's hard to describe. "So, did we pass through some sort of portal or something?"

"You could say that. But I think that would be a little misleading," He said. "We didn't go anywhere different. A portal implies that the two points on each end of the portal are different places entirely. We are still where we were. The car is a mile back, maybe two." I nodded for him to continue as we made our way through the forest. "We've simply entered a higher dimension in that same place. The only way to perceive the higher dimension is to enter into it with ritual. If someone came here without taking the proper steps or having a natural perception of the higher dimensions, they would see only a continuation of normal forest like the one we came in through.

"Dimension might not be the best word to convey it either. It's just the closest word in the English language to it. Here. Close your eyes," Nick said, stopping.

I stopped too and closed my eyes. Then my mind suddenly filled with an idea. An idea so complex, I couldn't understand most of it. It was the idea of "dimensions" that Nick was trying to convey to me through a shared thought. And he was right, it is impossible to communicate through the English language, even for someone who understood what was happening. There is no simple way to relate the idea Nick shared with me in that moment. I didn't even understand it all, but the idea of "layers" is what I took away from it.

"Unfortunately, your species forgot all about these higher dimensions, so they haven't been discussed in a millennium."

"How long have you been on Earth? You seem to know

so much about it for someone who isn't from here. More than I do apparently," I said.

"Some of these things are Universal. Higher and lower 'dimensions' are everywhere you go," Nick explained as he continued hiking through the hot, dense forest. "As for Earth, there is knowledge available throughout the known worlds through advanced technology. Earth as a planet is not new to the Universal community. Humans, however, are a different story. I learned all I could about humans on my way here."

"And how did you do that?" I asked.

"There are various ways to communicate information across the Universe," he said. "Radio waves and television signals mostly. You all are *quite* loud."

You're telling me. I knew what he meant, but in a different way. Recalling all those times I couldn't hear myself think because of the drowning volume of the thoughts of everyone around me. In this moment where Nick could hear all my thoughts though, I had sympathy for all those people for the first time. We are all constantly thinking. Some thoughts are voluntary and controlled, and some seem to be uncontrollable and involuntary. Just flying out of you before you have the time to catch it and decide whether you agree with it or not. There were so many thoughts constantly flying out of my mind while I was with Nick, and he heard every single one. Some of those thoughts, I didn't even necessarily agree with. But no matter what I did, I couldn't take them back or prevent Nick from hearing them. Maybe I was too critical of so many people for so long. Maybe all those thoughts weren't necessarily one's that they agreed with.

"Here we are." In the most audaciously cinematic way possible, Nick pulled back a layer of the vine in front of us to reveal the most adorable cottage I've ever seen, with tiny plumes of smoke coming from the chimney. The cottage sat in a clearing of the forest about an acre large. The whole vision looked so cartoony, it was nearly perfect. The sun was positioned in such a way that it was the late evening "golden hour" as photographers like to say, which typically happens between 5pm and 7pm depending on the season. But it couldn't have been later than one in the afternoon. We started walking at eleven this morning and it didn't take that long. Did it?

"And where exactly are we?" I finally asked.

"Tilda's," He said.

Nick waved his hand for me to go through the opening in the vines. The moment I stepped through and my foot hit the grass on the other side, I heard a loud shriek. "Cameron?!"

A small red fluff of hair was moving through a small maze of hedges in front of the cottage. "I'm gonna go out on a limb here and say that's Tilda?" I asked.

"Very insightful," Nick said, pushing me forward so he could come through the opening as well.

The little red fluff of hair rounded the final corner of the maze and up the small hill where I stood ending up five feet in front of me. Her eyes locked on mine with a smile that was growing larger by the millisecond. And...a tear? Her face was warm, her skin old and wrinkled. Her eyes were soft. Her lips, bright red with lipstick. She wore a selection of robes, each a different solid color. From the top layer down there was green, red, and soft orange. Those robes were covered by one blue robe that looked like silk. The pattern looked like that of some Hindu sacred shapes. A soft gold fringe all the way around. As she rushed towards me, I noticed that she had one quite large mole on her right cheek, just below her eye.

Before I knew it, she was clasped around me hugging me tighter than any bear ever could. "Oh I've been keeping a watch on you for so many years," she wept into my chest. I'm about 6' 1" and she must have been 5'2". "To finally lay my arms around you is a blessing that I am entirely grateful for. "

Normally if some random old lady that I didn't know decided to assault me with a hug, I would be entirely weirded out. But now, at this moment, I could feel her sincere joy. It was almost as if the relief she felt washed over me too. But relieved of what? I wasn't sure. "You've been watching me for years?" I asked.

"Oh yes." Her grip did not let up one bit. "That's me! Always hiding around a corner or just on the other side of a tree to catch a glimpse of you." She suddenly pushed away from me, looking me dead in the eye while clasping my arms in her hands. "I wanted to be there for you when your mom died. Believe me, I did. I was there the day that we buried her. Hers was the purest natural soul on this planet. You did right by choosing her."

A full tear now slowly ejected itself from my right eye, falling gracefully down my cheek. "You knew my mom?" I asked, chin quivering.

"Well of course I did! I know everyone!" she said, letting go of the death grip. "I only spoke with her once. When you were just a little baby."

"Oh?" I asked, too dumbfounded to come up with a follow-up question. All this new information was entirely overwhelming. I consciously tried to stop the unending flow of tears.

"Maybe we should head inside. Cameron had quite the

walk up here," Nick says gently, walking past us toward the cottage.

"I'm fine," I said, wiping my eyes. I couldn't put my finger on it, but everything in this moment felt right. "Could I have another hug?" I asked her, my voice still choked up.

"Of course, my dear." She stepped towards me and slowly placed her arms around me, leaning her head back into my chest. My heart was so full I thought I would explode. Then I did. You know that moment when you're trying to hold back tears, and then someone you really love hugs you to make it better and you just lose it? Well, that's what happened to me. Out loud, sobbing into the shoulder of a woman I'd never met. "*She would be so proud of you,*" Tilda thought directly to me. That made it even worse. I stood there and cried for a solid 60 seconds. It felt like an eternity.

*　*　*

The inside of Tilda's home was beautifully warm. Normally in June, areas like this would be hot and sticky from the humidity. Without air conditioning, going inside a building would be a nightmare. But Tilda's home had no air conditioning. Not even a fan. The cottage was well shaded by trees all around the perimeter of the property. You could still look out each window and see a beautiful view of the surrounding cut out, but the trees immediately around the house were quite tall and large, providing ample shade inside. It felt perfect.

The interior decor wasn't really decor. I would describe it more as a continuation of the nature from outside. Chairs, counters, and tables made of what looked like hand-fashioned wood furniture were spread across the main area. Plants crept in the windows from outside. The furthest wall from the entrance was covered in a purple vine that I had never seen before. The wall to the right of the entrance wasn't really a wall at all. Two large bay windows gave a view to the outside world with a large glass door in the center. A fireplace with a vine growing across the mantle adorned the left wall. It smelled of sage and moss, a lovely mixture.

"Quite the thinker you are," Tilda said to me as she gestured for me to sit down on a stool at the bar top counter of the kitchen.

"He sure is," Nick said, saddling up beside me.

My mind must have been screaming a million things a minute. This place was full of sensory overload. Not just from sight either. Sounds, smells, even emotions were palpable. "I'm sorry." I sighed.

"No need to be sorry dear," she replied assuringly.

"I don't mean to sound rude but who are you?" I couldn't think of a better way to formulate the question and I was sure she heard the many different attempts I made in my mind as I got my bearings.

"That will be quite a lot easier to explain after you have some basic understanding of who *you* are," she said.

Tilda now carried something over to us from the opposite side of the kitchen that looked like some sort of watermelon with a daisy coming out of the top. She grabbed a knife (one of the first normal home objects I had seen since entering the cottage) and cut into the watermelon-shaped thing.

As I looked closer I could see the markings which were quite different from a watermelon. The overall color was a deep royal purple. It reminded me of Nick's eyes. Then there was a trace of gold? It looked like gold leafing in one large infinity symbol had been placed along the lower base. Impossible to tell if that symbol was natural or painted on. The flower growing out of the top was evergreen.

"I understand this is a lot of information to process. Unfortunately, we don't have much time for explanation," Tilda said, handing me a piece of the fruit. "This fruit is called Immantium." I took the fruit into my hand. The piece that had been cut for me was a perfect triangle. The soft pink inside of the fruit looked absolutely delicious. My mouth was watering. "Immantium is one of the only fruits you can find throughout the Universe. Once a planet reaches a certain evolutionary capacity, it will begin to produce Immantium. Thousands of years ago, Earth was covered in it. Immantium contains a chemical that is capable of decalcifying any physical being's third eye in a matter of minutes. It will help you understand much faster. It is the God plant."

I sat there with my eyes going back and forth between Tilda and the fruit. My confusion wasn't because I didn't understand what she was saying. In my teenage years, I did a lot of research into why I could hear people's thoughts. The third eye, or Pineal Gland, as science has named it, is a part of our brain just up and back from the center of our eyes. Different religions and sciences have said that the Pineal Gland is our connection to something beyond. I had also found conspiracy theories that say America puts fluoride in our drinking water to basically ruin the Pineal Gland by calcifying it. I had always suspected though that if what different people through time have said about the "third eye" is true, then mine must not be calcified. Because I have no issue being connected to the "beyond."

"Your gift is not what you perceive it to be," Tilda said with a smile, clearly hearing my whole thought process. "Just

3,000 years ago humans were able to communicate tele-pathically. They still can! They just forgot how. You have a gift, Cameron. Hearing the thoughts of those around you is not it."

"Well then, what is it?" I asked.

"You're about to find out," Nick said, taking a large bite out of the purple fruit.

"The Immantium will help you through a process. It is not a one bite solution, but it will help," Tilda said.

I looked at the Immantium in my hand. My brain wants me to eat it. My mouth is still watering. I'm starving. This feels like the 29th time in two days that I've been in a situation where I'm going to do something that I don't know if I should do. But I knew deep down inside that I wouldn't trade the experiences I'd had so far to go back to waiting tables and hoping one day that I would be a Broadway star. Just the few things that I had experienced felt so immense and real. I was slowly opening the door to another world, and I wouldn't close that door now. With that, I took a bite. I hate to say that the flavor was underwhelming but it really tasted very similar to watermelon. Meaning it tasted like water. The purest water you've ever tasted, mind you.

"Now what?" I asked, expecting some sort of radiant energy to be pulsing through my veins or the ground to start shaking.

"Now, we meditate," Tilda said, exiting the kitchen and grabbing me by the arm on her way out the large glass doors to the back of the cottage.

* * *

Somehow daylight had given way to the moon and stars above. The way time moved in this place was strange. To my brain, it was no later than three in the afternoon. But it appeared to be midnight now. The effects of the Immantium had become noticeable about ten minutes after eating my slice. I could feel every smooth blade of grass beneath my feet. Even the slightest breeze sent the skin of my face and the back of my neck into a world of sensation. Leaves shuffling gently on branches sounded like the percussion section of a thousand bands in the far off distance. A light hum from Tilda, which phased in and out of my awareness as time went on. We were deep in meditation now. It was hard to remember a time before we were in this moment.

I'm no stranger to meditation. This one though, was something else entirely. From the moment Tilda started to guide us through breathing, maybe three breaths in, it was different. *It must be the Immantium effects.* I thought.

"*The Immantium only cleanses what you already have,*" Tilda thought to me in our meditative space. "*You could have come here anytime in your life through a strict practice of meditation and self-healing.*" In the times I had done meditation in the past, it had lasted for a few weeks at most. I always felt great when I had incorporated it into my life, but as soon as the anxious feelings had subsided, I moved on from meditation until I needed it again. "*Most people never see the results they seek from meditation because it isn't taught properly or followed through. It takes great dedication to get the experience you are having now. You've been given a fast track.*"

"*You could have come here anytime …*" I let that thought toss around in my mind. Where was here? Was it a good place to be? It was quite overwhelming to experience it, let alone connect with it or digest it. But I tried to anyway. Though my eyes were closed, I saw everything and nothing at the same time. A world of trapezoids and colors that melted together in the most serene yet intense way, but at the same time, complete blackness. The sounds of the world around me, yet no sound at all. An ethereal ringing, there one second and gone the next. Yet, somehow always there. The existence of these things coming and going with my awareness of them. A new existence and separate mindset, with a constant tug toward the idea that we were three people (well, two people and an alien) sitting in the grass somewhere in Pennsylvania on drugs, and when we stopped this, it would be all over. But…it wouldn't?

"*Good*," Tilda thought. "*You are caught in the middle.*" It was as though she was there with me, not only physically, but standing beside a "me" that suddenly existed within the vast space of glory. "*Now, you need to let go of the parts that are pulling you down. They are no longer your reality.*"

I didn't respond to her. I just thought to myself about what she meant which I had no idea.

"*Let go of the idea*," Tilda helped me along, "*that you are here by chance. Believe the idea, that you are here for a reason.*"

I had been 60/40 up until this point, that extra 10% and Nick's good looks pushing me up the hill each time I was met with a new challenge in this strange set of events that brought me here. The truth was that meeting Tilda took me an extra 20% at least. I couldn't explain why, but something about her made me feel safe. So now I'm 80/20. The Immantium took me another 10%. Now I believe with 90% of my mind and body that I am here, in this moment, for a reason. So what was that last 10% holding me back?

"*It's called being human*," Nick thought. That hit me hard. He was standing next to me too now in the void. I was glad he was there.

"*Say it*," Tilda thought to me. "*Say that you know this is real. That you know that you're here for a reason.*"

I know this is real. I know that I'm here for a reason, I thought. The colors became a little brighter. I felt a little lighter. I believed it too. Wholeheartedly. The little voice in the back of my mind saying that all of this was a lie or a dream was now nearly impossible to hear. I had always had a gut feeling that there was a reason for my "gift." Even more, that there was a reason for my existence. In this moment where I existed in a different reality, standing next to an alien, I was certain that there was a bigger story to my life. But no matter how hard it was to hear the voice that was telling me all of this was ridiculous, I could still hear it. It still had power.

"*You still don't completely believe it*," Nick thought.

He was right. I could feel that I was still in "the middle."

"*That is far enough for now*," Tilda thought. "*The most important thing is that you know you are here for a reason my sweet child. With time, as you learn more, you will be able to let go of that doubt.*" I believed her. "*Now, I am going to tell you part of that reason that you have come here. Once you understand, you will be able to believe even more. Do you think you can handle more?*"

"*I need more*," I thought. Quite loudly. Almost a sob. A rush of golden light seemed to swirl all around me within the void. The relief it seemed to provide felt amazing. I was aware that my posture had corrected quite a bit in my physical body that sat somewhere in a cropping of grass on Tilda's property. Tears were in my eyes in this alternate reality, and I could feel a tear roll down my physical body's cheek as well.

"*Come.*" Alternate Reality Tilda reached out her hand to me. In the distance, a small ball of light began appearing in a circular motion in front of us. "*It is time to tell you the most important story you'll ever learn.*"

I took her hand and followed her into the white spinning light, which had now become a portal of some sort. Nick walked close behind us.

CHAPTER 8
THE HISTORY OF SOULS

"**B**EFORE EARTH WAS even forming from the remnants of our home Star," Tilda's voice sounded through an empty void. Though our physical bodies sat somewhere in a grass covered area behind Tilda's cottage, inside this meditation, I stood inside a large expanse of blackness with Tilda on my right, and Nick on my left. "Sentient beings have existed on the physical plane. Different societies from different planets. All of them capable of more than just living. All of them able to ask the question: 'Why are we here?'

"Some looked like reptiles of different varieties," Tilda said. Before me rose a reptilian looking humanoid from the blackness. Tilda must have been using this meditative space as a way to visually represent the story she was telling. The being had green scales covering his entire body and face. His head was the same shape as a human, but that's where the similarities ended. The eyes were much wider than you'd see on any human with a harsh slant upwards from the center on the bottom. The mouth flicked out a tongue that split in two like a serpent. His nose was replaced with an indentation that had two small holes that I assumed were nostrils. I counted six *fingers(?)* on each hand, the shape of which was nothing like a humans. Four longer appendages that were reminiscent of fingers, and two smaller ones on the opposite side that must have done the job of a thumb. The most striking feature was a large tail that seemed to help in holding the creature upright. Stretched out, the tail must have been as long as the creature itself in total, starting quite thick where it connected to the lower back, and gradually shrinking down to the width of a penny at the end.

"Others were avian in nature," Tilda said as another being rose from the darkness. This one was like a man-bird hybrid, with blue feathers adorning it's head and body. A small beak replaced the mouth with nostrils at the top of it. I was amazed at Tilda's ability to make these visions appear in this space, assuming it was her that was doing it.

"This one has arms *and* wings?" I asked as I noticed the large set of wings that I assumed could carry the weight of the Avian creature.

"Evolution comes in many forms," Nick told me as I walked around the being to get a closer look. "This specific species of Avian evolved a new set of legs for walking over time. The original legs now are used as arms, with hands and fingers." He was right. The fingers at the edge of the "hands" were like those of the talons from birds of prey on Earth. The skin of them was gold in color. It appeared that over time, evolution had worked them out to be used as more of a hand. Five talons in all, with one opposable thumb.

The feathers stretched all over the Avian varying in size from some that had to be a foot long on top of the head, to tiny ones that were about an inch in size covering most of the body. I guessed that the wings attached at the shoulder blades would likely span out twelve feet when fully spread out. They were also covered in foot-long feathers across the top, shaving down to smaller sizes towards the inner area of the wing.

"Certainly," Tilda continued, "a fair share that looked like bugs." The final creature to emerge from the abyss looked nothing like a man at all. The only similarities it carried to the other humanoid beings was that the creature was biped-al. It's two legs were extremely thin compared to the massive beetle-like body that sat atop it's hip area. The upper half of the bug-like creature was six times the width of its legs. It's body seemed to be covered in a hard shell, which led me to believe it had an exoskeleton. It's eyes were black as night, and as it stood, I couldn't define where the mouth, nose, or ears were located. Of the three creatures that stood before me in the black abyss, this bug-like creature was the scariest to look at and comprehend.

"These are all real alien species?" I asked with concern.

"I don't love the word 'alien,'" Tilda said. "But yes. These are just a few examples of the thousands of different species to be found throughout our own galaxy."

I couldn't believe it. Not only were aliens real, but they came in such a different variety of shapes and sizes. So far, this would be the hardest thing for me to accept, that these beings actually existed. But the fact that I was witnessing their existence here in a meditative void ensured that the strangeness of it all wasn't too far out.

"Each of these beings' physical existence is powered by a soul," Tilda continued. The different alien figures now glowed in different colors from the inside out. The bird was blue, the reptile green, and the bug was an orange hue. "The souls within each of these different races are beings in them-selves. Each one existing on a higher dimension or frequen-cy long before they occupied the physical bodies you see be-fore you." The bodies now faded away, leaving only the colors of their souls. Each color had a different distinct formation of light within. A body in itself perhaps? I was now visually witnessing the ideas Nick had told me about on our drive.

"Everyone has a soul," I reminded myself aloud.

"Exactly," Nick said proudly.

"These higher dimension races within all of us have existed for ages before the creation of the physical dimension," Tilda went on. "When this reality was brought into existence, these races were tasked with filling the consciousness of sentient beings on the physical plane." The lights disappeared, and we were back in total darkness.

"As it is written, the first of these races to take physical form was the Hyamin." A white light appeared in the center of the abyss. If it was possible, the white light seemed just a bit brighter than the souls that had just faded. "The Hyamin are the oldest and wisest of the higher dimension races. They are considered to be the Original Souls. They manifested physical bodies before any species had evolved into consciousness on the physical plane." The light turned into an all-white figure that floated in the blackness. The outline of a human-like body was visible, but the light was too bright to perceive any of the features. "With their immense power of manifestation, they were able to help with the formation of galaxies. Adding just a little here and there to quicken the process of physical evolution across the Universe. Creation excited the Hyamin.

"The Hyamin employed the help of the other high frequency beings to fill the bodies of the first sentient beings on behalf of the Universe. They chose a reptilian race in one of the first stable star systems to be given consciousness. They called upon the Andar, an ethereal race well known for their power and cunning. The Hyamin wanted the first sentient race to develop rapidly. They chose the Andar with the confidence that they would see the results they desired." Before me, thousands of green lights entered the bodies of what appeared to be newts with arms and legs. The way the creatures floated in the abyss made me think they lived underwater.

"The second race to develop was the Blue Avians. The Hyamin called on the Reotion. Known well for their wisdom and truth. The Hyamin wanted the second sentient race to be one that would think about their creation, and perhaps appreciate it. The Blue Avians were just that. As they evolved over time they became the first species to question their creation. Even before the Andar. They were…beautiful." Tilda said honestly. The same Blue Avian creature flew in front of me in the void, it's blue soul glowed around it's feathers. I was amazed.

"The third race to develop was the insect races. For these races the Hyamin wanted obedience to themselves. Quite a few of the other races had already begun running amuck throughout the Universe, and the Hyamin wanted control. So they chose the Orenthea." The orange light of the Orenthean souls entered into thousands of small bug creatures that resembled a big horn beetle now. "These higher dimensional beings would only communicate with each other and the Hyamin." The bugs now marched in formation in front of us in the void with a few white souls hanging above them, which I assumed were the Hyamin.

"As far as we know, physical reality played out with these three types of souls filling the minds and bodies of sentient beings freely. Ten different races became hundreds. Hundreds became thousands. Eventually, the Universe was teaming with physical life. What has happened in the span of human history with man has happened a million times over before. Eventually, the Hyamin became bored with their creations. They sought to create a new set of races through mammalian evolution. This time though, they wanted to create beings with "Free Will." Enter, the Daemon.

"The Daemon, a high vibrational race unlike any other." A gold light now entered the abyss in my vision. "In the times before the physical plane of existence was created, other races would squabble over higher dimension issues. The Daemon though, were a race that liked things the way they were. They lived in abundant appreciation for all the Universe had given them and never sought more. The Hyamin secretly despised the Daemon. It is not known exactly why, but some throughout the Universe claim the Hyamin are not the Original Souls, that, in fact, the Daemon are. The Hyamin believed a great service was due to the Universe for what it had given them and all beings on every plane of existence. The Daemon believed that life was a gift, and the only service owed to the Universe for their creation, was to live life to the fullest. The Hyamin always believed the creation of the Daemon to be one of the only mistakes the Great Universe had made during its inception. The Daemon were quite ignorant to the Hyamin's distaste for them. This is why when the Hyamin offered to help create vessels for the Daemon to live physical lives, they jumped at the chance." The closest thing to a human yet appeared to the right of the golden light.

"Man was complex and beautiful. Created in a similar image that the Hyamin's first physical body was. The Hyamin knew the Daemon would take such an offer to fill their existence as a gift. They baited them in with the line of Free Will, only for the Daemon to be born into the physical reality under a veil.

"All other races conceived before this time were born into their physical bodies knowing of their soul," Tilda continued. "The proverbial contract that was signed between the Daemon and the Hyamin, included a clause that all beings born would forget their connection to their soul, and be forever stuck in a physical life cycle until they reach enlightenment, trapped in a loop of physical existence without any outside help.

"At most, higher frequency beings only allowed a small percentage of their souls to be sent into the physical reality. As their true home was living in the ethereal realms, and living a physical life was a short trip that only some volunteered for. The Daemon, however, were being pulled into physical realities faster than any race before. Because of the constant loop they were trapped in, the Daemon were dying off in higher dimensions at an alarming rate. This caused a war to break out between the Daemon and the Hyamin which lasted for ages. Eventually, the Hyamin believed they had extinguished all the higher frequency Daemon from existence, and they had won the war.

"However, two Daemon had escaped the Hyamin and remained in the higher dimension. By the will of the Universe, those two Daemon were saved from the grip of the Hyamin and brought to a place where they could survive." Two golden lights now hovered in the darkness before me. All other imagery had fallen away as Tilda continued.

"Those two Daemon not only survived, but they became the saviors of the race. They worked quietly to collect any souls that reached enlightenment. Slowly they grew by the hundreds. Then the thousands. They began to create a network of Daemon that would travel to planets that housed a large number of their souls inside physical bodies. Once they arrived on those planets, they would work to get as many souls to enlightenment as possible. Over time, their numbers grew again into the millions, and they established a home in the far corner of the higher dimension. Safe from the Hyamin, and the energetic pull of physical life.

"The Daemon had never had rulers before. They always saw each other as equals. But now, the two Daemon who survived it all became the leaders of their race. Daia and Ayan, breakers of the cycle. The first rulers of the Daemon race. They became lovers in their newfound bliss. The higher dimensions rang with songs of their passion." The way Tilda said this conveyed a sincere joy on her part. "To be free to appreciate the majesty of the Universe and also the love they shared for each other was enchanting for any Daemon who witnessed it.

"The Hyamin learned of this newfound success within the Daemon race. The war they thought they had won was not over. They needed a new plan to exterminate the Daemon from the Universe entirely.

"Ayan had been pushing many different high capacity enlightenment trips to physical planets where large numbers of their souls were trapped." Before me, a planet appeared covered in golden lights which I assumed were Daemon souls. Then, ten golden souls travelling through space seemed to dive into the planet. "Each trip would yield hundreds of thousands of new souls being released from the cycle via enlightenment." The ten golden souls then left the planet with a large number of additional souls following behind. The planet then faded away.

"Their numbers were growing quickly," Tilda continued. "The Hyamin knew that to eliminate the Daemon forever, they'd need to stop the flow of enlightenment at a rapid rate. The Daemon once numbered in the quadrillions. Though they were a few million strong now, the overwhelming majority of Daemon were still trapped in a physical existence cycle. The Hyamin knew that the only way to eliminate a soul's life entirely was to destroy the planet in which it is trapped while the soul is in a physical body. The Hyamin needed to destroy as many planets with Daemon souls trapped on them as possible, and they intended to.

"Only the Hyamin were busy with other things further out into the Universe. So they requested the help of their most loyal creations, the insect races, to begin destroying man-inhabited planets on a large scale. The most esteemed of these recruited insect races were the Tahn." The beetle-like humanoid creature appeared before me once again. Sending chills down my spine.

"The Tahn amassed an army so large, they could blot out the sun from the sky of any planet they came to destroy. Over the last hundred thousand years, the Tahn destroyed hundreds of planets with trillions of men inhabiting them, ending the precious lives of so many Daemon souls forever." Tilda's voice wavered with sadness. "The possibility of total extinction for the Daemon race was once again headed towards becoming a reality.

"Just one thousand years ago in Earth time, the Daemon had three defenseless planets remaining that were inhabited by their souls. Ayan was distressed by this news. The love that Ayan had for the Daemon race was immeasurable. Ayan wanted to go to one of the planets and live a physical existence to help the Daemon trapped there. To fight for the people living on it. Daia begged Ayan not to go. Daia said that Ayan had fought enough battles in their time. That a simple enlightenment journey wouldn't yield enough souls to risk Ayan's own life.

"Ayan knew that a simple enlightenment trip wouldn't

be enough, and that the Tahn needed to be stopped. So Ayan gathered a group of ten of the finest Daemon warriors who worked tirelessly to create a plan to fight the Tahn before they destroyed another planet. When Daia found out about Ayan's plan, Daia threatened to leave Ayan forever. Ayan finally promised Daia that they would not leave to save the remaining Daemon souls. But Ayan broke that promise shortly after when the group of warriors made their way to begin their plan to destroy the Tahn.

"Of the three planets remaining, one had more Daemon souls trapped than any other. With just over seven billion, Earth was not only the best place for the job, it was the next place on the Tahn's list."

* * *

"And that's why you're here," I heard Tilda say back in reality as I opened my eyes to a dark night sky, the moon looming over us closer than usual. I took a deep breath and felt my legs to see if I was still hypersensitive to everything. It appeared that the effects of the Immantium had finally worn off.

"So…" I said blinking, "I'm a Daemon?"

"Most beings on Earth are powered by a Daemon soul," Tilda said, "The difference is, you have not lived a thousand existences on this planet like everyone else. You came here for a reason."

"I'm one of the souls that Ayan took with him?" I asked.

"Not technically a 'him' per se," Nick said, rubbing his face to aid in coming back to reality. I almost forgot he was there. "There is no gender amongst the higher frequency beings."

Interesting, I thought. "Okay, so I'm one of the souls that Ayan brought here?" I asked.

"Yes," Nick answered quickly. It looked like Tilda was going to answer but she was cut off by Nick's quickness.

I toyed with this thought. It would take some more letting go to accept it. It was the most foreign idea brought to me yet. It didn't make me uncomfortable, but it wasn't fitting right in my head. The idea that my soul had come to Earth across the vastness of space to fight in some intergalactic war was intimidating to say the least. I couldn't process it. "And there's a swarm of bug-people coming to Earth right now to destroy it?" I asked

"You could say that," Nick said.

And what am I supposed to do about it?

Tilda reached forward and grabbed my hands. Hers were warm and made me feel comforted. "Right now all you need to do is to learn."

CHAPTER 9

THE FIRST THING I smell is...forest. It's not until a few moments after opening my eyes that I remember where I am. Two nights in a row, waking in new surroundings. Sure I had seen the room where I slept before I went to bed last night, and I had seen the interior of the car I slept in the night before too. But it took my brain that extra second to process where I was, because I had never seen either place in the light. Tilda's home was even more beautiful in the daylight. And the smell of fresh, forest air was immense throughout. It was a drastic change from the harsh, polluted air of New York City I had become accustomed to waking up in. But it was a vastly more pleasant odor than even Colorado.

I sat up in the bed onto the mattress that was more comfortable than anything I'd ever slept on. I studied the room in the cottage with the sunlight pouring in on the opposite side of the room from where my head laid. How lovely it was to finally wake up without the "help" of the sun for once. Cream-colored walls with a light-toned pine trim lined the baseboards and door frames. There were plants *everywhere*. Not house plants either. There were beautiful ferns, growing from the walls themselves. With their foliage hanging low over the dresser mirror. Vines set with purple flowers grew in through the window and up the walls, creating the illusion of a headboard for the bed. It was stunning. Clusters of five or six flowers each that I had never seen before sprouted from the floors themselves on each side of the bed where the nightstands would normally be. The sconces above them were glowing lights that looked to be flowers themselves. At this point, I wouldn't be surprised if they were.

I moved my feet to the floor and set them in something that I thought was carpet the night before. This morning I could see that there was a rug of...moss? Beautiful moss if it was. Five distinctly different colors woven into gorgeous teardrop designs. *Who is Tilda's decorator? Cause I want her...or him for my future home.* The rug felt cool and soft. It left no residue or moisture on my feet when I lifted them. Incredible.

My ears were the next sense to come into play. The forest just outside the windows was *alive*. At least ten different birds made their distinct chirps that sounded quite harmonious. A fountain in the courtyard behind Tilda's home splashed gently outside the window. All these different sounds came together to create a Disney-like start to my morning.

"*Breakfast is ready when you are dear.*" A thought that belonged to Tilda came into my mind. Another direct message. I definitely couldn't hear Tilda's normal thoughts, only the ones she chose to share with me. In my experience, thoughts are so rarely directed *at* someone. I mean, you think about people all the time, and you think about things you will say to them. But you really don't try to send a communicative message with your mind. This whole "direct message" situation was going to take some getting used to. On top of that, the idea that I couldn't hear Nick or Tilda's thoughts would take even more getting used to. I was starting to realize how privileged I had been to gain an extra insight into people's minds when I was with them. Being able to hear someone's thoughts is like knowing the answers to a test before the questions are asked. There would be no cheating when it came to communicating with Nick or Tilda. In a way, it was like I was a child, learning to communicate all over again.

I wore a grey t-shirt and shorts. Nick's, apparently, from the last time he had been here. A little big on me, because even though I was just a little taller than him, he was…thicker than I was. Not chunky or anything, just burlier. His chest was huge. Sometimes you could see the defined curved line of his pec while he was driving. Sorry. Moving on. I looked for the clothes I had before changing last night. I left them on the chair in the corner, but they didn't seem to be there anymore. Seeing the chair in the light for the first time, I saw that it was absolutely gorgeous. It appeared to be Victorian by all accounts, save the thin white vine growing up its dark wooden legs. *I guess I'll be wearing these in front of people*, I thought with concern. *They do smell good.* I shook my head fiercely as soon as I realized that I was sniffing Nick's shirt. *Ew. Gross. He's literally an alien.*

"I heard that," Nick said, standing in the doorway to my room. I didn't even hear it open. I stood before him stunned, replaying all the thoughts I just had to see how bad the damage was. Then I realized he was hearing all of that too. "Okay well, when you're done talking to yourself, breakfast is on the table. You're gonna need all your strength for what we've got ahead of us." He slid slowly out of the doorframe towards the kitchen.

In an effort to prevent myself from thinking ANY-THING else, I followed directly behind. The smell of warm oats filled the air of the kitchen. *Maple and brown sugar*, I thought pleasantly. The smell took me back to my mother's homemade oatmeal. It was my favorite when I was a child.

Tilda came into view in a comical fashion, popping her head up above the counter of the kitchen island as I walked in. Today she looked a bit more…normal? Hard to say if that was the right word to use because I didn't consider her previous outfit to be abnormal…for her. Her robes had been replaced with a simple set of pink corduroy overalls and a light purple sweater underneath. I could see her hair now, red and curly. The vast majority of it stuffed up under a pink bonnet that matched her outfit perfectly. She almost looked like a hipster if I'm being honest. A sixty-ish-year-old one, but a hipster nonetheless.

"I made your favorite," she said as she approached me, carrying a bowl of what looked exactly like my mother's oatmeal. "It's your mother's recipe. She gave it to me to make it for you. I ground the peanuts for the peanut butter myself though. So it's a little different."

My heart immediately throbbed. My gut clenched. And my chin started an unstoppable quiver. I was going to cry.

"No dear, don't cry!" Tilda said, touching the right side of my face. "It's meant to be a good luck charm from her to you. It's a good thing!" As she said this, I detected what sounded like a very slight Scottish accent. So subtle that I hadn't noticed it before. It luckily distracted me enough from my emotions and I was able to nod and smile, taking the bowl of oatmeal from her.

I sat next to Nick at the kitchen bar counter. The kitchen itself was quite unique. In that it wasn't really unique at all. It was quite an astonishingly 'catalog kitchen' from Ikea. All brand new and updated. The rest of the cottage looked like it had been standing for at least a hundred years. But this kitchen looked like it was installed yesterday. Glass cabinet doors that opened and closed automatically with a tap of the corner. Updated stainless steel appliances and a standard coffee maker. The green theme throughout was the only tie into the rest of the rooms.

"Listen, I'm a simple woman," Tilda said, looking at me with a half-smile. "I don't need a lot in this world, but I do enjoy a well-equipped kitchen." Clearly she had heard my thoughts.

"What? Oh no! It's really cool actually," I said, discerning my thought of difference to not be perceived as negative. Something I wished more people would have done for me throughout my life.

"Kaylee had the same thought the first time she walked in this kitchen," she said.

Then I remembered! Kaylee said I was going where she had been all this time. Even though I realized this, and Tilda had just confirmed it, I still blurted out: "You know Kaylee?!"

"Of course. She came here looking for me all those years ago. Many of the Daemon souls that came here with Ayan do without me saying a word to them. Except you." She pointed at me softly. "How's the oatmeal?"

I hadn't taken a bite yet. It smelled welcoming. "How do they know to come to you?" I asked, blowing on a bite of breakfast to be respectful and at least start eating it. It was hard to be distracted by food when I was currently enamored in the conversation I was having.

"They just know," she said. "Different ways I guess. Depending on their gifts."

So other Daemon souls have gifts too, I wondered

"All ten of the Daemon souls that came to Earth with Ayan have gifts, yes. But all humans that are filled with Daemon souls have gifts too."

"Kinda like not all hot tubs are jacuzzies but all jacuzzies are hot tubs," Nick said looking at me without any humor in his face. I was sure that it was a joke. I stared at him for a moment deciding whether to laugh or not. "I heard that over the radio waves on the way to Earth."

"Your soul is a part of the most ancient group of souls in the Daemon race. These souls are…much more powerful than your average soul floating around in a human. Your soul has lived thousands of physical lives. Throughout all of which you've learned to…manage very well in the physical dimension."

This is a lot before breakfast. Before my mouth could utter the filter sentence I really wanted to say, which was much less sarcastic, Tilda followed up on my thought.

"You just wait until we get to dinner."

* * *

Breakfast continued without much of an event. Tilda had asked me to meet her in the garden after I finished eating. I wasted no time but noticed on the walk there just how truly overgrown with beautiful plant life the entire property was. The wooden planks I had walked across the night before, which I assumed were just a lifted patio, had seas of wild grass growing taller than me on each side. I had no idea that it was there last night as I walked through it.

I followed the path to where Tilda sat on the mossy ground under a gazebo covered in, you guessed it, vines all the way to the top. "It's so beautiful out here," I said to her as I approached, sitting in front of her just a couple feet away.

"There's beauty everywhere," she said with a smile. "The beauty that overcomes this entire property is everywhere. But it can only be viewed by those who are willing to see it."

"When we came here, Nick said that we had to cross the river into a higher dimension," I recalled. "This must be it then?" I asked, still looking at everything around me.

"The river cleansed you so that you would be able to witness it. Not everyone who stumbles across this area would see it the same," she said as she was lighting some incense which she seemed to do with such care. "To others who don't come here with the proper intention, it would look like another bit of forest. The cottage would appear dilapidated and in ruins."

"Would they be able to see us?" I wondered.

"If we wanted them to," she said, looking into my eyes. "The forest would let me know long before anyone was close enough. I've had to hide out from hunters just passing through before."

I feel like I've said this before, but with everything else going on, this actually made sense to me. I asked a few more questions and Tilda answered almost excitely. "So we're in a different state of awareness of our surroundings?"

"Exactly!" Tilda could barely contain her enthusiasm for my understanding. "At least by human standards, that's how you would define it."

"How would you define it?" I asked.

"Not with words," she said. A small knowing smile crept on her face.

I'm no physicist. But I had spent my fair share of time smoking weed, watching videos, and reading books on aliens, dimensions, and everything in between. Something about the theories behind how our universe worked had always intrigued me. From what I understood, Tilda's home existed in another dimension. It also existed in the standard reality that humans perceive all the time. Just in a much different state. It took a certain level of awareness to be able to connect with this reality where the foliage was alive and breathing. Where fairies seemed to dance in the glimmers of light around us. Perhaps they weren't fairies, but regular bugs that gave off a beautiful light. Either way, I could imagine this exact place as it would be to any normal person walking through the area. It wasn't a quarter as magnificent.

"What about cities?" I asked, thinking of New York. "Do they have a different appearance in other dimensions?"

"Of course," Tilda said. "However, each city is different depending on how it was constructed. The humans who built Hong Kong, for example, took into consideration the higher dimensions while they were constructing it. They call it *feng shui*." I had heard the term before many times. Tilda continued, "They built most of the city to bring good luck and fortune. If you were to go to Hong Kong and perceive the higher dimensions, you would see the beauty of nature working alongside the man-made construction. You'd see spirits flying through its streets. Even giant dragons flying through the gaps in the buildings, and down the mountainside into the bay."

I pictured what that must have looked like in my mind. But then I realized I had never been to Hong Kong, and I certainly didn't have enough of a mental image of what it looked like to put this image together. Tilda shared these images with me via a connection in our mind. It was stunning. The red dragons of Chinese folklore soared through the skies, performing beautiful acrobatic tricks. "Beautiful, isn't it?" Tilda asked.

"Gorgeous..." I said, my eyes wide open but not looking at anything they could see. I was focused inside my mind.

Tilda took the image away, and my awareness switched back to the forest around us. "What about New York?" I asked.

"New York is…a bit different." Tilda said. "There are a few buildings that were created with the harmony of nature in mind. But only a few. New York was developed at the height of man's industrial age. Consideration of the forces outside the human dimension were minimal, to say the least." Images of New York now flooded my mind. Only the city was much darker than the one I knew. "The *dimension* we reside in now is a cultivation of the natural beauty of the world. It sings with nature, it dances with the animal spirits. Not all dimensions are so beautiful.

"Some dimensions are fueled by greed and anger. Power even. New York City is one of the most beautiful man-made accomplishments on Earth. I truly believe that. But the energies running through it, created by those in power, are anything but positive." The city appeared to be overrun with a black moss of some sort. A dark cloud hung in the sky just above the buildings that I knew so well. There were also spirits flying around in the sky. Perhaps even dragons? But these dragons looked much more mischievous and evil than the ones above Hong Kong.

"What is that cloud?" I asked Tilda, totally unaware of her presence, trapped in the vision. I knew she was there from the sound of her voice. But I couldn't see her. Even though her physical body was sitting right in front of me.

"Energy," she said. "The energy that is cultivated in that city is overwhelmingly negative."

I looked around from what must have been a high rooftop in midtown now. There were several small blooms of colored smoke arising from the streets and buildings. Not at all from chimneys, but from what appeared to be people? Some were orange, bright, and vibrant. Others were a bold blue. Purples, pinks, reds. All different colors of the spectrum, rising into the sky.

"What are those?" I asked.

"More energy. But these energies are much more positive. Creative individuals. Doing something great within the city and so vastly contrasting the dark soot of the sky."

It was almost beautiful in its own way, seeing so many different peoples energies competing with this overall gloom that pumped from the buildings. With that, the vision ended. Tilda sat in front of me again, and my eyes adjusted to the bright sun.

"I can't believe I never knew that all of that was right there this whole time," I sighed. Something about the whole experience was discouraging. Knowing that a place I loved to live so much was filled with that energy hanging overhead made sense to me, but I didn't want to believe it.

"You are not to worry about that Cameron," Tilda said, gently touching my face. "Human evolution will take many paths and many tolls on the greater species. But that's part of growing up. Humans will eventually access their knowledge of the higher dimensions, see the error of their ways, and hopefully correct it. But that is not why you're here on Earth."

I let that thought turn around in my head. Quite a bit actually, before Tilda finally reached out and touched me again. "It's time to get that mind of yours under control."

Meditation Journey #1

I took a deep breath in. *One, two, three, four, five, six,* I counted in my mind. And then the exhale. *One, two, three, four, five, six, seven.* Tilda told me to try and make the exhale one count longer than the inhale. I repeated this for what seemed like hours, but in reality was probably five minutes.

"Calming the mind is the most important thing any sentient being can do. Yet, so few people on Earth care to do it anymore," Tilda said calmly. Her voice was like a waterfall in the blackness of my mind. "Whenever a new thought pops in, I want you to see it without acknowledging it. Be a witness to it, and let it go."

My mind was rushing with things as usual. From thoughts about everything Tilda had told me about the death of the human species. To me being an alien soul sent here for a purpose. To Nick. That last one held on a little longer than it should have. I was slightly embarrassed when the thoughts of him started to roll in, because I knew that Tilda was hearing them all. I did what she asked and tried to see each thought without participating. I had learned from videos on the internet that you should treat your thoughts like small clouds in a bright blue sky. Always passing, always moving, never there permanently. I tried to treat my own thoughts now like those clouds, blowing them through the sky until it was as clear as it could be.

"Good." Tilda said, listening to my thoughts as they slowed down and more than ten seconds of silence were able to pass between them. "Now I want you to scan your body. Starting from your head. Visualize each muscle in your head and face relaxing. Your eyebrows, your nose. Now unclench your jaw." I did as she said. "Now scan down to your neck, relax the muscles that hold your head. Imagine your head is a weightless balloon with no need for your neck to work hard to hold it up."

Tilda took me down the rest of my body. Shoulders, arms, chest. My stomach, legs, and even my toes. When I finished, I realized I hadn't thought about anything other than what was happening in the current moment for a while, which caused my brain to start thinking of other things. This time, the vision of a blacked-out New York City.

"Just witness, and let go," Tilda said. With that, I imagined the thought getting smaller and smaller until it disappeared. "Good. Now I want you to see a source of light, just above your head. A small orb of white light, that hangs above you." I could see the light in my mind's eye. A small orb floating magically above me. "Now when you breathe in, I want you to breathe THROUGH that light, bringing the light down into your body."

I did as she said, and I could feel a rush go through the skin of my skull. It seemed as though every atom in my body vibrated as the light entered into it. I could see the light being pulled through the orb above my head, down into my skull, flowing all the way down until it reached my stomach. "Again," Tilda said. I did it a few more times, and at one point I thought my body would lift right off the ground from the vibration.

"Now," Tilda started, "you have cleaned your body of negative energy. This will need to be a daily process for you as it should be for everyone." It felt incredible, and I was aware of it. "I want you to visualize your mind. Inside it, there is another glowing orb. What color is it?"

I focused my attention inside of my head. There was another ball of light. "Red," I said.

"I want you to focus on making that light turn blue," Tilda replied. "You can do this by asking it to. It's as simple as that."

Confronting the light, I asked, *Please turn blue.* The

orb swirled around in a circular motion. Its color began to change from red to purple.

"Breathe," Tilda said because I had almost forgotten to.

With the next exhale, the orb shifted from purple to a dark indigo. For some reason, I wasn't satisfied with this change. *Lighter blue*, I thought to the orb. It settled and cooled into a soft pewter blue with my next inhale.

"Great Cameron. Absolutely perfect," Tilda said. "Now I want you to picture yourself standing in a hallway." I did. "There are doors to your right and left in this hallway. Two on each side." The hallway began constructing itself in my mind with astonishing detail. "But the door directly in front of you, at the end of the hallway, is the one I want you to step towards." I took a step. Then another. "As you get closer, you notice this door has a label over the top. It says 'basement.' Reach your hand out, and turn the golden knob of the door and push it open."

I reached my hand out, felt the cold temperature of the knob, and gave it a solid turn to the right. The door gave way easily. "You see a staircase descending downward." It was as if the staircase was forming out of thin air as I looked at it. "There's a light at the bottom. Take the steps down to the basement of your mind." I began to start down the staircase. "Pay attention to the sounds. What do you hear?" I suddenly became aware of the sound each step made as I headed down. The wood of the stairs creaking ever so slightly. The light at the bottom creeping closer. "When you get to the bottom, you enter into the basement of your mind. Which is a beautiful library."

She was right. Like something out of *Beauty and the Beast*, the basement of my mind was the most regal library I had ever set foot in. A sliding ladder was there to get you to the topmost shelves. A little messy though, if I'm honest. Books were thrown from some of the shelves, lining the corners of the great room in tall piles. "Snap your fingers, and clean it up," Tilda said. And so I did. With the snap of my fingers, all the piled-up books began to make their way to their proper spot on the shelves, whirling around the room in a gorgeous tornado of flapping pages until each book was where it belonged. The sun now came creeping in through the skylights above. Showing the majesty of the old cherry wood that the shelves were made of. The rugs on the ground were some of the most intricate I had ever seen. Made of red and gold fibers. "Isn't it beautiful?" Tilda asked.

"Yes," I replied in my vision. Wondering if she could hear me outside of it.

"I want you to make your way to the back of the library. To the fireplace." I started to head further back through the rows and rows of bookshelves. I could see the fireplace already, surrounded by gorgeous white marble, a cushion for seating placed just in front of it. "Is the fireplace open?" she asked.

"Yes." Its cast iron door hung open with a fiercely burning fire inside.

"I want you to close it."

I leaned forward and reached for the door of the fireplace. Though the fire was raging, the door was not hot to the touch. I pulled the handle, shut the door, and locked the handle down. It was closed.

"You will see beneath the fireplace, a lock with a key made of cast iron," Tilda said. I saw the lock. "I want you to put that lock onto the fireplace doors, and lock them closed." I lifted the lock off the ground, surprised at its weight, and began to weave it through the notches in the doors. "As you close this lock, I want you to know that by doing this, you are locking off access to your mind from anyone else." The lock was now through the notches about to be pushed closed. "You are safeguarding your thoughts from those around you, as your thoughts should be only yours to hear." I locked the lock. "Now place the key in your pocket. In doing this you know that you hold the key to your mind, and who is allowed inside of it." I placed the key in my pocket. "Now turn around, head back up the stairs, and open your eyes."

I lingered in the library for just a moment longer. It was beautiful. The golden chandelier that hung from the glass ceiling flickered in candlelight. Part of me wanted to stay here forever and read every book. I knew that wasn't an option, but I let the idea of it fill my mind with joy. Each step on the rugs back to the staircase felt plush and soft. For some reason, before exiting the library I said "I love you" to the open space. I then ascended the stairs. opening my eyes back to the reality of the courtyard with Tilda halfway up.

I felt lighter than air.

* * *

"Tilda, where are you from?" I asked as Tilda tended to her garden around the meditation area. I don't think I had ever been so relaxed as I was after completing that last round. I laid in the grass and watched the clouds float by.

"That depends on who you're asking," she giggled. "Do you mean the physical being you see in front of you, Tilda? Or do you mean the soul that powers this body, Tilda?"

I thought about it. "Yes." I couldn't decide which answer I wanted first.

"Well, Tilda ME Tilda, is from Scotland. I was born in Edinburgh three hundred years ago."

"Three hundred years ago?!" I shot up from lying in the grass with great surprise.

"Yes," Tilda giggled. "I was the first soul of the ten Daemon souls sent to Earth by Ayan to arrive."

"Forgive me for saying this, but—"

"I know, I know. I don't look a day over sixty-five." Tilda teased.

"How is that possible?" I asked

"Solving the problem of aging will be one of the first advancements humans will make in their evolutionary journey. It's quite a simple thing to do. You just need to have total control of every cell in your body."

I sat in shock. Was it really so surprising that Tilda could control the aging of her body with everything else she was capable of? I mean, we were sitting in a higher dimension after all. That alone was hard to wrap my brain around. This realization made me feel discouraged about my ability to grasp onto the knowledge that I needed to have for the journey ahead. Tilda could see it on my face.

"You don't understand now, and you won't understand when I tell you this," Tilda started as she sat down next to me. "But you already know all of these secrets. You just forgot them the moment you were born into this physical body. But that doesn't mean you won't ever be able to remember." She now rubbed her hand across my back to comfort me. "Don't feel discouraged. Feel excited about the things that you will remember over time. It took me the first sixty years of my life before I finally remembered everything."

"Is that how long it will take me?" I asked.

"Not at all," she assured me. "I didn't even get a start until my sixtieth birthday. You haven't even turned twenty-one yet. Something tells me that you'll remember everything in no time. So it's better that you start preparing yourself for that moment, rather than assuming you won't. Understand?"

"I understand," I said. I tried to shake off the doubt and dismay that I was feeling. I could only trust Tilda, and I had no reason not to. I believed that she knew the truth about who I was, and why I was here. I resided within myself to continue optimistically. Because going back to anything before this moment seemed like a nightmare.

* * *

The day flew by. Tilda told me to enjoy the peace that I felt after the meditation as long as I could, so I spent the rest of the day relaxing in the sun of the courtyard behind the cottage. I was so relaxed that I dozed off for a couple of hours. Normally, falling asleep in the midsummer sun would be unbearable for me and my skin would surely burn and blister. But for some reason, the temperature was perfect for a nap and my skin didn't burn at all. Just another interesting thing about this higher dimension that I had stepped into.

Dinner was about to be served now, and Nick sat across from me at the massive dining room table while Tilda finished in the kitchen. "So, what did you learn today?" he asked me.

Wouldn't you like to know, I thought. After a few moments, I realized Nick hadn't replied. *Oh shit!* My thought continued, *You can't hear what I'm thinking!* I let another moment pass, and nothing on Nick's face indicated that he could hear my thoughts. *Nah nah boo boo Nick's a big old asshole!* Tilda and I immediately burst out into laughter.

"That." I said to him mockingly. He couldn't hear my thoughts anymore. "*This is gonna be GREAT*," I told myself.

"I thought it was quiet in here," Nick teased. He looked almost...proud?

* * *

After dinner, I accidentally snuck up on Nick and Tilda having a conversation at the dining room table. I had gone to my room right after to read a book I had borrowed from Tilda's library, *Concessions of the Dome*, which outlined the details of the Hollow Earth. That's right, according to this book (and Tilda), the legend was true. Earth was hollow and contained an entire civilization inside. A city called Agartha was apparently the capital. I had just started reading it when I needed to use the restroom. But hearing Tilda and Nick's voices through the hallway, I paused to listen.

"The man who attacked Kaylee was asking where *he* was," I heard Nick say.

"And you think they meant Cameron?" Tilda asked.

"I don't see who else they could be looking for."

"I just don't understand why humans on Earth are after him," Tilda said. Her voice sounded genuinely concerned.

"It must be a separate issue entirel," Nick said. "They can't have any knowledge of what's going on in space right now. I spent a few days when I first arrived here listening to the thoughts of some higher-ups in the American government. Nothing about the coming war. Nothing about him."

"There must be someone else searching for him., Tilda said. "But who? Is it possible that the Tahn know we've come here to fight?"

"I don't think so," Nick countered. "Even if they did, they wouldn't communicate with any humans about it. The Tahn don't exactly fear anything, and it would be beneath them to have humans do their bidding for them. It's possible he's been discovered through use of his power. He hasn't exactly been subtle with it." That comment stung. I knew what Nick meant, but it wasn't as though I had ever purposefully used my power before. Would he prefer I didn't stop a massive jumbo jet from killing hundreds of innocent people?

"You think they would want to harness it?" she asked.

"Can they?" he asked back.

"Whether they can or not, I'm not sure that would stop them from trying." Tilda knew the human race all too well.

"We just need to keep his level of activity to a low enough amount that they don't find him."

"Did Kaylee say anything to you about the man?" Tilda asked.

"We didn't have time to discuss anything. She ran off just minutes after the attack." Nick told her.

"And what about the Tahn? Where are they?" Tilda asked earnestly. Thoughts of the bug-like sentients came to my mind.

"They have just taken Tiepe. No survivors. Three billion souls lost." Nick's voice carried a tone of regret.

"There's only two unprotected planets left now," Tilda sighed.

"They will be here within a year," he told her.

"Poor Tiepe…"

"Let's hope the *great* Ayan's plan to save Earth instead was the right one." Nick sounded almost sarcastic.

"The only plan." Tilda sounded firm with him. "Ayan did what needed to be done for the Daemon."

"I pray the cost doesn't outweigh the profit." I could hear a chair scooting away from the table. I tiptoed as quietly as possible back to my room so they wouldn't know I had been listening. I closed my door silently behind me and crashed onto the bed.

I looked at the book in my hand, half wanting to read it, but half knowing that wasn't possible with as much as my mind was racing. It was becoming more and more real to me, that my life was in danger. People were after me, and we didn't even know who. Alien bugs were coming for the whole planet. And three billion people had just died on a planet called Tiepe. I wondered what Tiepe was like. Did the people know the Tahn were coming? Did they stand a fighting chance? How did the Tahn destroy the entire planet? Why had Ayan chosen to save Earth and not Tiepe? What would the Tahn do when they arrived here? More importantly, what would I do to help stop them?

CHAPTER 10

ON MY SECOND morning with Tilda, she had taken me on another meditation journey to further get control of my mind. This time though, instead of locking my thoughts out from other people, which I had to do again first (and every day), she taught me how to resist the thoughts of others if necessary. The metaphor of this meditation was to change the frequency of a radio that was playing in the basement on my mind. Not to tune it to any specific channel, but to gain the knowledge that I could control the dials at all. Tilda assured me that now I would be able to pick and choose which thoughts from people I wanted to hear. Or, that I'd be able to tune them out entirely if I chose to, as long as I regularly practiced meditation.

Part of me was thrilled to give this a shot next time I was near people. Never in my life was I able to be around others without being bombarded by their thoughts. But the other half of me was so immensely frustrated with myself that I hadn't learned this earlier. For twenty years I had been living with this unpleasant way of life and all the while the keys to "tune the frequency" were inside my own mind. I had resolved to try and not be so hard on myself, knowing there was nothing I could do to change the past. But the negative thoughts kept itching at the back of my mind.

Tilda was muddling around in her garden after the meditation journey while I sat in the grass next to her pondering these things. My attention then turned to the conversation I had eavesdropped in on the night before.

"Tilda..." I started as she was watering a section of flowers.

"Yes, dear?" she replied, sweetly as ever.

"What is the *plan*?" I tried to ask in a way that didn't convey I had been listening in on their conversation the night before.

"Which plan, dear?" Tilda asked.

"How are we going to win a fight against the Tahn?" I asked bluntly.

"Ah...That plan," she said with a sigh. "It's still a little early on in your awakening to discuss that."

I hated being told that I wasn't ready for more information, and this time was no different. I was grateful for the fact that Tilda couldn't hear my thoughts of frustration. "Please," I said earnestly, "I can handle it."

Tilda put down her watering can and looked at me with a serious expression. She made her way over to me slowly. "You're right," she said. "You can handle it. I can't baby you along forever." She then sat next to me in the grass. "There were two plans. The ideal solution would have been to gain the help of 'The Collective.'"

"The Collective?" I clarified.

"Yes. The Collective is an interstellar group of societies that have come together to form a sort of galactic government. At least that's how they would be defined in human terms," she explained. "Once you join The Collective, you have the resources of the entire group at your disposal, within reason."

"So The Collective could help us fight the Tahn?" I asked.

"Theoretically, yes they could. However, humans would have to join The Collective in order to receive that aid."

"So why don't we join?" I was confused.

"It's not that simple unfortunately." Tilda looked down at the grass. "In order for any society to join The Collective, the specific species must reach the ability to do so themselves. Humans don't know about The Collective yet, nor have they even broken the tip of the iceberg when it comes to space travel. Even if we 'borrowed' technology from another species to get a few humans to meet with The Collective, they would be given a test that they would surely fail. The test is quite easy to pass if your species engineered technology to get to The Collective on their own, and impossible to pass if they cheated their way there. It would be obvious immediately that humans weren't prepared to join their ranks."

"But surely they would care about the destruction of our planet?" I pleaded.

"Care? Perhaps…but the long-standing role of The Collective in the Universe is not to 'help' just any civilization. Each individual species has to prove themselves as viable individually. To help just any civilization anytime they needed it would allow that civilization to advance further than they are naturally able to, which would create chaos in the Universe. They must pass all of The Great Filters along their evolutionary path on their own."

"Great Filters?" I asked.

"Throughout the evolutionary process, every intelligent species will come to incredible milestones. Some of those milestones are rather dangerous. Humans have already passed the filter of nuclear fusion, a technology with the power to destroy the entire human race if handled improperly. Even then, humans may have passed the original test of nuclear technology, but the threat of mutual destruction still looms over us today. Nuclear fusion is the first of *many* filters humans will have to face.

"The Collective will not welcome or aid any civilization that hasn't passed their Great Filters on their own. Because the beauty and devastation that is evolution weeds out those worthy of being part of an intergalactic society. Humans haven't advanced enough and are still quite volatile and dangerous to be deserving of the attention of highly evolved physical beings."

I sat with this new knowledge for a moment. I understood everything Tilda was saying. Who are we humans to deserve the help of super-advanced species from throughout the Universe? As a whole, humans are selfish, greedy, and destructive. Nick said last night that the Tahn would be here within a year. There was no chance of getting the human race up to speed on technology within that time frame. As of now, most funded science had a weaponizing or financial purpose. If there was no way for someone to make a profit off the research, the science wouldn't be funded. There was a small batch of advancement that was for the good of all people. I reminded myself of Prince Amjad and the many projects he was involved in that seemed to have no ulterior motive. I knew that wasn't enough though.

"The Collective easily has the power to stop the Tahn. In fact, when the Tahn made a move towards destroying Valnor, The Collective immediately put a stop to that," Tilda said.

"Valnor? Where Nick came from?" I asked.

"One and the same," Tilda answered. "One of the first and few man-inhabiting planets that has joined the great allegiance."

"So the Tahn can just go around destroying planets that haven't joined without repercussion? That doesn't seem like a very evolved viewpoint of things. I understand that species can't join without making their own progress but surely there must be something against destroying species entirely before they get the chance?" I said. Emotion seemed to overcome me now.

"They would have consequences," Tilda replied. "But the consequences of destroying a civilization outside The Collective is like a slap on the wrist for members of The Collective. The Tahn, as well as most of the insect races, never bother to be part of such an organization. And because they are not part of it, they are not beholden to its rules. The Collective won't start an all-out war with the Tahn over their disagreements either, as it's not a guarantee that they would win. The Tahn believe instinctually that they are more advanced than The Collective could ever be. Most of the time, creatures like the Tahn won't even communicate with other species. The only reason Valnor was saved was because a Collective force, that was quite a bit larger than the Tahns, was waiting for them upon their entry to the solar system."

"They didn't do anything to Valnor?"

"Nope," she said flatly. "They simply turned around and headed for their next target. Valnor is one of only four planets where beings filled with Daemon souls are safe in the physical dimension. For now at least."

"So...if there's no hope of The Collective helping us, then how is that one of the plans?" I asked.

"That's why I said it *was* one of the plans. I assume that a few of the ten Daemon souls that came to Earth are here with the intention of advancing humanity as quickly as they could. But time seems to be running out for that option to have a chance. I haven't seen any significant advancements that would say otherwise," she said somberly.

So there was no hope of getting humanity to be a part of The Collective, and equally as little hope of getting The Collective to care. "What is the other option?" I asked hopefully.

Tilda sighed as she looked up at the sky. She didn't say anything for a moment, and then, "Fight."

That much was obvious to me. "Yes, but how?" I asked.

"The truth is, Cameron, I don't know."

Her comment made my stomach sink and my mind whirl off into a million mile an hour panic. "So there is no plan?"

"I was the first of the ten souls to come to Earth when the planning had begun. I was sent here to scout Earth and keep tabs on humanity until the rest of the souls arrived."

"Surely the other souls must have kept you up to date?" I asked.

"It would be far too risky to disclose such a plan unnecessarily. The information could get into the wrong hands."

"So who does know?" I asked.

"Ayan is the only one who knows the full plan. The rest of us just have to be ready to play our part when it is revealed to us."

I didn't have any follow-up questions and Tilda seemed to know it because she returned to her afternoon gardening. Once again I was left with more questions than answers. Half of me wanted to know more about The Collective and the amazing societies that formed it. Ever since the confirmation that life existed outside of Earth, my mind speculated about the different species out there. But the other half of me was terrified trying to figure out what my part to play would be in this war.

After a few moments of contemplation, I had one more question to ask Tilda. "Has anyone ever defeated the Tahn before?"

Tilda didn't even turn towards me from her plant watering to say, "No."

* * *

I lay in bed after finishing the book on Agartha, the city at the center of the Earth. I had finished the whole book in just two nights, and now I contemplated whether or not I should grab another gem from Tilda's library. I knew that I needed to get some sleep because Tilda and Nick said we would be getting up at dawn the next morning to continue my practice. At the same time, I knew there was no chance I would be falling asleep anytime soon. My mind ran wild with all the different situations I had been through in the past few days. From that moment of first seeing Nick on the train, up to my meditation with Tilda today. I strained to grasp any sort of reasoning I could for everything to no avail.

I grabbed my cellphone which hadn't moved from the spot underneath my bed since I put it there on my first night here. After turning it back on, I was surprised to see that it actually had a small signal of service here in this higher dimension of the Pennsylvania forest. I thought if the dimensional difference didn't affect the reception, the distance from civilization surely would. I made a mental note to write an email to my service provider to congratulate them on their dimension traveling signal.

I decided to check the news to see what the rest of the world was up to outside of this bubble I now lived in. The majority of the stories were covering the US election that would be happening later this year. Most of those stories I skipped right through. *Who cares about an election when the planet is about to be destroyed*, I thought to myself.

Then I came across an interesting headline: "Space Elevator Construction Rushed Significantly." I had heard about the "Space Elevator" before. Another one of Prince Amjad's ingenious plans to further the human race. The elevator would be a structure so tall that nothing that had been constructed yet could even compare. Reaching into low Earth orbit, the incredible piece of architecture would be used to carry massive payloads into space without the need for rockets or fuel. Prince Amjad said it would change the way humans went into space forever.

According to the article, construction was set to begin this year and be completed within three full years. Typically with such large construction projects, you would expect an impossible amount of delays which would ensure the project to take twice as long. Apparently though, Prince Amjad had prioritized the elevator so immensely that construction was set to be completed in just six months.

Prior to learning about some of the vast secrets of the Universe, you know, like the upcoming war with an alien race, this would have seemed like quite an astonishing advancement for human civilization. It did now too, but there was an air of it being a useless move on our part. I'm not sure why I had such a pessimistic view of the situation, and I told myself that I would resolve to be a bit more optimistic about it. My entire reason for coming to Earth, allegedly, was to save it from destruction. If I didn't start putting some hope behind these thoughts, what good was I going to be when it came time to "play my part" as Tilda said.

The article continued, and there was a video embedded within that was an interview with Prince Amjad about the updates. I tried to play it, but the signal was too weak and the video was quite grainy. So I continued to scroll until I came to a photo of Amjad at the groundbreaking site for the elevator. I paused for a moment to study his handsome features. I wondered what such a strong man like Amjad would do if he knew about the upcoming doom that Earth would face in the next year. I figured that he would probably have a much more hopeful view of the situation than I did. He would fight for this planet until his dying breath. In fact, that's what he was already doing as far as I could see. As I continued to admire him, I thought about how he was just a regular human guy who was accomplishing so much. And then there was me. A stubborn gay guy from America who hadn't done much for the world at all, but was supposed to take part in some massive plan that I still knew very little about. *He's the one who should be here*, I thought. *He would take this much more seriously. He'd be much braver than I am.*

I was about to log out of the browser and try to get some sleep when another headline caught my eye in the "Related Articles" section of the page. "Spontaneous Combustion or Murder in Central Park?" My anxiety began to peak as I read the title. I clicked on it as quickly as I could. I could count several heartbeats for each second that it took for the page to load. The article read as follows:

"Runners in Central Park were greeted with a foul smell on Monday morning that seemed to be coming from the dense area of forest near the southeast section of the park. Investigating police were shocked when they found thousands of pieces of human flesh spread throughout the forested area. Autopsies revealed that the flesh had been decomposing in the park for approximately three days.

"The source of the flesh is still unknown. However, foot-

age from the CCTV system within Central Park which showed three suspects fleeing the scene late on Friday evening has police asking for anyone with knowledge of the suspects to come forward."

Panic surged through my body as I continued to scroll until I arrived at the picture of the "three suspects." Sure enough, a highly pixelated photo of myself, Kaylee, and Nick was posted there for the world to see. It wasn't a good picture, and it would be hard to tell who any of us were unless you knew specifically. Knowing that didn't comfort me at all, and I began to contemplate whether or not I should wake Nick to let him know. Then I began to worry about Kaylee. I had no idea where she had gone, and I began to fear that the police had caught up with her. My fear for Kaylee's life pushed me to make the decision to wake Nick with the news.

The room where Nick stayed was just down the hall from mine and I was out of bed and knocking on his door within a breath. He didn't answer after the first few knocks. Deciding that this information was too important to wait until morning, I pushed his door open without permission. "NICK!" I yell-whispered into the darkness of his room.

He sat up quickly in his bed and looked at me. "What?!" he said in a confused state. I realized immediately that he had been sleeping without a shirt on. The moonlight that came in through the window seemed to perfectly reflect the ridges of his chest and stomach. Though he may have been an alien, his chest was one of human perfection.

I was stunned for a moment by the sight. "Look at what they're saying on the news." I handed him my phone that lit up a small portion of the darkness.

Nick read through the article silently until he came to

the picture of the three of us. He looked back up at me with a face that spelled irritation. "It's nothing," he said.

"Nothing?! They have our picture! They are going to look for us!" I yelled through a whisper, trying not to wake Tilda.

"They won't know it's us. Even if they did, they won't be able to find us here," he said calmly.

"What about Kaylee? They could have already found her!" I wasn't understanding why he wasn't taking on any of this panic that was taking over me.

"She will be fine. Trust me. She would know if something was going to happen to her, and she would avoid it."

"How do you know that?" I asked.

"You'll have to ask her when you see her again," he said.

"*IF* I see her again." My whisper faded.

Nick rubbed his eyes and then looked back at me dead in mine. "You need to calm down," he said firmly. "No one is going to find you OR Kaylee right now. You're safe and so is she."

Something about the earnest way he said this made me want to believe him. But then I realized. "Are you using your soul to talk to mine and convince me of what you want me to believe?" I remembered that he was able to communicate directly that way. Though he said it was always trustworthy and honest, I couldn't be sure that there wasn't a level of manipulation involved.

"No," he said. "I'm talking to you with my mouth. Now can you please go back to sleep?"

"I never was asleep," I said, embarrassed.

Nick stood up out of his bed revealing the boxer briefs he was wearing. I wondered to myself if they had come from another planet themselves, until I saw the Hanes logo around the waistband. He made his way towards me and began pointing at the door. "Go," he said.

I turned around to make my way out of the room thinking that he was going to walk me back to my bed. But as soon as I made it to the hallway and turned around to speak to him about more of my concerns, the door to his room closed in my face. I could hear his footsteps back to his bed where he fell back in. Something about the way he had just pushed me out of his room hurt me in a way I couldn't explain. It wasn't just that he was rude in the way he did, it hurt more than that.

I turned away and headed back towards my room. Before I got into bed though, I did something I hadn't done since before my mother died. I kneeled down on the side of the bed, folded my hands in prayer, and started talking.

"Dear Universe…or God…or soul guides…anyone really." I didn't know how to begin so I tried to include everything possible. "Please keep Kaylee safe. I lost her once, and I can't lose her again." I was infinitely less worried about myself and Nick than I was about Kaylee. Out there all on her with no way of getting in touch with anyone as far as I knew. Tilda didn't have a phone here. Neither did Nick. And Kaylee didn't know my number. "Obviously I want everything else to work out well too," I continued. "But please…just take care of Kaylee right now. Please don't let that be the last time I ever see her." In my mind I envisioned her running down the streets of New York City away from me. Sadness filled my heart. "Amen…Or thanks…"

I reminded myself that three days had passed between the explosion of the man who had attacked Kaylee and the time his remains were found. That was more than enough time for her to get far enough away to not get caught. I don't know if that thought was my own, or if the Universe or God or whoever was sending me comforting thoughts. But I tried to hold onto that idea as I closed my eyes, falling asleep faster than I expected to.

CHAPTER 11

I T HAD BEEN ten days since I first arrived at Tilda's. All the different lessons and meditations were really starting to compound. Ten days felt like a lifetime. Aside from a few pleasant memories of family and friends, the life that I lived before this felt totally separate from who I was now. Moving to New York City on a whim changed my perspective on everything. This change I went through at Tilda's was different though. I felt...happier.

Every day I noticed more and more that I was living in the moment. I wasn't getting lost in thought like I normally would. Overthinking everything until I sent myself into a spiral. In moments when that would happen, I was able to stop, take a breath, listen to the sounds around me, and pull focus back to the present. If I ever did go off on a tangent, it was usually out of concern for the future and what would happen.

Even with all this progress, I still had doubts. Getting my head wrapped around the idea that Nick was an alien was hard enough. Even with those purple eyes that were clearly out of this world. Getting my head wrapped around the idea that my soul was not only an alien, but an ancient spirit that had come to Earth to defend the human race...was something I still didn't identify with personally. I wanted to, but

I just didn't feel special enough to have that kind of responsibility placed on my shoulders. Throughout my entire life, I had experiences that made me feel "special." If you define special as different than everyone else, that is. But none of those experiences made me feel like I was strong or wise enough to be a hero of the human race.

Tilda assured me that with more practice and meditation, I would soon awaken to the reality I had come here for. That didn't make much sense to me either. Was there some sort of light switch that I had left off in the basement of my mind? That once flicked on, I would realize this million-year history that my soul allegedly carried with it? And what would that look like? Would the Cameron that was here and now disappear entirely? Would my soul take over the operation of my body, and I just become a bystander?

Tilda had been working with me daily through different meditative practices. After she was sure that I knew how to keep my mind locked out from those around me and keep their thoughts at bay, she moved onto harnessing the powers that I had unknowingly used throughout my life.

"Every one of the special Daemon souls that came to Earth brought a gift with us into our physical bodies," Tilda started explaining in the courtyard behind her cottage. The majority of my "training" was done here in the grass under the perfect sunlight that cascaded through the air, showcasing the full spectrum of rainbow colors. "You are no different, and it's time we start unlocking those gifts."

"What is your ability?" I asked. "I'm guessing it's that you can stop yourself from aging?"

"Not at all," she giggled. "Even a standard human with an entry-level Daemon soul can learn cell regeneration and total body control. Though it would take an awful lot of discipline that I'm not sure the current human race possesses."

"Well then, what *is* your gift?" I asked.

"All of this." She gestured around her. She could tell by the look on my face that I was confused as to what she meant.

Tilda then reached her right hand up into the sky and pulled it down slowly in a waving circular motion. Something began appearing in the area her hand was swirling around. In a matter of seconds, a red rose hovered there just above her hand. She then grabbed the rose with her left hand and handed it to me. "My gift is the ability to create things in this higher dimension."

The rose in my hand felt as real as any other. As I looked back up to Tilda, she once again gestured around her at the entire property. It was then that I realized, "You created this whole place? The cottage? The meditation area?"

Tilda smiled at me. "Who else would have done it?"

I considered that for a moment. As Tilda and Nick had both told me, this place wouldn't exist to those who didn't take the proper steps to see it. So how then did I suppose Tilda's home existed? How did her kitchen that seemed to be completely modern in every way get installed? Had each delivery person or handyman gone through the proper steps of going through the cleansing river carrying appliances and all? I decided that seemed even less likely than Tilda doing it all herself. I took a look around again, astonished by Tilda's abilities.

"So you really did design that kitchen yourself, huh?" I asked with a joking tone.

"No one could have done better!"

"But is it all real?" I asked.

"It's as real as this dimensional frequency is. If you're asking if that rose could survive outside this dimensional frequency, the answer is complicated."

"I'm listening."

"It takes a certain amount of time for things to manifest from the higher dimension into the physical world. That rose was created with my thoughts. Thoughts create in higher dimensions and eventually manifest into the real world. That's why 'manifestation' is such a growing practice in today's day and age amongst some humans. Creating things with thought or manifesting what you want causes the Universe to conspire in your favor. If someone wants to be wealthy, they imagine themselves surrounded by things and feelings of infinite wealth. Eventually, the Universe will give them that wealth if they do a little work to get there and clear the pathway to make their visions become reality.

"My gift allows me to create anything within this higher dimension from my thoughts. After a certain amount of time, those things will manifest in the physical reality as well."

"So eventually your cottage will exist in the physical world?" I clarified.

"Eventually, yes. In fact, I believe some of the foundation has already begun appearing there. Hard to tell since I never check. That rose in your hands, though, could be taken with you into the physical reality in just a few hours."

I stared at the rose again as I contemplated everything Tilda had just told me. It was as beautiful as any rose could be. The only indication that it wasn't "real" was the stem that appeared to be closed. This rose hadn't been cut from a bush; it had been created out of thin air and thus there was no cut mark. The things I was learning here on a daily basis couldn't compare to anything I had learned in school.

"Is there a limit to what can be created?" My mind ran wild with endless possibilities.

"I haven't found one yet," Tilda smiled.

"And what about the other Daemon souls? What are their powers?" Visions of superheroes came to mind.

"A vast range, no doubt. Some of their abilities I am unaware of myself. You know I haven't met *all* of the ten remaining souls. Eleven if you count Ayan. My knowledge of the different abilities that were brought here is limited to those who I have met," she answered.

Interesting. I had assumed up until now that Tilda knew all of the souls. "Who have you met?"

"Well let's see." Tilda stood up from her seat on the grass as if to stretch her body which had been sitting too long. "There's me." She lifted one finger in the air. "Nick." Two fingers now.

"What is Nick's power?" I interrupted.

"Didn't he tell you? He can communicate with the souls of physical beings directly with his own soul."

He had told me, but I wanted to hear Tilda confirm that he hadn't lied to me. I still didn't trust him for some reason. "Oh yeah. Who else?"

"Kaylee, of course."

Kaylee! I thought excitedly. I'm not sure why up until now I hadn't made the full connection that Kaylee was one of the Daemon souls herself. It should have been blatantly obvious the minute Tilda explained the souls to me, but for some reason, I hadn't grasped the entire situation. "What is her power?!" I asked excitedly.

"I'm going to leave that for her to tell you," Tilda said with a smile.

"I'm going to see her again?" I asked.

"Well of course you are!" Tilda laughed at that, which reassured me. To Tilda, it seemed so obvious that Kaylee and I would be reunited. I took comfort in that, and my anxiety that had been building since seeing our picture slammed all over the internet lessened. If Kaylee had a power, she would be that much safer.

"Then there's Barry." Tilda held up a fourth finger without noticing my own inner turmoil dissolving.

"Barry?" I was confused.

"He must not have introduced himself when you met." I tried to think about who Tilda was talking about. No men came to mind that had made a significant impact on my awareness besides Nick. "Surely you remember getting the ticket to the play?"

Then it hit me all at once. The man who had disappeared after giving me a free ticket to *Chicago* that day when I found Kaylee. *I couldn't hear his thoughts*, I reminded myself. "So that's Barry…" I said out loud. I was shocked that I had forgotten that interaction so quickly. Remembering back to the day, it was no surprise that he didn't leave a huge mark on me because of all the other insanity I witnessed that day. If it had been only that one interaction with him next to the memorial, I surely would have remembered more. "How did you know he gave me the ticket?"

"I told him to," Tilda said matter-of-factly.

I tried to decipher what she meant by that. But Tilda interrupted my thought process before I could reply. "All of the elements were in place that day to ensure you would run into Kaylee. We just had to give you a little nudge to *pay attention*." The memory of those last two words sent a shiver down my spine. That entire day of "paying attention" had been spent in fear. I constantly looked over my shoulder and overanalyzed everything. The thought of Nick's words reverberating in my mind for that entire day was not a pleasant memory at all. But, it had led me here, and for that I was grateful.

"So you know Barry…" My speech drifted off with my contemplation.

"Know him? He's been my life partner for over 200 years!" she exclaimed.

"Life partner?!"

"You know, boyfriend, lover, soulmate…whatever you kids are calling it these days."

Partially offended with myself over the shock that Tilda had a boyfriend, I quickly changed my tone for my response. "That's amazing!"

Tilda could tell I was overcompensating. "I wouldn't say it's 'amazing.' It just is what it is."

"Well where is Barry now? Why isn't he here with you?" I asked.

"Barry and I spent plenty of time together over the last 200 years. Heck, we spent even more time together before coming to Earth. Now that the main event is here, we both have our separate parts to play." Tilda sat back down beside me. "He's out in the world trying to find more of the souls to awaken now. I stay here and train the souls he sends to me."

"Don't you miss him?"

"Every day," she said. I could tell that she meant it.

"What is his power?" I asked.

"Simply put, he can heal people." Tilda studied my reaction, which spelled confusion. "He can control energetic frequencies that are used to manipulate organic matter."

"What types of things can he heal?" I wondered.

"I've only seen him heal simple flesh wounds myself.

Once when I was out gardening just there," Tilda motioned towards the flowery area of her courtyard, "I pricked my hand on a thorn. It wasn't too bad on its own but the way I pulled away after the initial prick caused a gash that ran the length of my hand." She mimed the gash that went from the base of her fingers down her hand nearly hitting her wrist. "Within a matter of seconds, Barry had my hand sealed back up as though nothing happened. Not even a scar remains.

"Theoretically though, he can heal much larger issues. Cancerous cells, virus-ridden bodies, things like that," she concluded.

"That must be the strongest power of them all," I thought aloud.

"Hardly." She smiled at me. "That's enough talk for now. It's time to work on *your* powers, Cameron." Tilda rose next to me and reached out her hand as if to offer an aid in standing up. I took her hand even though I didn't need it.

"What are my powers exactly?" If my ability to read minds wasn't a power, then I guessed it had something to do with the ability to blow people up or stop a jumbo jet from killing hundreds of people. But I didn't know how to quantify that power into words.

"What do you think your powers are?"

"Telekinesis?" That was the best guess I had put together to define my abilities.

"It's not telekinesis you seek, my dear." Tilda told me. "Telekinesis is a power that any human *can* possess. Bending spoons in the physical reality is nothing more than a show of the power of the mind. You could do it if you wanted to, I'm sure. But your ability comes from your soul."

Tilda spent the rest of the day trying to get me to lift small river rocks, sway the branches of the trees, and other small movements using the power of my soul. None of them worked, and I became more and more frustrated. I couldn't understand how I had been able to stop that plane and save Kaylee's life when I needed to, but not in the moments that I wanted to. I left the day's training feeling defeated, questioning more than ever if Tilda and Nick had the right person. If I truly was one of the Daemon souls that came to Earth to save humanity.

"Your soul has protected you and those you care about most for your entire life," Tilda had explained after my multitude of failures. "It has acted on your behalf in moments that you needed it. Altering the physical reality around you through a higher dimension. All you need to do is connect with your soul so that you can become one."

All I need to do, I thought sarcastically, thankful that Tilda could no longer hear my thoughts.

* * *

I thought about what she said as I laid in bed. I pictured my soul jumping out of my body, hands thrown in the air like a superhero, stopping the plane from wrecking into the ground that day at the air show. I tried to imagine how I could have... *helped* my soul at that moment. Would it be a conversation between myself and him? Or them? I remembered Nick explaining that souls were free of gender. Then I began to trail off into a thought pattern of how higher dimension beings communicated. Was it even with language? I caught myself trying to fantasize about communication without pronouns. Knowing that I had gone off track, I focused my attention on the picture of my mother on the dresser next to me. Tilda had brought it to me on my second night here. "I've held onto it for you," she told me.

The picture was framed with a brass wire that looped around it in a beautiful weaving design. In the photo, a black and white version of my mother smiled wearing a cowboy hat. She looked so happy, even if it was just a pose for a photographer. *Come here*, I asked the picture in my mind. It didn't move.

I took a deep breath. Cleared my mind. Still staring at the picture. *Dear… soul? If you're listening right now, which you probably are because you are a part of me*, I thought into the air. The words "a part of me" lingered in my mind. *Can you please bring me that picture?* That felt wrong as soon as I thought about it. I knew that wasn't the right direction. I was separating myself from my soul, and that wasn't the goal.

I sat up in bed and took another deep breath. This time, I tried to imagine the light of my soul within my chest. Just like how I could now identify each chakra along my spine and above my head through meditation, I knew I should be able to see the light of my soul. A gold light illuminated itself within that immediately reminded me of the Daemon souls I had seen. *Is that you?* I asked.

"*Yes.*" A reply came into my clear mind.

How do we…connect? I stumbled for the right word to use.

"*We are connected.*" Hearing thoughts that came from somewhere inside my own mind that I had not created freaked me out a bit, but I calmed myself and took another deep breath.

We are connected…But what does that mean?

"*Know it,*" came the reply.

A thought came to my mind of all those beings I had seen when Tilda told me the Greatest Story in Earth's History. How their souls were a part of them. Just like their hands, their feet, their brains, and their hearts. It made understanding a little easier. My soul was a part of me? Not different or separate. Not some spirit that was only there from time to time. My soul had been with me since the day I was born. So, my soul was me? And I'm just a version of my soul being expressed into this body?

"*Yes.*" Came a strong thought into my mind.

The lightbulb had been switched.

I lifted up my hands to see the gold light flowing like a river through the tips of my fingers and up my arms. Constantly flowing. I looked again at the picture on the dresser. This time, not visualizing its movement with my mind's eye. Instead, I just knew that my soul had the power to do it. With this new understanding, I reached the golden light of my soul, which I now controlled, over to the picture on the dresser, and it lifted into the air. It hovered there in space for a moment before dropping back down gently. I was worried it had cracked but fought the desire to get up and check. Instead, I continued, this time pulling the picture with the golden light of my soul into my hand.

The light stretched out from my arm towards the picture. Lifting it up, and bringing it towards my body. *My soul is an extension of me*, I thought. At least that's what it sure seemed like. The picture floated along the golden river of light directly into my hand. The golden light subsided from my view.

What is your name? I asked hopefully, staring at the beautiful image in my grasp.

"*Ayan.*"

* * *

The next morning I awoke to the familiar sounds of birds

chirping in the wilderness outside the cottage. I had no recollection of falling asleep last night. I remembered hearing
the name "Ayan" and that's it. As I remembered this mental
conversation, I had a feeling that my soul had something to
do with my immediate departure to dreamland. *Too much
for one night?* I wondered.

I hopped out of bed and ran outside. My bare feet slap-
ping the stone that leads to the wooden path through the
wild grass. I stopped in the center of the wooden path and
saw the golden light radiating through my arms. I pressed
the light out over both sides of the wild grass and brushed
across it gently. Causing a wave in the green sea. I smiled the
biggest smile I think I ever had.

I ran past the meditation area to the river where the
rocks that had previously teased me with their inability
to move. Reaching the golden light out underneath them,
I raised one large rock with each arm of light. And then I
thought, *It can't just be two arms.* And with that, the light
split into six different bands, grabbing four more rocks from
the river and holding them up. I lifted them up high above
my head and the water that coated them rained down on
me. Refreshing, cool, and blissful. My smile could be seen
for miles. I couldn't believe that I had struggled for this long
with my connection to my soul. It was so simple. It was there.
It was part of me.

"Oh my!" I heard Tilda's voice behind me. I turned to
look at her when suddenly the rocks came crashing down
all around me. One just a few inches from where I had been
standing in front of me which caused us both to laugh.
"You've done it!"

"Tilda!" I yelled as I ran towards her. "I AM AYAN!" A
small part of my brain was concerned with the ease at which

I made that statement. No fear, no worry about what that meant of the future. Just pure excitement that I had connect-ed with my soul.

Tilda pursed her lips as a tear ran down her right cheek. It glimmered in the morning light. "Of course you are," she whispered.

CHAPTER 12

TILDA HAD LEFT me in the courtyard almost hysterically. She needed to pray and give thanks, she told me. Though I was concerned for a moment, I could feel her genuine elation at my revelation. I walked back towards the house to get something to eat. Moving things with your soul could be physically taxing, apparently! I brushed the golden light over the top of the wild grass again as I walked along the old wooden pathway back into the cottage.

Nick stood in the kitchen, ignoring me when I walked in the back door. "Hey!" I yelled, a little loudly.

"Morning," he said, still not making eye contact. I felt like he had been avoiding me after the night that I woke him up in distress about Kaylee. He had always been short with me, but I felt like I had reached a new level of annoyance with him.

"I thought you didn't like coffee." I gestured towards the steaming mug on the counter.

"Rough night of sleep," he said. His eyes finally met mine. Oh, those purple eyes…

"Well, guess what?" I said, taking a seat at the stool on the other side of the kitchen bar from where he stood.

"Oh, I think I know this one," he said, turning towards me. "Chicken butt?"

I all but lost my composure entirely. But instead of laughing at him like I wanted to, I chose to make a sad face. "That's literally the cutest thing you've ever said." *Damnit*, I thought. *That one was supposed to stay in your head.*

"Is that not how the joke goes?" he asked sincerely. "I've heard it on television multiple times." I was glad he had chosen to ignore my comment.

"It is a joke, and you did get it right. Only I wasn't joking. I was really trying to get you to guess something."

"I'd rather not," he said.

"You really love to pick and choose when you get to play games with people, don't you?" He always had a way of grinding my gears.

"It's a talent." The jokes were back.

"I'm Ayan." I said, completely changing the conversation before it got so bad I wouldn't want to tell him anymore.

He stopped himself from taking a sip of his coffee, and locked his eyes on me. He didn't say a word for a few moments. I wished so badly that I could hear whatever he was thinking right now inside his head. It surely didn't look like a *good* thought process. His face looked… disappointed?

"What else do you know?" he asked, casually returning to sip his coffee.

"I can do this." I tilted the cup of coffee with the golden light of my soul. A little of it dumped onto his shirt. I immediately felt bad for doing it. He reacted swiftly and looked at me with…disgust? Really hard to tell here but definitely not a positive reaction. "I'm so sorry," I said hastily. "I shouldn't have done that."

"What else?" So seriously he asked this question.

"I can do it with rocks too?" I said, trying to lighten the tone.

Tilda came crashing in through the back door suddenly, drunk with happiness. "It's time to go," Nick said, causing Tilda to stop dead in her tracks with confusion. She looked back and forth between Nick and I to try and understand what was happening.

"Go where?" I asked sharply

"It's not time yet, Nick," Tilda said, looking at him. "He's just getting a grip on all of this now! If you leave now, he won't…he just doesn't know enough yet."

Know enough? What else don't I know?

"He knows plenty," Nick said firmly as he stared at me. My happy mood from the morning suddenly shot in the face.

"Nick," Tilda said even firmer. "I'd like to talk to you outside for a moment." She pointed to the back door. Nick didn't have a fighting chance at arguing with her. I know that I sure wouldn't. With that, they both vanished out the back door.

* * *

"Don't mind him," Tilda said as she led me out the back door of the cottage. I had no idea where Nick had gone after their conversation which seemed pretty tense. But judging by Tilda's response to me asking where he had gone, my assumption of the tension was correct. She seemed grumpy in a way that I had never seen before, and that I never considered possible for someone as delightful as Tilda.

I followed her into the courtyard out of the house, peeking around to see if Nick was still there. But there was no sight of him. Tilda informed me upon her return to the house that my training would continue today, so we made our way back to the usual grass spot just beyond the wooden walkway through the field of wild grass on each side.

"Earth is alive," Tilda began with a tone of frustration that I hadn't experienced from her before.

"Should we start with meditation?" I tried to convey a kindness in the way I asked so as to not offend her.

"No," she said firmly, causing me to recoil a bit. She must have noticed because she then took a deep breath, then another, and said, "In the situation that we are all going to be put into in the coming months, there won't always be time to meditate. It is very important to meditate every single day if you can. For today though, let's see what you can learn without your usual grounding exercise, because you won't always have that chance."

"Okay," I said. I was fine with continuing on without meditating. I had suggested it for her sake. I hadn't known Tilda long, but she didn't seem like someone who held onto tension very often in her life. Seeing her this way hurt me, because I felt like it was my fault. Should I not have told Nick about my discovery last night? Was he not supposed to know? Now my mind was whirling with guilt.

"Keep up and pay attention." Tilda headed off towards the forest at a faster rate than I guessed her small frame could manage. She dived into the forest as she started the lesson again. "The Earth is alive. She lives and breathes just like you and I."

"She?" I clarified as I stumbled through the woods, not making nearly as effortless a journey as Tilda was.

"The physical dimension calls for a duality of gender for creation. Some planets throughout the Universe hold a male energy. Mars for example, is a male energy planet within our own solar system. But Earth carries with her a strong female energy." Tilda was moving so quickly that I could no longer see the cottage behind us, only forest ahead and behind.

"That's why humans call her 'mother nature.' They've picked up on the feminine energy that resides within her." I tried to process the information she was giving me while keeping up with her. A tall order that I wasn't doing well with.

"Earth has a soul of her own," she continued. "Not a soul like the Daemon, the Reotion, or the Andar. The souls that fill planets are called the 'Plutong.' They are even more ancient than the Hyamin. But like their physical counterparts, the Plutong are large and slow moving ethereal bodies. In the higher dimensions, the Plutong souls are so large that smaller souls can exist within them. Any soul that inhabits the space of a Plutong soul shares their knowledge with the Plutong soul, and is gifted the knowledge of the Plutong as well."

"Let me get this straight." I said more for actual clarity than disbelief. "Planets have their own souls?"

"Correct." Tilda darted under a bush that I had to find an entirely different way to go around. Our height difference definitely affected how rapidly we were able to move through the brush.

"The souls that inhabit planets are called the Plutong?"

"Exactly."

"And the Plutong, as they exist in the higher dimension, are much larger and slower moving than the average soul."

"You got it." She must have been a full ten feet ahead of me now. I raced forward to catch up with her before my final clarifying question.

"And in the higher dimension, other souls can live and reside within the Plutong souls, just like how humans live on Earth." I was just behind her now, not having to shout that question, but having to catch my breath between every few words.

Tilda stopped dead in her tracks, looked all around her, and turned to me to answer, "Precisely."

I waited for Tilda to instruct me on what to do next. I didn't know why she had led me into the forest or why we had stopped at this point. There didn't seem to be anything obviously significant to me about this place. But then I realized that the summer sun was pelting me with heat in a way that had never happened at Tilda's. The higher dimension area of the cottage was always the perfect warm and balmy temperature, but it was never too hot like this. The way the light hit the air at the cottage caused the eye to see a spectrum of the rainbow hovering wherever you looked. In this place now, the light was nothing more than that, just light.

"We left the higher dimension," I observed aloud.

'That's right." Tilda's calm tone seemed to have returned.

The trees around swayed in the gentle breeze. But they didn't breathe with me anymore. The bushes and moss that scattered the forest floor were a simple color of green. They were lovely, but the colors didn't take your breath away. The ground was just brown in the areas that weren't covered in brush. The gold sparkle of Earth was no longer visible to my naked eye. I had spent such a significant amount of time existing in the higher dimension of this forest that the drastic change was almost sad to witness. Before I had known anything about the higher dimension, I might have thought this forest was beautiful. But now, it felt dull and grim.

"It is still beautiful," Tilda told me.

"You were listening to my thoughts?" I had meditated first thing that morning. I thought for sure that my thoughts were contained to my own mind. Tilda's clear knowledge of what I was thinking caused me to panic slightly because I must have done it wrong.

"You don't need to hear someone's thoughts when their face says all that needs to be said." She was right. I could feel that my face showed a look of disappointment. "This *is* the reality that everyone on Earth lives in. It *is* beautiful in its own right, and you'll need to learn today's lesson here."

My mind began filling with dreadful thoughts the minute that I realized we had left the higher dimension. Thoughts of things, people, and places I hadn't considered much since arriving at Tilda's. In this moment, it felt like the world I had left behind that night when Nick took me out of the city had come crashing back into my mind at a million miles an hour. I couldn't tell if it was the higher dimension protecting me from those thoughts, or if the reality of this world still existing had made me realize what I had been pushing off. Either way, it didn't feel nice.

"Perhaps we *should* do some meditation." Tilda must have noticed the stress that seemed to be overwhelming me now. "Here, let's sit down and get started."

Tilda guided me down into a seat on the forest floor and then sat in front of me with a small space in between us. "Let's start by taking some big deep," she inhaled sharply, "rejuvenating breaths of this air that you haven't interacted with for some time."

Tilda took another deep breath, and I followed shortly after. The air I brought into my lungs felt different than the air in the higher dimensions, if that was possible. It felt... heavier; ever so slightly harder to draw in large breaths. *Has it always been this hard to breathe?* I wondered to myself.

"Now close your eyes..." I did as she told me and continued the deep breaths and after a few of them my heart slowed back down, and the overwhelming sense of anxiety seemed to relax. After ten full and deep breaths, the anxious thoughts and fears were slowly replaced with the reminder of what I had discovered last night. I reminded myself that my soul was Ayan, that I was Ayan. Knowing and realizing this made the concerns of being back in the normal world for the first time seem much smaller. The idea that I had such a negative reaction to being somewhere I had already spent most of my life now made me giggle a little.

"Okay," I said through a smile, my eyes still closed.

"Feeling better?" Tilda asked. I could feel that she was still meditating as well.

"Much," I said with an exhale, so grateful that this process of meditating constantly was really working well for me.

"Keep your eyes closed," she said. "What do you hear?"

I listened for a moment to the world around me. "Birds," I started. "Crows, I think."

"What else?" she pressed.

I took my time to listen beyond the sounds the birds were making. "The leaves on the trees?"

"Good. But what are you really hearing if you can hear the leaves moving?"

"The wind," I said calmly.

"What is the wind saying?" Tilda asked.

I thought for a moment as I continued listening to the wind blowing through the trees. I didn't know exactly what I was looking for. "I don't know…"

"Open your eyes." Tilda still sat in a meditative pose in front of me. Her welcoming green eyes sat above full cheeks that were dazzled with freckles. Her cartoon-like character-istics hadn't dulled a bit in leaving the higher dimension. "Earth is alive. Not only is she living and breathing just like you and me, but she's communicating with us all the time. She uses the elements to act as her voice. She speaks to us through earth, air, water, and fire. Not every blow of the wind has a meaning, but if you never learn to listen, you'll miss the song in every storm."

"How do you know what she's saying?"

"You already know what she's saying. You just have to set aside the idea that you need to 'understand' what she is saying. Anyone can understand her with a calm enough mind. All humans, ourselves included, are a part of Earth. Communication with her is instinctual. Just like the souls in the higher dimensions that existed within a Plutong soul. They could communicate with the Plutong, and the Plutong with them. But they never communicated with words, they communicated through their minds. Close your eyes again, clear your mind, and be willing to receive a response. Tell me what you *hear*."

I closed my eyes and took a couple deep breaths to clear my mind. The wind rushed through the trees once more and the first thought to pop into my mind was that the wind was greeting me, as if saying "Hello." But I thought that was entirely too simple. "I don't know…" I said, defeated.

"What was the first thought that popped into your mind when you were listening?" she asked.

"The word 'hello,'" I said.

"And that's exactly what she said to you." I opened my eyes again to see Tilda smiling. "Communicating with nature works the same way as trusting your intuition. The first thing that comes to mind, that you did not create, is the communication. It may seem a bit simple for the Earth to simply tell you 'hello,' but a welcome greeting to any of the beings that live on her surface is the first natural step of communication for any scenario. Why don't you try and greet her back?"

I closed my eyes again and took a moment to ground

back into my focus. Once I felt that my intention of communication was set in the right place, I thought, *Hello*, to
the world around me. In an instant, a rush of wind that was
entirely stronger than anything that had happened all day,
swirled around me causing my hair to blow in all directions.

"Did you understand that response?" Tilda asked.

"There wasn't a word this time. But I could feel something…"

"And what was that feeling?" she asked.

"Love?" I answered questioningly.

"Precisely."

* * *

The moon hung low and close to Earth. The creatures of the
higher dimension jumped through the forest ahead of me
as I dipped my feet into the cleansing river. Tilda spent the
rest of the day teaching me about connecting with Earth.
Having me expose myself *thoughtfully* to the different elements. She said I needed to learn to listen to what they had
to say. She told me that Earth would communicate with me
via whichever element most available to her, so I needed to
be able to understand each one. Water was the only element
we hadn't worked with today, and I told Tilda I would take
some time alone to try it on my own after dinner, hoping the
Earth would have some answers to some of my remaining
questions about everything.

It made sense, and somehow since discovering that I was
Ayan, everything made sense. I still had no recollection of
my existence before this life as Cameron. I had no idea if I
would ever remember life as Ayan the soul. But each idea
that I was learning now seemed to be easier for me to understand. Less of a lesson, and more a reminder of something I

already knew deep down inside. I felt more in control of my mind than ever before. As the water in the river seemed to rush over my feet, it was almost as if the water was...proud of me? *The water of this stream can't possibly have an emotional attachment to my progress*, I thought. The water rushed just a bit faster and higher, reaching past my ankles for a moment. *Okay...I guess it can.*

The Earth is...proud of me? I wondered. I think that had to be the weirdest thing I had learned yet. Surely Earth has better things to do than toot my horn?

My attention was pulled away suddenly when a commotion in the bushes behind me caused me to turn around. I wasn't worried, my gut was calm. Another revelation of the training. "Your intuition will never steer you wrong. If something is bad, you will know inside before your physical senses tell you. You just have to learn to trust it," Tilda told me. The cause of the noise turned out to be Nick. I hadn't seen him since this morning when Tilda dragged him away after telling me that we needed to leave. Quite angrily, I might add.

"Mind if I sit?" he asked, standing over me.

"Go ahead," I said, shifting my focus from him back to the water.

As Nick sat down and removed his shoes, I thought about my opinion of him. All jokes of me trying to convince myself otherwise aside, he was handsome. Not handsome in the way that a supermodel or lead actor of a soap opera would be. Handsome in the way that he could be the best looking guy at the mechanic shop, or some other blue collar workplace. Rough around the edges, with the most symmetrical facial features a man could possibly have. And although Nick was handsome, I still didn't trust him completely. I couldn't put my finger on it, but the way I felt about Tilda since meeting her was completely different from how I felt about Nick. The interaction this morning pushed my distrust for him even further. His anger seemed to come out of nowhere because of a revelation I previously assumed he would be happy about.

"Water telling you anything special?" he asked as he dipped his feet into the water to the left of my own.

"I think so…" I said. I wondered if he knew what Tilda had taught me today. "Hard to be sure."

"The trick with nature," he explained, "is to clear your mind. Whatever the first thought that pops into your head that you didn't create is usually the answer." Tilda had already told me that, and I didn't feel like poking the bear from this morning. He continued, "Most people never get to communicate with their planet. Because they never learn to separate their own thoughts from the thoughts of others or from the Universe. You got a head start being able to hear everyone else's thoughts. You're lucky. Trust yourself."

I knew what he meant. The average person on Earth doesn't get to experience the thoughts of everyone around them. They don't know the difference between their own thoughts versus thoughts from outside their own head and how to interpret them. "Did you get to communicate with your planet? Before you came here?" I asked.

"Of course," he said. "Valnorians are raised from birth to have a respectful relationship with nature."

"Is there water just like this there?" I asked.

"Just like this," he said, kicking a small splash of water in my direction.

Is he flirting? I wondered. "What things are different

about it from Earth then?" I asked, wiping the drops of water from my legs while trying to hide my smile.

"Many things." He looked up to the stars in the sky. "For one, Valnor has a close relationship with its sister planet. For half of the year, you can see her as close as the moon is to Earth. Only it is much farther away and quite a bit larger."

"What is it called?" I asked, genuinely intrigued. I pictured what it would be like to have another planet in view where the moon was.

"Serena," he answered.

"Are there any people on Serena?"

"Yes. An Avian race called the Iwanta. Our two species developed in a similar pattern and time. Around the development of telescopes, they were able to see each other's structures. The knowledge that there was already another race on another planet allowed for rapid advancement for both species."

My mind pictured a world with another planet on the Horizon. Ancient Grecian-era people looking through telescopes to see bird people with telescopes staring right back. The thought made me giggle. Nick looked at me oddly. "Sorry, just a funny thought," I said.

Nick continued, "You laugh, but the Valnorians and Iwanta were trading goods from planet to planet in the period of time that humans had barely figured out the wheel."

Touché, I thought. "I wasn't laughing at that. I just pictured a bird person looking through a telescope at a human person looking through a telescope."

Nick laughed. "I see it now," he said.

"Are we leaving?" I asked him softly.

"Not yet," he said. But he didn't sound as defeated as I expected.

"Why were you so insistent that we should go this morning?" I asked, thinking back to the anger in his voice.

"I was just…frustrated at the moment." It felt like that wasn't what he was thinking, or what he wanted to say. But that's all he could muster. I've heard plenty of thoughts get filtered down immensely before a completely different set of words get spoken. I can see it a mile away.

"Why would you be frustrated?" I asked. "Isn't this what you wanted? For me to discover who I am?"

"Of course. But…you've learned a lot. There's still a lot more to learn. And I don't think you'll be able to learn all of it here. I worry there isn't enough time," he said. That didn't make sense to me. But if I had learned *anything* from communicating with Nick over the past two weeks, it was that he doesn't give out information easily. Either way, I didn't care. I wasn't ready to leave Tilda's. And Nick seemed to be somehow resolute with the idea of staying.

"So, how did the Valnorians get involved with this Earth conflict?" I asked, changing the subject. "What made you come here?"

"They didn't…necessarily," Nick said, smiling at me. "The Valnorians are mostly occupied with Daemon souls. We are a closely distant relative to the human DNA strand. We are also the most spiritually advanced of the remaining human-like species. By being born into a Valnorian life, you're guaranteed a world where you won't forget everything you knew before you came under the physical veil."

"So you are one of the souls that went with Ayan to save the Daemon?" I asked.

Nick paused for a moment before answering, his attention on the moon's reflection in the river. "Yes," he said casually, "but I was sent to Valnor to be born and raised so that I would know my purpose for living a physical existence much more rapidly. My parents raised me to know who I was from an extremely young age. They had consulted with my soul before it entered the life of their unborn child."

"So you were given a head start?" I clarified.

"Someone needed to remain awake. In case the rest of you stayed asleep," he said

I let that thought turn in my mind. *Asleep…is that what I've been this whole time?*

"So we knew each other before this?" I asked, not sure of where the question came from. I hadn't given much thought to my previous existence yet fully knowing I had one. Processing this one was still a confusing nightmare.

Nick didn't answer right away. Which basically gave me an answer. When he finally said, "We did," I began to wonder how we knew each other exactly, and what that would have even looked like. "The main difference between Valnorians and Humans," Nick said, changing the subject, "Is all in the eye color." He turned and looked me in the eyes. Somehow the gorgeous royal purple bounced off the moonlight. "Humans have a wide range of eye colors. All Valnorians share the same purple eyes."

"That's cool but…isn't there a certain lack of diversity in that?"

"I don't make the rules." he joked. "But I will say, seeing beautiful blue eyes for the first time after all these years of only seeing purple was enough to take my breath away."

I looked at Nick. He looked at me. At that moment I realized… *I have blue eyes.*

"How did you get here?" I asked, changing the subject myself now. I was nearly certain he wasn't talking about my eyes, so why bother focusing on it.

"I assume you mean to Earth?" he clarified, looking over his shoulder at me with a small grin. This had to have been one of the best conversations I had ever had with him.

"I actually don't have a sarcastic response for that so… yes," I said.

"I took a portal from Valnor to the nearest exit in Alpha Centauri, and from there I took a starship to Earth." I love how he says it all so nonchalantly. He made it sound like it was akin to hopping on the freeway to head home after work.

"Okay so how do portals function exactly?" I asked, mocking my own stupidity for not knowing the inner workings of the Universe.

"You know, you could just work on your meditation more so you can let go. You already know everything. You just need to unlock it." He didn't mean it rudely. He was right. Every other step of the training with Tilda had been going so well. Since learning that I was Ayan, everything had progressed so well. But at the end of each day during my deep meditation to "let go" and unlock all the secrets my soul had to share with me, I could feel myself holding on to something. Some tiny shred of doubt with the clarity just above my head, but I can't pull myself up to see it. It looks beautiful though.

"Yeah, I could. And I will," I agreed. "I could also just go inside and ask Tilda which book will teach me about Portals and Alpha Centauri." I started to push myself off the ground next to him.

Nick grabbed my shoulder gently and pulled me back down. "Portals don't function in the reality of this dimension. To explain them without you knowing how the higher dimensions work, wouldn't work," he said. I was still focusing on his hand that hadn't left my shoulder. He suddenly realized and pulled away. Not awkwardly though. "That being said, explaining any higher dimensions to beings that can't see them is pretty hard as is. The simplest way to explain it is it's a hack. Distance doesn't exist in much higher dimensions. The beings within those dimensions create portals for lower dimension beings to cross large distances."

"And how long does it take?" I said, still mocking, but more joking.

"Nearly instantaneous," he said. His eyes locked in a gaze with mine.

I dropped my smartass attitude and asked seriously, "So beings like the Daemon put the portals in place?"

"No," he said grinning, "WE Daemon are some of the most powerful beings in the known dimensions. Daemon can technically travel anywhere in physical space-time instantaneously in their ethereal form. But physical beings in the physical dimension have to take portals. Portals are created by beings in dimensions that are not comprehensible by even the Daemon."

"Why didn't you come through a portal to Earth?" I asked.

"Earth doesn't have any portals set up yet. It's still a relatively new planet in the grand scheme of things."

"Thanks," I said.

"For what?"

"For explaining that. Sometimes you can be an asshole." I smiled at him. "I appreciate you actually taking the time to explain that to me, as rudimentary as you might think it is."

"It's not rudimentary for anyone," he said. "But it is rudimentary for *you*," he said, talking about my soul.

"So how exactly did we know each other before?" I pressed. His statement made me feel small, and I wanted to get him back with some discomfort. Even though I didn't understand why that question made him uncomfortable.

"What's the expression on Earth?" He twisted his head up inquisitively like a dog. "Oh yeah! That's for me to know, and you to find out."

"You know, for an enlightened alien who has mastered the art of mindfulness you really are an asshole," I said, getting up to leave. It was crazy to me how quickly this conversation had turned from flirty and pleasant to irritating and annoying.

"Enlightenment doesn't have anything to do with withholding information from people who can't handle the truth!" he yelled as I walked away.

* * *

I slammed the door to my guest room behind me and went directly to the wood frame bed to meditate. I sat down and fixed my back up straight, aligning the chakras that Tilda had been teaching me about, and began to breathe. *Fuck him. I will get my own answers.* My mind raced a mile a minute as I took deep and furious breaths in through the nose, and exhaled like a dragon through my mouth. My thoughts still spiraled. *That's so cute to just hide information about someone. If I knew someone that had amnesia and they asked me if I could tell them about themselves I WOULD. IT'S THE RIGHT THING TO DO.*

My mind continued to spiral into frustration. But I pressed on through my meditation anyway. In my mind, I was back in the space just between the darkness below and the bright passionate warm happy light above. I reached for the light and pressed away from the darkness holding onto me. Giant hands reached out from the blackness below and grabbed onto my legs and waist, pulling me back down. *I CAN DO THIS!* I screamed in my mind. What felt like hours and hours of pulling myself up finally ended with a gentle tap on the hand of my mind's eye. I looked up towards the light and saw a face leaning over the edge looking at me. A woman with a beautiful head of hair. That's all I could see. The light behind her blinded my eyes from focus. I wanted to look away. It was so bright. But I couldn't. The woman leaned forward and as her face came into focus my heart sank.

"Cameron, wake up from this meditation right now," my mother said forcefully into my face. I paused everything and looked into her eyes. "NOW!" she screamed, pushing me and causing me to lose my grip.

When I opened my eyes, everything was in chaos. The entire house was shaking and Tilda's trinkets were crashing to the ground from the shelves. I looked to my right and saw Tilda holding my arm and crying into it. "What's happening?!" I screamed. But just as I did, everything settled. The rumble passed. "Was that an earthquake?!"

Tilda pulled herself off my arm and wiped her tears. She looked scared. Then Nick came crashing into the room. "Did he do that?!" he asked Tilda, pointing at me.

CHAPTER 13

I CAUSED AN *earthquake. I caused an earthquake! Did I cause an earthquake?* That pretty much sums up my thought process for the last twelve hours. After helping Tilda and Nick clean up the mess, they went to bed. Me? I stayed awake, eyes locked on the ceiling repeating that same set of questions over and over again.

I've never experienced an earthquake before, and while I only experienced five seconds of this one, it was intense. The intensity didn't stop there. Nick checked the news and found that the quake had stretched across the eastern seaboard. No deaths had been reported. Only a few very old buildings collapsed.

"There's no way I did that. That's impossible," I said, looking into Tilda's concerned eyes.

"Cameron," Tilda said sweetly, grabbing my hand. "Lots of things that seem impossible now are going to become more possible. The less you fight it, and the more you accept it, the sooner you will be able to let go."

Tilda explained to me that what I had been doing when the earthquake started wasn't actually meditation. It was something else entirely. "Meditation," Tilda said, "Is the art of turning your mind off to access your soul. What you were doing was something between manifestation and conjuring."

She went on to explain that this ability is not something that has yet been seen on Earth. There were comparisons that she pointed to, like the witches of old times that still exist today. Who use spells and potions to work their magic. Tilda described these practices as a whisper to the Universe with the tiniest bit of cheat code for the Universe to listen. What I was doing as far as Tilda explained, was manipulating a physical space in the Universe with my soul's power. Cheat code vs. back end hack. Tilda said that she wasn't surprised by this, many souls just like mine on other terrestrial planets had been given these same abilities. She had even met one before. A whole subject that I almost allowed to derail the conversation out of my inquisitiveness about who/what/where/when/why this person existed.

"Your soul has a special relationship with this Earth." Tilda grabbed me by the shoulders. "Upon your entering here your two souls agreed. She is here to fight the war with you."

"With *me?*" I asked. The way Tilda said that felt different than the way she had described my existence here before. There had been many times throughout our time together that she had referenced who I was before this life. Some things made sense. Others didn't. This sounded heavy.

"You can never do that again," Tilda said seriously. "Frustration can never be the key to using this gift." I'm not sure how she knew that I was frustrated.

"I saw my mom," I said, looking down at the ground. "She stopped me."

"Well thank the Universe for that." Tilda sounded disappointed.

Great, now I've made Tilda hate me too, I thought.

"I am not mad at you. I'm not disappointed," she said.

I looked up at her with concern. "And I'm not reading your mind. I can tell by the look on your face." She put my chin in her hand. "I love you more than you will ever understand. Because of this love, I will do whatever I can in my power to stop you from conjuring up anything like that ever again." Her tone firmed as she spoke. "You WILL learn to control your abilities. I don't care if it's the last thing I do."

My relationship with Tilda had become something otherworldly. That much was obvious. I hadn't felt a connection to another person like that since my mother was still here with me. Her compassion made me feel safe. Like I could say anything or be anyone and Tilda would still love me. Having someone on your team like that is a gift from the Universe directly. I knew it. For Tilda's sake if nothing else, I would master my abilities.

Meditation Journey #53

The next morning I decided to try and take myself on a journey on my own. Up until now, Tilda's voice had guided me to all the beautiful pastures, lighthouses, and even basements of my mind. Today it was time to visit a place I had longed to go to ever since my first guided meditation. I knew that if I could properly create it within my mind, she would be there.

I took deep breaths, ensuring that I wouldn't start my journey to this new land until I was totally clear in my mind. Once I came to a place where everything was mostly blank, and any thoughts that remained were far away and tiny, I began, creating the start point in my mind. Detailed pictures. Smells, feelings, tastes, and all.

I'm in New York City. It's steamy hot. The humidity causes my skin to perspire gently. The sidewalk beneath me is twelve different colors of cement, gum, debris, and tar. The air smells like piss. Horns honk obnoxiously throughout the area. I reach out and touch the red brick of the building to my right. It's rough. The grout hurts to rub my knuckle against. Looking forward I see the New Amsterdam Theater, currently showing Chicago, *as it mentions in all the signage on the Show box.*

I step forward. I step again. Paying close attention to the sounds my loafers make on the ground. Loafers? I think. I'd much rather wear Vans. To which I quickly shrink the thought, and say goodbye. I look down again and my shoes are now... Vans. Beautiful red ones at that.

I reach my hand forward to pull on the large iron door handle. Much larger than a handle really. More like an arm. It's swiveled all the way down like an ice cream cone. It's cold to the touch. I pull on it and the door gives way easily, though I can feel its weight. I step inside to the lobby. It's astoundingly beautiful with marble sculptures of Shakespearean Scenes. Ascending up the staircase to the actual theater, I'm overwhelmed at the beauty. The theater was originally decorated specifically for its first show: A Midsummer's Night Dream. *This theater in my vision is all brand new. The reds pop like they can't anymore. The golds flourish. The seats are all empty, but I hear a faint round of applause that has greeted this building so many times cascading through the air.*

The stage is bare, save two chairs sat facing each other. They won't need to face the audience, as there won't be one for this show. The big red curtain hangs in place behind them. The stage is lit, and a slight layer of dust can be seen floating in the lights stream. I approach the stage along the right side, hearing voices and songs sung in this place over the years. All of them are beautiful, at least the ones I can hear. I walk up the first step to the stage, and the wood beneath my foot creaks slightly.

The next step does as well. But not the third. By the fourth, I'm on stage.

I make my way towards the chair nearest me. The chair is made of metal and has a thick top rung which I wrap my hand around. It's cold to the touch. My hand leaves a mark on its shiny surface when I move it away.

I sit down. I feel the bones in my butt push right through the lack of fat and touch the chair. It's not the most comfortable, but that's okay. Suddenly, both chairs have a cushion. Both red. Now, mine is white. My mind is getting a little out of control as other things in the theater begin to change at random.

I take a deep breath, press the thoughts away, and ground myself in the moment. I close my eyes and take another breath. I open them and reach out to the curtain beside me. Its velvet softness is remarkable. I sit straight up, and I say, "Mom. Would you mind coming to talk to me?"

I sit. Noticeably nervous. Perhaps not nervous. Hopeful? Yes. Hopeful. I sit up a little straighter. Then I hear it. The indistinguishable sound of high heels clicking down on a stage floor. My mother appears next to the red curtain, stage left. She's beautiful. At first, she's in a Roxie Hart style getup. Dressed for her show that she's starring in. But then I think about how much I loved her as she was, and suddenly she's in front of me in jeans and a red turtleneck. Her hair no longer in a roaring 20s bob, but in her natural wavy curls that flow past her shoulders. Her heels swapped for a comfortable pair of white tennis shoes. And the showiest thing she ever wore, a pair of gold earrings that dangle down about an inch of her ear. Finally, I notice her necklace hanging across her neck, which I am also now wearing suddenly.

I look back up at my mother as she sits. She eliminates the foot of distance between us by reaching out with her right arm and touching my right knee. She looks me in the eyes. I'm on the verge of tears. I reach down and touch her hand with mine. She's smiling at me. And suddenly we are alone in my childhood bedroom sitting on my bed. We are both sitting still facing each other, with my right leg hanging off the bed and her left.

"Thank you for coming," I say softly, my voice choking up. "And thank you for...stopping me."

"Oh, sweetie." Her voice is just as soothing as it always was. "I know you didn't want me to have to see you like that for the first time. But honestly, I'm just glad I could finally get through."

Tears started falling down my face. I could also feel the real me, outside this vision in meditation, begin to cry. "I won't ever do it again. I promise," I say sincerely, trying my best to remain focused on the vision.

"Honey, you wouldn't have done it in the first place if you knew what you were doing. It's not your fault. There's so much more to the Universe that you could have never known before. You're still learning, and you're doing a great job."

I wipe the tears from my eyes but they continue to flow gently. "Come here." She says, pulling me with her onto the bed. She lays down on the right side of my power rangers comforter and pulls my head down into the crook of her left arm. She smells just like she did when I was a kid.

"Did I ever tell you the story about how I came to Earth?" She asks casually.

"Huh?" I - I wanted to say "what" but my mouth moved faster than my brain.

"What, nobody told you?" she asks. "I thought you would have figured that out by now."

"*I have no idea what you're talking about…*"

"*That's one of the reasons your soul asked me to be your mother,*" Her fingers are now gently caressing my hair.

"*Really?*" I ask. *This type of comment from my mom even a month ago would have warranted a million other questions.*

"*After your dad and I got married, he really wanted to have a baby. I did too but he REALLY wanted to have a baby, and we tried and tried and tried.*"

"*I get it,*" I quickly urge her to press on.

"*But no matter how hard we tried, I couldn't get pregnant. Then one day I was meditating in the park next to the apartment we lived in when we first got married.*" I close my eyes and I can picture my mother, young and beautiful, sitting in the park. Meditating on beautiful plush grass. "*During that meditation, I was visited by a golden spirit. A soul. A Daemon soul to be exact. It said that it knew that I was trying to have a child with my husband. The soul then told me it had come to Earth for a purpose. To help mankind. And if I would be willing to help raise this soul with love, an open mind, and patience, they would help me conceive the child with my husband.*"

"*So…*" I start with nowhere to go.

"*So, I said yes. And after everything I had gone through, coming to Earth…having a baby that would help all of mankind, that made it extra worth it.*"

"*Huh…*" I'm speechless.

"*I never told your father. I didn't want him to worry about it. I just thought I'd see if we actually got pregnant. Then we did! Like the next day if you go by an exact nine-month count. Then you were born. With all your gifts that you had before you probably even realized.*"

"Like what?" I asked. Always a sucker for a little self-indulgence.

"You basically got whatever you wanted when you were little. Cookie jars came down off of counters before you could walk. Or the time a little boy pushed you off the swing set when you were four! Oh, man. That poor kid."

"What happened to him?"

"Let's not talk about it," she says passively.

"Did I kill him?!" I panic.

"Oh God no!" she laughs. "Not even close."

I relax again back into her arms. "So where did you come from?"

"It's hard to say really." She sounds somber. "The planet I was born on doesn't have a name. Or at least, it doesn't anymore. Whatever the native people, my people, called it, is unknown. When I was a baby I was taken by an Avian race called the Blue Avians. They saved all the young children from our planet just days before a cataclysmic event. They then took us all to a planet called Zanthor in the Alpha Centauri galaxy. I grew up there in an orphanage for beings whose home planets had been destroyed."

"They didn't bring your parents too?"

"No," She says curtly. "The Blue Avians only rescue the youngest from doomed planets. They believe it's the only way to give the species a good chance for future survival. Because typically the parents would have already been plagued with issues that caused their planet to end in the first place. Most sentient species don't go extinct from natural causes. Ninety-nine percent of the time, they destroy themselves. That's likely what happened on the planet I was born on."

I sit up and look at her. She sits up against the headboard. "Wow," is all I could muster.

"*I came to Earth with a few other human-related beings and some who disguised themselves as such when I was thirteen. I learned to speak English along the way. I started high school the day after we landed. At the time, it was such an incredible gift. Earth was beautiful. I was happy to be a part of it.*"

I always knew that my mom was an orphan. The only grandparents I ever had were my dad's parents. But my mom never really talked about it or let it show. The topic had been discussed less than a handful of times throughout my life.

"*You'd better get back,*" she says, touching my leg. "*You've spent a long time here. You can come back anytime. I don't want you to get stuck here.*" *She's right. Hours have gone by. Time moves so much faster when you're truly lost in a vision.* "*Is there anything else you want to know before you leave?*"

"*Did my soul tell you anything else?*" *I ask.* "*Did it tell you why I was here?*"

"*All they told me, was that if you never woke up to who you truly were, it would mean the end of the human race on Earth.*"

"*Cameron?!*" *A voice yells outside my vision. My mother looks concerned. Then suddenly my real physical body is being shaken. I reach for my mother but before I can touch her I'm ripped back into reality.*

"Cameron!" A face yelled directly into mine, shaking me back into consciousness.

"Kaylee?" I said sleepily.

CHAPTER 14

"I'M SORRY FOR interrupting your meditation," Kaylee told me as I sipped the water she had given me. I don't think I had ever been in such a deep meditation on my own before, and being jogged back to reality so harshly took me a second to adjust. I could tell she felt bad for it.

"No really it's okay!" I said with extra reassurance. I was truly thrilled to see her, but the way I left my mom so quickly hurt just a little.

"You must have been deep in there…Where did you go?"

"Somewhere awesome." I smiled, thinking once again of my mother holding me on my childhood bed. I hoped that wouldn't be the last time I saw her. "Where did you go? The night we left the city?"

"I went home actually." She smiled softly.

"Really?" I asked in disbelief.

"Well, not home to Erie. But I went to see my dad."

"What?!" I nearly spit out my water. "Why would you do that? Did he freak out?" I couldn't see how it was a good idea for her to go see her dad in the middle of everything that was going on. Not to mention how emotionally jarring the experience would have been for him after all this time.

"He didn't actually. He took my explanation for it all quite well," she said calmly. "And I went because I had to."

"Had to?"

"My visions told me I needed to."

"Visions?" I asked. I was having a really hard time following along with this conversation.

"Tilda didn't tell you about my 'gift?'" she asked with air quotes.

"She told me you had a gift, but she wouldn't say what it was," I told her. "What kind of visions?"

"Visions of the future. Or…possible futures."

"You can see the future?" I asked, dumbfounded.

"Parts of it." she said. "I started having them right before my sixteenth birthday. They started out as dreams. I assumed I was having some horrible nightmares for a few nights in a row. Then they started happening when I was awake. I would just be sitting there studying and suddenly I'd lose track of reality and slip into them. Everything was so real in the moment. Like I was really there."

"What did you see?" The way she described it reminded me of when Tilda would show me visions through her mind in meditation.

"The worst thing that I could never even imagine. Everything was on fire. People screaming in the streets. It looked like hell on Earth. Giant insects killing people everywhere I looked."

"The Tahn," I thought out loud.

"Right. But I didn't know that then," she reminded me. "Then there was a second vision that would play every time just as the first one ended. It would start with me on a bus. Just waking up from a nap. I get up to go to the bathroom and look in the mirror, and realize it really is me in the vision. When I return to my seat the bus exits the highway somewhere in Pennsylvania."

"Tilda's…" I thought aloud again.

"Right! But I didn't know that then either," she continued. "I had the vision a few times and eventually I decided to look up the exact exit number. Turns out it was real. Then I looked up the Greyhound bus routes through Pennsylvania, and there was one straight from Denver to the exact exit leaving the next morning."

"So you went?" I couldn't understand how she had actually been brave enough to just do that.

"You don't understand. The visions were so real, and they were happening more frequently. I was starting to have a hard time knowing which reality was the real one. I had to get on that bus. And I couldn't tell anyone because they wouldn't understand. They'd think I was crazy."

"I know what that's like," I said, my eyes meeting hers. "You could have told me."

"If I told you, you wouldn't have been able to lie for me. You're really bad at that." She was right. I was terrible at lying. "I knew my dad would call the police, and I knew they would question you first. Besides, I didn't know that I wouldn't come back after I left. I just knew that I had to go to the place in my vision."

"Well, what happened after you got on the bus?" I asked.

"The visions finally stopped coming so abrasively. I had just one as I got on the bus. It was the same vision of me arriving in Pennsylvania, only it continued a little further to me going into the farmers market that was there. Then, before the bus finally arrived, the vision continued a little further to me meeting a short and gangly man with a beard. Someone you also met."

I tried to rack my brain to understand who she was talking about. Then I realized, "Barry?"

"Turned out to be, yes," Kaylee confirmed. The same man that had randomly given me the ticket to see *Chicago*, and apparently had a romance with Tilda, was the same man Kaylee had met upon her arrival.

"And what happened? What did he say?" I was still very much enthralled in the story.

"He didn't say anything. He didn't know who I was or why I was standing so close to him. The vision didn't tell me what to say either, so I just said, 'I think I'm supposed to be here.'"

"And then what?"

"He looked me dead in the eye and said…" Kaylee built the intensity as I leaned in closer. "'I'll be right back.'" Then she laughed and I rolled my eyes. She knew that she had reeled me into the story and did a great job of bringing some levity to the situation. Same old Kaylee. But a Kaylee I was grateful for in this moment. "Then he came back with Tilda and she started crying and yelled my name from across the room…You know, the usual Tilda stuff." That made me smile even harder. Though our stories were different for how we got here, there were probably a lot more similarities than either of us knew.

"And then what? You came back to the house, walked through the cleansing river?" I teased.

"All that. Learned to meditate," she joked. We hadn't had a conversation in years. The last time I saw her was one of the most adrenaline filled moments of my life and it happened so quickly. We really didn't get to talk much. In this moment I was reminded of the friendship we once had, and it was nice to have that rapport with her now amidst the chaos our lives had taken on recently. "The visions stopped for a while after I got here," she said, getting a little more serious. "Tilda said it was because I had taken the first step in getting here, and I had a lot to learn before the next phase of the plan."

"The next phase?" I asked.

"The visions started again about six months ago. They started the same way. That awful scene of death and destruction. The worst part is you can actually smell it. Like burning fle—" Kaylee looked at me and my face of dread. She noted it and continued, "But the second one was of me getting on a plane."

"A plane where?" I said with jealousy. I had always wanted to fly on a plane. That seemed like a minor dream now compared to the Universal war we were now involved in.

"Dubai," she said. "But I actually didn't know that until I got to the airport and saw the next part of the vision."

"Dubai?" I asked. Why would she need to go to Dubai?

"The one and only," she said.

"What did you do in Dubai?"

"Stuff."

"Care to elaborate there, Captain Mysterious?" I joked.

"You know their new prince? Amjad Al Beziin?"

"Of course!" I said a little too excitedly. Images of Amjad's handsome face rushed to my mind, and a smile filled my face. I looked back at Kaylee and she was looking at me with concern.

"Yeah…" she said, trying to brush off my excitement. "Well, he has a new space program that I'm sure you've heard of then."

"Oh yeah," I said, trying to calm down. "Where they're building the new space ladder."

"Right. And I figured that must have been the reason

that the visions sent me there. Something to do with, space seeing as how this war that's coming our way is set to begin there," Kaylee said.

"So what happened?"

"Nothing too crazy, except…" she thought about it. "When I entered the museum portion they had open to the public, I had to walk through a metal detector. I set the thing off even though I didn't have any metal on me. I had watched at least fifty other people go in before me when I was checking the place out. Not a single one of them set it off. When I did, the security guards pulled me off to the side and asked if I would come to the back room."

I was hanging on every word of her story.

"I didn't want to throw a fit or make a scene. Generally, if the visions doesn't tell me exactly what to do in a situation, I try to go with the flow. So I agreed and they led me into a room that was hidden from the naked eye by a trick door in the wall."

"That sounds terrifying," I said.

"Not really, actually," she continued. "The guards were really polite, and they offered to get me any beverage I wanted after I sat down. I thanked them and told them I wasn't thirsty, and then I waited for about twenty minutes before anyone came back. The surprising part was that Prince Amjad himself was the next person to enter the room."

"YOU MET PRINCE AMJAD?!" My excitement was visible, my jealousy was not.

"Uh huh…" Kaylee said, studying me, trying to figure out the reason for my outburst. She had seen the way I lusted after guys in school. I was sure she could see that same energy from me now.

"Sorry," I said, realizing how crazy my outburst had seemed. "So what did he say?!"

"He asked me who I was, where I was from, and why I had come to visit the space center."

"And what did you say?"

"I said I was Britney Masterson, from Arizona in the US, and I had always wanted to be an astronaut. I told him I wanted to see what they were accomplishing there."

"You look literally nothing like a Britney," I laughed.

"He bought it," she said.

"Well, then what happened?" I said, pulling more of the story I needed to hear from her.

"He gave me a private tour of the space station. Showed me everything. He was actually really nice."

"A PRIVATE TOUR?!" I exclaimed. "What did he smell like?"

"Wasn't paying attention to that," she said with a hint of judgment in her tone. "There was one weird thing, though."

"What? Did he hit on you?" I asked.

Kaylee looked me dead in the eyes with all the seriousness she could muster. "No."

"I KNEW he was gay."

"Do you want to know the rest of the story? Or do you need me to leave you alone for a moment with your thoughts?" Kaylee joked.

"Go ahead," I said, calming myself.

"He said if any of my friends ever wanted to come to tour the space center, or meet him, that I should feel free."

I gasped loudly.

"He even gave me his private phone number," she said.

I jumped up from the bed I sat on. "WHAT?! YOU

HAVE HIS PRIVATE PHONE NUMBER?! LET'S GO RIGHT NOW!" I shouted with excitement.

"We can't," she said flatly.

"Why not?"

"Because he sent someone to follow me. That night that I was attacked and you saved me, that was one of his men who had been trailing me since I left Dubai."

The memory of Kaylee pinned with the knife against her throat flashed into my mind. A shiver was sent down my spine. "Why did Prince Amjad send someone to follow you and attack you?"

"I have no idea. I've been trying to figure it out since that night and I got nothing. It has to have something to do with that metal detector…" She became lost in thought.

"When did you find out that I was a part of all this?" I asked her. If Tilda had always known me, I assumed she had told Kaylee about me too.

"The same day you did," she said. "I had a vision while I was seeing a show in New York. That I would leave that show, be attacked, and that *you* would save me."

"Tilda never told you before?"

"Nope. I was just as surprised to see you that day as you were surprised to see me. Actually, I *did* have an hour head start," she laughed again.

"So…you think your visions are alternate futures?" I almost felt bad for asking her so many questions. But I needed to know.

"Not alternate futures necessarily. Because the first vision seems to be further into the future than the second one ever is. The way Tilda explains it, is the second vision is always a step that I can take on the path away from the first vision. Like a warning. If I don't do step two, then vision one will become a reality."

"The first vision has never changed?" I asked.

"Not since this morning when I had my last one, no."

"What was your last vision?"

"Coming here from the airport and waking you from your meditation." She smiled.

"Interesting." I smiled back. Apparently I did need to be woken up from that trip to see my mother. It made sense. I could have stayed there forever.

"Where did you go in that meditation that was so amazing anyway?" she pressed.

"To see my mother." I smiled shyly. I didn't understand why saying that was nearly embarrassing, but it was.

"Was she as beautiful as I remember?" Kaylee asked. I could tell she sensed my concern. Her response alleviated that entirely. If there was anyone I could talk to about my mother, it was Kaylee. She knew her when she was alive.

"Just as beautiful." I said smiling. "Oh, and apparently from another planet…"

"Not surprising after everything I know now," Kaylee laughed. "She was truly a cut above everyone else."

"That she was…" I trailed off, thinking about her smile again. "Did something happen in Colorado?" I asked.

"What do you mean?"

"Why did your visions send you back to see your dad?" I asked.

"I think the Universe wanted me to see him one last time…" Her response sent shivers down my back.

CHAPTER 15

"I RECEIVED A message last night in a dream," Nick said to Tilda and me as he entered the kitchen where we were having breakfast. Oatmeal, as usual. Kaylee was out meditating ahead of us. "From my mother. I must go to see her."

"You're leaving?" I asked, a hint of fear in my voice. I was really starting to get used to Nick. His presence became less and less irritating as the days had gone by.

"Not exactly," Tilda said, reassuring me. "What did she say?"

"Asteros is coming to Valnor." Nick said. Tilda made a face of shock.

"Who is Asteros?" I asked, not wanting to be left out of the conversation.

"Asteros is the only Hyamin currently living a physical existence in the Universe," Tilda said. I recalled the part of the story about the Hyamin, the oldest and wisest of the higher dimension races. The image of their white light souls came to mind. "You must go to him. Seek his aid!" Tilda pleaded with Nick.

"I know," Nick said flatly. He sat down at the table with us.

"Are there no other Hyamin left?" I still wanted to get a firmer grasp of the concept of what was happening.

"I thought they were the ones sending the Tahn to destroy Earth?"

"The Hyamin are a smaller numbered race in total for sure. But they are far from extinct. They stopped entering the physical dimension thousands of Earth years ago when the uprising of the Daemon began. They didn't want any of the Hyamin souls to be destroyed along with their planets if the Daemon were to retaliate. So they left their physical lives behind until the war was over.

"It is said that Asteros disagreed with the ideals of the Hyamin greatly," Tilda continued. "He held a soft spot in his heart for the human races and more importantly, Daemon souls. He was one of the souls who originally helped man to evolve."

"He's visiting Valnor during the passing of Dineyhs," Nick said "Every one hundred years, a large asteroid passes by Valnor that we call Dineyhs. Close enough to see with the naked eye," he explained to me. I appreciated the knowledge.

"He loves a ceremony," Tilda said of Asteros. "The one time that he visited Earth was during the completion of the Great Pyramid."

"So...he can help us?" I asked.

"It's impossible to know without trying." Nick looked at me. "No one ever knows where Asteros is or will be until just before he is there. I searched my entire young adulthood trying to find him."

"It's fate," Tilda said.

"How will you get to Valnor? When will you come back?" My mind reeled with the idea of losing Nick. Even though he sometimes pissed me off, and was mostly a smart ass, I knew that he was essential to saving the planet. Even more...I knew he was somehow essential to me.

"He will travel there astrally, my dear," Tilda said, touching my hand to comfort the rising worry she felt coming off of me. "His consciousness will go, and his body will remain here."

Astral projection? I wondered. I had heard of it before. People walking through the world, without their bodies. Witnessing real experiences that they weren't physically there for. A co-worker in New York at the French bistro told me she could do it when I told her I could hear people's thoughts. She was one of the very few people that I ever told, but I felt like I could trust her. That or, no one ever took anything she said seriously, so if she decided to tell anyone else, they wouldn't believe her.

But Nick going to Astrally travel to Valnor to see his family, and speak with this Asteros…Something inside of me screamed with a desire to go. My mind tried to quell it, thinking I had no idea how to astral project. But the force inside won the argument and I blurted out, "I wanna go!"

Tilda and Nick both looked at me. Tilda, with a smile. Nick, with confusion. Then they simultaneously spoke.

"No way," Nick said flatly.

"I think that's a great idea!" Tilda said even louder.

* * *

Tilda and Kaylee carried the Imantium into the kitchen. Two large melons in each arm. "What do we need the Imantium for?" I asked.

"The Imantium will aid in getting your body to a place where it can let go of your consciousness for an extended period of time. It will also help to mitigate the *risks*."

I nodded. The risks? Oh, no biggie. Just that my consciousness could get lost in space forever. Never able to find its way back to my body on Earth. I would remain in a coma physically, for the rest of my life. More importantly, I would fail to save Earth from the Tahn. Tilda made me aware of these risks. The risks that Nick mentioned were far more severe:

Apparently, no one knew for certain why Asteros had left behind the Hyamin way of life. There were rumors, and most of them favored him as sympathetic to the Daemon plight. However, some speculated he had been forced out of the Hyamin. Cursed to live a physical life alone. If the latter was true, Nick feared that Asteros would take any opportunity he could to get back in favor with the Hyamin. What better opportunity than the leader of the Daemon people standing before you, separate from his body? He could single-handedly end Earth's chances at fighting the Tahn. A sacrifice Nick was willing to make himself, but not for Ayan.

Tilda thought that Nick's concerns were slightly unfounded. Asteros had spent millennia visiting different human civilizations in times of celebration. He may from time to time knock up some young beautiful girl, but aside from pleasures of the flesh, he had been nothing but good to them. Nick finally agreed that I would go, and lay low. I would go for the experience of seeing another world, and for mastering the art of astral projection. Which could be very useful in my future, Tilda told Nick. I would not take part in any conversations with Asteros, and I would avoid him at all costs. If something were to happen to Nick, one of his family members would aid my consciousness in finding its way back to Earth.

Another notable point of discussion here is the distinction between my consciousness and my soul. Originally, I had thought them to be the same thing. Tilda had explained to me though, that my consciousness was everything I am inside my mind. My soul would participate in the travel, as a part of my consciousness. Basically, Cameron entirely, but in spirit form, would travel across the Universe. The same as I am now, just...lacking in physical matter.

Nick entered the kitchen where Kaylee and Tilda were now chopping the Imantium on the counter. Its golden circles seemed so much brighter in the daytime. It was now afternoon and Nick had spent his morning mapping a way for us to get to Valnor. Apparently, since planets and star systems are always moving. Getting lost could be way too easy.

"It's time," he said. Everyone turned to him. "If we leave now, we will have a relatively simple flight. If we wait much longer, things are prone to change."

"Kaylee, open the hatch," Tilda said, gesturing to Kaylee. "Cameron, follow her down there with this platter of Imantium."

What hatch? I wondered. But I grabbed the platter and followed Kaylee around the kitchen bar top. She then scooted out the stool closest to the window, where I sat almost every morning, and bent over to remove a section of the wooden floor. It came out pretty effortlessly and revealed a ladder heading down into an abyss. Kaylee swung her leg onto the ladder, then the other, and headed down.

"Hand me the Imantium." She said once she reached the bottom. I lowered the heavy plate down to her gently and stood back up. Turning around, I saw Nick and Tilda standing behind me. Clearly waiting for their turn to walk down the ladder. For some reason, I hadn't thought we were going down there right away. But apparently, we were. I grabbed onto the ladder and descended into darkness.

Only a second after my foot hit the hard ground, a match

was struck. Kaylee was lighting a candle. By the time she had lit a second one, Tilda had come down, and I could now see that we were standing inside a cave, smooth rock on all sides of us. In the far section, there was one large rug. Kaylee lit the candles all around it, and I could see now that the rug was purple. There was a large circle in the center of the rug, large enough to fit two people lying down, painted in white. Symbols traced the edges, the origins of which I could not tell.

"This has been here the whole time?" I asked Tilda

"Yes!" she giggled. "It's where I hide whenever people from lower dimensions come through the property. This cave can't be found there."

"You two will be safe down there in case anything goes wrong while you're gone," Kaylee said, handing us both a wedge of Imantium. "We will take turns watching over your bodies to make sure everything's okay."

"Thank you," Nick said to Kaylee. Weird to see my best friend and my crush interact like they know each other.

Ew. Did I just think crush? He's not my crush. God, I was glad no one could hear my thoughts.

The Imantium tasted exactly how I remembered it. Like the purest water, I had ever drank. There were no seeds inside of it either. I finished my first slice as Tilda gestured towards the rug. "Both of you lay down here."

Nick sat down first, and then he looked at me. At that moment, the weirdness of everything that was happening caught up with me. This vision of four people underground in a secret cave about to meditate for days on end was a bit cultish. That little voice of doubt inside my head had all but faded since I realized that I was Ayan. But it still would pop up every now and again. Usually in the most extreme of times. It was just me being human I guess. But that part of me was still holding me back from knowing everything I needed to know. I sat down next to Nick on the ground. Kaylee handed me another piece of Imantium.

"Don't get lost out there," she said as I took the piece.

"I won't," I assured her. Truthfully I didn't know if I could say that though. I had no idea where Earth was in relation to the rest of the Universe. If I had any more time than just this morning to think this over, I might have reconsidered. The risks weighed in my mind now.

The Imantium was already buzzing through my system. The lights of the candles danced in front of my eyes as I focused. The veil between this world and the rest thinned quickly. "Lay down," Tilda said. Her hand guided my head backward to prevent it from hitting the rug too hard. I then heard her light another match. Moments later the smell of incense came creeping across my nose.

"I am going to walk you both through the exit of your bodies," she said. Her voice echoed in the cave. As the Imantium took hold, it sounded further and further away. Nick of course knew how to do astral projection. Probably had been doing it since he was a small boy on Valnor. But for my sake, he waited to leave his body until I was ready. Tilda would help me get there. "Inhale for as long as you can. Count it. When you exhale, try to last one count longer. Repeat this five times." This was a process of calming the body and mind that I was familiar with. We both breathed. I could hear Nick next to me. I could feel his warmth, our arms only a couple of inches apart at most on the ground.

"Now, I want you to feel your body get heavier and more relaxed with each exhale. Feel each point of your back that is touching the ground, and ask your body to relax into it." For

being a rug on a cave floor, it was surprisingly comfortable
to lay on. My body relaxed and after a few breaths felt like
it was 400 pounds. "I want you to remind yourself that it is
safe for your consciousness to separate from your body. Tell
yourself now,"

It is okay for my consciousness to separate from my body,
I thought. This part of the process was important apparently,
as your body really doesn't want to let go of your consciousness. For good reason I supposed. A little convincing had to
be done for your body to let go.

"You will be safe on your journey," Tilda said.

I will be safe on my journey, I repeated mentally.

"Now just breathe." Tilda said. Breathing louder than
both of us so that we could follow along.

We stayed like this, calming and breathing, for I would
guess twenty minutes. It felt like an eternity. At times, I could
feel my spirit wanting to jump out of my skin. Like a little kid
who completes that math puzzle his first-grade teacher gave
him before anyone else, I could feel my soul ready to jump.
Just when I thought I would leap out before I was supposed
to, Tilda said, "There is a rope hanging above your eyes. See
it with your mind, but do not open your eyes. When you're
ready, grab that rope without moving a muscle." And just
like that, my spirit reached up and grabbed onto a rope. Pulling itself up out of my body.

I stood over myself now, my lifeless body resting on the
cave floor. Tilda's eyes closed beside me. Nick's body to the
left of mine, I looked up and could see his spirit standing
right next to me. He smiled softly. It was him, only a slightly holographic version of him. I reached out to touch him
without thinking about it and was able to grab onto his arm
and feel it. Just like he was really standing there. He gave me

a weird look in response and I quickly retracted my arm. I knelt down next to Tilda and reached my arm out to touch her shoulder. It immediately went right through her, but she turned and her eyes looked directly at me.

"You made it," she said.

I hovered over my body for a second longer. Waving my hands through the points of my feet. My spirit went right through them. no feeling attached to me whatsoever. I reached over again towards Nick's spirit leg and tried to wave my hand through it. It stopped and I hit his chin.

"Ow!" he yelped. "We are in the same dimension right now. Yes, we affect each other." Clearly, he understood the connections I was trying to make in my first time out on a spirit walk.

Maybe I should have tried this before we attempted a Universal crossing… I thought to myself.

"Time is of the essence," Nick said, gesturing for me to stand up. "We should be on our way. With that, Nick lifted himself off the ground completely and ascended through the roof of the cave back into the kitchen. Directly through the floor.

How does one fly… I wondered. *Seems like we should have covered that before.*

"Just lift up," Tilda said. I realized she was looking directly at me still.

"You can see me?" My spirit asked

"Of course, dear." she replied, another one of her signature tears of pride rolling down her cheek. "Many people where you are going will be able to see you too. Remember, you're not invisible everywhere."

Noted, I thought.

"Now, just lift," she said with a smile.

It's hard to describe to you, the reader, how this worked, as it's hard to describe most things that happen in another dimension. But I simply lifted my astral body off the ground with the same ease as I would lift my arm to grab something. I hovered above the ground about a foot for a moment, just taking it all in. Tilda was gleaming. I looked above me at the solid rock between myself and the kitchen and lifted. I must have overshot the speed, because as I came flying up into the kitchen above, Nick grabbed me by my leg and pulled me back down.

"Slow down, tiger," he said. "Remember, you don't want to get lost."

Kaylee stood in front of us in the kitchen. She definitely had no idea we were there. I knew that because she looked extremely concerned. A face I hadn't seen Kaylee make since we were kids. She was worried about us, me…I could tell. The main thing I noticed though, was an overwhelming pink light that surrounded her. It must have been her aura, because her soul was a Daemon one that would glow gold. I noted how interesting that was that I had always thought of her as a pink ball of energy, because she actually was.

I approached Kaylee and leaned in close to whisper in her ear. "I love you…" my spirit told her. "It's going to be okay."

Kaylee sighed. She couldn't hear me, but my words had noticeably calmed her down. She turned around and started washing the cutting board in the sink.

"Let's go," Nick said. He was already in the doorway to exit the cottage. I followed behind him into the yard. Once outside, Nick flew forward over the sea of wild grass towards the meditation area, landing in the center of the circle. I lifted myself again and brushed over the top of the wild grass. It was amazing. I was…flying.

When I landed next to him he said, "You're going to need to take my hand for this next part." His spiritual hand outstretched towards me. My spiritual heart beat a little faster. My cheeks blushed if they could. I reached out and took his hand. "Time to go up." And with that, he lifted off the Earth again with an amazing force, dragging me along behind him by the hand. By the time I could comprehend what was happening, Tilda's property was a spec in a mass of forests. I could see the nearest highway, probably fifty miles away, coming into view now like a toy race car track with little dots all along. I looked up to Nick, who was focused on looking up as well. I willed myself to fly up next to him, so that he wasn't dragging me along, and we were more flying hand in hand.

The forest below melted into a large green blanket as I could see the outline of the entire East Coast of the US. The Atlantic ocean, with its dark blue hue, now coming into view. An airplane nearby came rushing towards us, but we were up above it before it could get close. I watched the airplane shrink smaller and smaller. When I finally removed my focus, I realized that I could see a black edge of space along the edge of Earth. Looking up above us, it was all black. We were in space. All of this happened so quickly that it was hard to process. In just moments, we were surrounded by total blackness. The big ball of blue light that was the Earth now a separate entity from us entirely. I saw the moon begin to peek around the edge of the globe as we moved even further away.

"Wait!" I yelled to Nick.

He stopped immediately. "What's wrong?" He looked concerned.

"Nothing!" I said quickly, almost apologetically. "I've just never seen the Earth like this before." I looked back again at this huge ball just floating there. My mind was blowing over and over again. My consciousness was almost not able to process what was happening. She turned slowly, and I noticed her movement forward through space around the sun ever so slightly. "It's beautiful," I said.

"I sure hope you think so," Nick laughed. He seemed to be in a good mood. "Because that's what you're fighting for." As I looked back at him again, he smiled. "We'd better get going."

I took one last look at the Earth and looked back at him. "Okay," I said.

"This next part is going to require you to will yourself forward just as quickly as I am." He said. "If you see any planets or asteroids in front of you, don't mind them. You'll go right through."

I gulped. "And you're sure we're just gonna go through them?" I asked for double confirmation.

"If you even see them at the speed we will be traveling," Nick said with a laugh. "We're just going to go this way," he pointed forward in a continuous direction from where we had left, "for a very long time."

"Okay," I said. No other words came to mind. And with that, Nick launched forward, his hand in mine, and I raced alongside him to keep up.

* * *

I had no idea how much time had passed. Two hours? A day? A week? There was no way to tell. But I guessed it had only been a few hours at most. I could still see Nick's spirit next to me constantly, but that was all. At the speed we were traveling, space warped around us. Everything was black. At some moments there would be a bright flash of orange, and one of blue. But only for a split second. I wondered if we were passing through other planets when that happened. I wanted to ask Nick if we could stop for a moment to get a view, but I knew that he would say no. He was in a huge hurry, that much was for sure. There would be no sightseeing adventures today.

"We are going to stop on the count of three!" Nick yelled at me. I could hear him perfectly well, but I understood the need to yell as the sound of this travel was mute yet deafening. "One! Two! Three!" And just as quickly as it had all started, it came to an end. Our bodies hovered in space at a complete stop. Nick grabbed me slightly to keep my spirit from jetting forward too far. I noticed his grip on my hand, and looked up at him and smiled. His gaze was focused on something behind me though. I turned around to see the most beautiful sight I had ever seen.

CHAPTER 16

THERE BEFORE ME floated two planets suspended in space. My first thought was that they were frighteningly close to each other. Then I remembered Nick telling me about the planet Serena. Valnor and Serena orbited each other around their small red dwarf sun. A look to the left at a deep red star burning confirmed that we had arrived in their system.

I couldn't say for sure which planet was which. But I had a feeling that the planet to my right, slightly larger with a purple hue to its atmosphere, was Valnor. Two separate land masses, one on top and one below, were connected by a smattering chain of islands. The land looked orange from here, with very little green in sight, except at the top of the upper land mass. The purple atmosphere must have been the reflection of the purple...ocean? The planet to the right was smaller and resembled more of an Earth-like color palette. Deep green forests lined the equator and most of the northern hemisphere, with a blue atmosphere and ocean.

"Welcome to Valnor and Serena," Nick said next to me. I couldn't take my eyes off the planets.

"Let me guess," I started. "That one there is Valnor." I pointed to the purple-hued planet.

"Correct," he said.

"I thought you said the water was just like Earth? Those oceans look purple."

"They aren't always that color. We've come at the time of year when the smallest creatures in our ocean are hatching. They are so abundant in the seas it causes our oceans to turn purple and it alters the reflection of the atmospheric line as well. The Iwanta of Serena thought it was a sign from the gods in the old days. They now have annual holidays to celebrate the happening, even though they now know the reason behind it."

"It's beautiful," I said.

"Do you see that over there?" Nick asked, stretching his arm out to point past the planets.

A glowing white light flew through space just a little further off behind the planets. "Is that the asteroid?" I asked. Before we left, Nick had explained to me in depth the significance of the asteroid ceremony that we and Asteros would be attending that night. The asteroid, which very well may not be an asteroid, was the only one in this system that glowed a bright white light of its own. In ancient times, the Valnorians would worship it's passing. They referred to it as the "small sun." It seemed traditions for both the Valnorians and Iwanta held strong, even when the myths behind them had been debunked.

The myth of the asteroid Denyhs had actually never been debunked officially though. The Valnorians were a very advanced society, the most advanced of the man-like races. But Nick had explained that they were more spiritually advanced than anything else. Most of their architecture and technology came from manifesting in the higher dimensions, rather than created within the physical dimension like on Earth. Space travel was abundant on Valnor through portals and astral projection. But spaceships and space travel were not a thing they found to be important to their society.

"To think that we traveled through space faster than it is pretty amazing. Don't you think?" he asked, turning away from the asteroid to look at me.

"Amazing isn't enough of a word for it," I said.

We approached Valnor slowly. A million questions ran through my mind but I couldn't bring one to my lips to ask. So I decided to just watch. We entered the atmosphere, descending gracefully, and I wished so much that I was able to smell or breathe the air here. I suppose even spirits that are astrally projecting have limits. The land below took more shape and it reminded me of a lot of canyon country in Utah, a place I had been camping multiple times as a child. With slick red rock formations jutting out of the land below, there did seem to be a canyon here as well, but quite different than any I had seen on Earth. The area we were descending on contained one large canyon. The purple sea hugged the west side of the canyon. It was impossible to tell from this height but I would guess the sea was about ten miles away from where the canyon began to descend. Within the canyon were hundreds of pillar-like formations made of the same rock as the canyon walls reaching into the sky. The top of the opposite side of the canyon from the sea gave way to a desert that stretched on for as far as the eye could see.

We descended near what appeared to be a city center within the canyon, amongst the pillars. I say city, but it was almost anything but. Aside from the fact that you could tell a large group of people lived here, there were no signs of the definition that make a city. Buildings and homes seemed to be carved out of cave walls. They reminded me of the cave dwellings that were carved out in Southern Colorado I went to as a child. Only much more elaborate.

"Did the people here carve out all of those rocks?" I asked.

"Not at all." Nick smiled. "Some of the more high frequency Valnorians manifested these places into existence over years."

"How long did that take?" I asked. I was reminded of Tilda's explanation of manifesting things into the physical dimension and how it took a certain amount of time.

"About a hundred Earth years. Which was the perfect amount of time for the entire Valnorian civilization to move here," Nick said. "This is the final city of the Valnorians."

"The final city?" I asked.

"At some point in our evolutionary process, my ancestors decided to give the planet back to the wild, reserving only a small space for the people to live that was created in harmony with nature. We call it the 'Final City' because this will be the last place people inhabit on Valnor before we move to other corners of space or decide to die with the planet."

"Who would decide to die with the planet?" I asked with concern as we flew through the sky.

"Some consider it to be the right thing to do spiritually." He didn't mean to, but he made me feel quite ignorant with his response. A good reminder that I wasn't just visiting another country, but I was visiting another planet entirely with a much farther advanced species. Culture shock to say the least, but I made a point to remain respectful. There was no way I could understand the decisions of such an advanced species, and I needed to be willing to learn rather than judge.

As we came closer, people came into view, all wearing

white clothing made of what looked to be heavy fabric. Similar to how the ancient Romans dressed, but longer tunics that reached the ground. The Valnorians resembled humans in every way from this distance.

Suddenly, our spirits came to rest on the ground at the base of a cliff face that bordered the purple sea. The sounds all around were incredible. Avian creatures soared above the ocean. Much more massive than anything on Earth. White-winged beasts that somewhat resembled birds, only more mystical and majestic. Their tail feathers looked like streamers in the wind that extended twice the length of their own body.

The "city" lied just ahead of us beyond a set of gates that were carved out of rock. I finally let go of Nick's hand for the first time since Earth.

"So this is your home?" I asked.

"In this lifetime, yes." He smiled at me. His purple eyes gleaming against the backdrop of the Valnorian sky. On Earth, he was always a little out of place. But here, now on Valnor, he fit. I could feel that, and so could he. "Time to meet the parents," he joked.

I knew from the moment it was decided that I would join Nick that I would be meeting his parents. Never in that entire time did that idea make me nervous. Until now. I mean, it's not like we were dating or anything. So that's not why I was nervous at all, I swear. But the idea of meeting two new aliens from an entirely different planet that had raised this alien I had a crush on was daunting. *I do NOT have a crush!* I yelled at myself internally.

Nick started forward to enter into the gates of the city. The Valnorian people were everywhere, all dressed in their white tunics, their shoulders exposed, and their purple eyes hard to look away from. The air was full of excitement for the night's celebrations. I suddenly realized this was my first time around other people since leaving New York, and amazingly…I couldn't hear any of their thoughts. The spiritual awakening was apparent on Valnor. *How do we get humans on Earth to get this much control of themselves?* I wondered. It was an entirely new sensation for me to be out in public and be able to live in the moment. Normally my mind would have a hard time appreciating anything that was going on because of the loudness of the thoughts around me. I stood for a moment and soaked it up with a smile. Never in my life had I experienced such peace in a crowd of people.

"Cameron!" Nick yelled at me. I opened my eyes and looked at him, now a few feet ahead. "What's rule number one?"

"Don't get lost," I said, jogging slightly to keep up with him, realizing moments later that I didn't actually have to jog and that I could just float forward. But it felt more real to move like everyone else, and Nick was too. So I decided to keep moving that way.

Some of the Valnorians noticed Nick and me as we walked. They looked at us with confusion and concern. Well, at least they did that with me when they saw me first. When they noticed I was with Nick, clearly a Valnorian man, they settled. I could understand their concern. Seeing an apparition of an alien walking through your city streets must be striking.

Businesses and homes lined the streets. They were all beautifully placed inside the different sections of cliff. This place was like the hanging mountains in China in the environment of the Grand Canyon. Each little sliver of mountain contained a business on the bottom, and dwellings that went all the way up. They seemed to all be open to the elements too, with their "windows" wide open. A Valnorian sold purple shells, which I assumed she found by the sea, from a cart that sat in front of a cliff dwelling. Children laughed from the carved out windows above. I doubted they could see us. It was mostly the older Valnorians who would pause to look.

We rounded the corner of a street labeled with symbols I could not read, and a voice shrieked: "Daharun!" I turned to see a beautiful Valnorian woman with deep purple hair cropped just above her shoulders running towards us.

"Mother," Nick said as he approached her. He knelt down in front of her and she placed her hand exactly where his spirit hands were. Not falling through, but not making contact. I realized she could definitely see him.

Daharun? I thought directly to Nick.

"*It is my given name here*," he thought back. Interesting. That would require some follow up later.

"And you must be Cameron," Nick's mother said, approaching me. I didn't know whether to kneel in front of her as Nick did, or if I should hug her, so I just stood there. "I am Ophelia." She stood about six inches away from me, taking in all my facial features. Then, she took a deep breath in. "I see you, great soul," she said. Then, in a move that truly shocked me, she kneeled down in front of me and reached her hand forward.

Is this the typical Valnorian greeting? I thought-asked Nick. *Should I kneel?*

"*Just take her hand in yours, and thank her*," He thought back.

I did as he thought, and she stood back up, holding my gaze for a moment.

"Your father is busy helping Asteros get set up," she said,

turning her attention towards Nick. "He hopes to make great favor with him to get you an audience."

"I will have to thank him," Nick said to her. He and Tilda spoke before we left about how hard it would actually be to get a private word with Asteros. Everyone wanted to meet with him. Everyone had some favor to ask. I didn't realize it was so intense that Nick's father would need to do some of the biddings for him.

"Come inside. Your sister is dying to see you." We followed her into a carved doorway in the rock face into what I assumed was Nick's childhood home. The outside would not tell you at all what the interior of these dwellings looked like. All around the ceiling hung what looked like papier-mache decorations. Upon closer inspection I could tell they weren't made of paper at all, but something like a stiff silk. They moved with the wind that came through the front entrance and went out the back, breathing with each gust. The rest of the dwelling looked pretty similar to the ones you would see on Earth, save the walls and floors being made of carved cliffs. A simple white rug laid in the center of the living area with white seating on each side. They were very similar to couches, framed with rustic wood and cushioned with fine white pillows. A young Valnorian girl with light blonde hair sat on the farthest couch. Her attention jutted toward her mother as we entered.

"Are they here?!" the girl asked excitedly.

"They are here," Ophelia said smiling. "Cameron, this is my daughter Serena."

Serena approached and nearly walked right through us before her mother stopped her to point us out specifically. Clearly, Serena could not see us as her mother could. Nick had mentioned that not everyone would be able to see our spirits moving through a higher dimension. She was absolutely beautiful, and unlike everyone else I had seen on Valnor, her eyes were not the same deep purple. Hers were more of a soft lilac color. She must have been about eight years old, I suspected. Although I had no concept of how aging worked on Valnor.

"Hello, Serena," I said as I kneeled down in front of her.

"Hello!" she replied.

"She can hear me?" I asked both Nick and his mother.

"Of course I can hear you!" she giggled.

"Serena was blessed with the gift of clairvoyance. She can hear many things from outside of our physical dimension," Ophelia said. "One day, if she practices hard enough, she'll be able to see you too. Just like Mommy." Ophelia nuzzled her face against her small daughter.

"Hi, Serena," Nick said from behind me.

"Daharun!" she yelled, standing in place and looking all around.

"How have you been?" he asked her lovingly.

"Great! But I miss you." That sent a sting of sadness through my heart. Nick or, I'm sorry, Daharun had left this beautiful little girl behind just to help me. I felt my chin start to quiver as the emotions welled over me.

"I miss you too, little sis." He came in front of me and knelt in front of her, wrapping his spiritual arms around her. "I'm giving you a BIG hug right now."

Serena cheered in excitement and wrapped her arms around herself in an attempt to hug her big brother back. A single tear ejected itself from my eye now. *Spirits can cry. Noted*, I thought to myself. I looked back at Ophelia and saw that she had been watching me wipe the tears from my eyes. She smiled lovingly at me. I stood back up.

"You've got a long night ahead of you," she said to me. "And you've traveled a long way. Best for you both to rest before the night's events. Even spirits cannot live without sleep." An interesting idea. I had no idea naps would be taken in spirit form.

* * *

We slept for nearly two Valnorian hours on the floor of the cave-dwelling. Ophelia was right. Crossing the universe, even in spiritual form, was a taxing journey. Nick and I both needed the rest. Before we fell asleep, I was concerned that my spirit would simply fall through the Valnorian ground, and that I would get lost. "Your spirit goes where you tell it to," Nick told me. "The same way that we flew here with our will, if you tell your body to lay here and relax, it will do so."

During my slumber, I had a very specific nightmare that I was having a hard time recalling the details of when I awoke. Something to do with bugs. Infestations. Death. It reminded me of what Kaylee described in her vision of the future. I wanted to mention it to Nick, but when I turned over to wake him, he wasn't there.

My spirit jerked up off the floor with a start. There wasn't anyone else in the room with me. Although that in itself wasn't a reason to panic, I was a little worried being on a whole new planet all alone whether anything could actually hurt me or not. I took a couple of deep breaths of, not air, to try and calm myself. There was surely a good explanation for Nick leaving the room. I just had to go and find him.

"You're up!' Came Nick's spiritual voice from behind me. He floated in through the opening that lead to the outer back area of the dwelling. A strong-jawed Valnorian man followed behind him. He was older, and it showed, but just barely. Quite handsome with a striking resemblance to Nick. "This is my father," Nick said to me. "His name is Oseiden."

Oseiden bowed to me gently, coming back up after a moment. Then he spoke, but in a language I didn't understand at all.

"He says he is grateful for your visit and honored to meet you," Nick clarified. I hadn't realized up to this point that Nick's mother and sister spoke English. For some reason, I thought my spirit was just interpreting the different language, similarly to how I can universally hear thoughts. But no, his mother and sister must have learned to speak English when Nick had.

"He doesn't speak English?" I asked the obvious question.

"No. My mother and sister learned with me on my long voyage to Earth. It gave them something to focus on besides the fact that I had left," he said earnestly. Another pang of sadness in my heart from feeling like I was a homewrecker.

"Please tell him that it's an honor to meet him as well, and an honor to be in his home," I said.

Nick spoke back to his father in a Valnorian language that had the essence of Spanish, though not the same at all. His father once again bowed in front of me. "*Welcome*," a thought came to my mind. It had to be from his father. He must have known as well of the universal language of thought and wanted to communicate with me directly.

I didn't know exactly what to say, and without considering it too much, I thought back, *I am so grateful for your son.* To which he looked at me and smiled.

What an interesting experience. To be somewhere without really being there. To be seen by some and invisible to others. To be heard by a beautiful little girl, but unable to touch or hug her with real warmth. This was by far the most surreal moment of my experience since leaving New York City yet. I had to pinch myself to be sure it was real. I pinched my spirit skin. Sure enough, this was not a dream. Not one I was waking up from any time soon anyway.

"The ceremony is getting started," Nick said. I noticed the sun setting behind him through the opening, Serena visible on the horizon as well. It was breathtaking. "We should probably head over there if we want to get a good spot."

Nick's sister and mother were now on the other side of the main room, holding bags with a few items to bring to the ceremony. "Everyone ready?" Ophelia asked. And with that, Nick and I followed Ophelia and Serena out the door. Oseiden followed close behind.

* * *

As we ascended an even higher cliff, one overlooking the whole city, I saw droves of Valnorians making their trek upward. "Does everyone always wear white?" I asked Nick. "Or is this just for the ceremony."

"It's just for the ceremony. Everyone is usually naked." I stopped dead in my tracks and looked at him. Oseiden nearly falling back to stop himself from running into me, or walking through me rather. Nick laughed. "I knew that would be a hard one for your human brain to get around."

"The white robes are in honor of the white-passing asteroid. But every other day on Valnor, people walk around here buck naked. It's certainly not even something to give a second thought to if you grow up here. Coming to Earth, I was rather shocked to see how ashamed people are of their bodies. Always needing to cover up."

I tried to imagine what this hike up the cliff would be

like if everyone was naked. I really couldn't get there in my mind. "It seems less evolved to you," Nick said. "But it's really more evolved if you think about it."

"I'm sure trying," I said.

The top of the cliff was now in sight. White flags flew all around in a circle formation around another outlined circle on the top of the cliff. Valnorians gathered around the edges of the circle, but no one stepped inside. On the right side of the circle from where I stood, I could see a large purple chair. Its base structure was made of gold.

"That is where Asteros will sit," Nick said. "Everyone else here will remain standing until the asteroid passes, at which point they will get down on their knees to pray. Asteros, though, is quite old. His ability to stand or kneel went away a long time ago. So my people built this chair special for his arrival."

"He really is a special guy huh?" I asked.

"More God than guy," Nick replied. "This is his first visit to Valnor. Everyone is incredibly excited to have him. His visits have been taken as a sign of prosperity for whatever planet he chooses to go to."

"Is he here?" I asked, trying to get a better look at the chair.

"Not yet. You will know when he is," Nick said.

"And how are we going to speak to him? There must be ten thousand people here."

"The right opportunity will present itself if the Universe is on our side," Ophelia said ahead of us confidently. She had been listening to us the whole time.

We found our place amongst the mass gathering of Valnorians. To my surprise, we were able to make it to the front row of the circle, just across from where Asteros would be sitting. Apparently, Nick's father was held in high regard by the rest of the society, because as he walked ahead of us, everyone let us come through until we were in the front. Everything was settling and the sun was now out of view. The view of Serena was gone as well. Nick told me that Serena hid behind Valnor every night. The only way to see her glow in the night sky was to make an adventure out to sea. I thought about how nice it would be to do that one day with him when he told me.

Nick's mood was surprisingly cheerful since arriving on Valnor. More than I had ever seen before. There wasn't an ounce of sarcasm or assholeness in anything he said to me. He was loving to his mother. Kind and patient with his sister. Respectful with his father. I was honestly seeing him in an entirely new light. Little did I know, that light would become even brighter tonight.

At three o'clock to our six o'clock around the circle, a group of Avians came to the front of the crowd. "Are those?" I asked.

"Iwantans," Nick said before I could get the name out. "Probably here to request a visit from Asteros to Serena." He laughed.

"They always want everything we have," Ophelia said.

Oseiden then muttered something in Valnorian that I could not understand. "What did he say?" I asked Nick

"He says that the Valnorians always want everything the Iwantans have too. He's not wrong." Two civilizations evolving around the exact same time and witnessing each other's growth with the use of telescopes was so astonishing. It must have made for a race to evolve and grow faster than the other. Competition had driven the evolution of humans into a race as well. But because we were all on the same planet and competing with each other, the advances made were more defensive than anything. These two species raced each other to the stars.

The Iwantans moved gracefully forward. There were four of them, the one in the center right carried a golden box. Their arms were actual wings. Fully stretched out they must have been six feet long each, with fingers that had evolved at the midway point of the wingspan, opposable thumb and all. Their faces were covered in orange feathers. They resembled the parrots on Earth. Their heads were a little more human-shaped than your average bird, but a beak sat where the mouth and nose should have been all the same. Their eyes were a yellow color with a black center.

"Can they really fly?" I asked Nick.

"Not here on Valnor," he said. "But the lightened gravity and dense air of Serena is a different story. Their homes are built high in the trees of the dense forests. They fly everywhere there. I suppose it's their preferred method of travel."

"Have you been to Serena?" I asked, still watching the Iwantan. They were looking around as if thinking, "When will this all get started?"

"Only once," Nick said. "On a student exchange program when I was sixteen Earth years old."

"Such a time," Ophelia said, staring off into the darkness of space, reminiscing on her younger son before I stole him away from her. Why did I feel so bad about it?

Then suddenly, I heard the beat of what sounded like a drum. Then another one. The beating became faster and the crowd of Valnorians started to cheer. The drumming was sharply joined by other instruments, and music washed over the crowd. It was still too early to tell, but the music being played reminded me greatly of Latin samba music. The beat moving back and forth, it was hard to keep my hips still. I wasn't the only one either. The crowd moved in unison swaying back and forth to the music. The energy was high and exciting as the first song ended, and the people cheered.

"Well, somebody's got to get this party started!" Ophelia yelled over the sound of the second song starting up. She grabbed Oseiden's hand and pulled him into the circle.

"The circle is for dancing!" I realized out loud.

"What else would it be for?" Nick asked. I guess prior to now I assumed the circle was meant for some sort of ceremony for the asteroid. But then, is dancing not ceremony?

A few other Valnorians jumped into the circle to join the beautiful couple. The way they moved their bodies was too close to Samba dancing to not be mentioned. "It looks like they are dancing the samba!" I yelled to Nick

"I'm not familiar," he yelled over his shoulder, gleaming at his parent's love.

"It's a specific dance from Latin America. Very similar music too!"

"Well, that makes sense seeing as how the Valnorians played a huge part in ancient civilizations there when we were big into space travel. I believe on Earth they were known as the Mayans?" As the words left his mouth, it all suddenly made so much sense. The cliff dwellings, the art, the language. It was all an alien version of the South American culture I had learned so much about. Thoughts of Valnorians on Earth with early human civilizations filled my mind. I smiled at the thought of it.

As the second song came to a close, the crowd cheered again. Ophelia made her way back to the edge of the circle where I, Nick, and Serena stood. Well, technically only Serena stood there. Nick and I just somehow existed. She laughed as she caught her breath. Small beads of sweat glistened on her forehead in the reflection of the fire. "Too old to dance with your momma?" she asked Nick. I thought it was cute that she used the word momma instead of mother or mom. Clearly somewhere she had picked up on the casual version of the word.

"Never," Nick said to her and reached to grab her hand so perfectly that it didn't go through. He followed her into the dance circle. The song that was playing now had a very jumpy and happy rhythm to it. People cheered Ophelia and Nick on as they danced in perfect symmetry. It seemed they were always in tandem, Nick never passing through Ophelia. His hands always hitting the exact right space of air to appear as if they were actually dancing together in physical reality. It was clear that not everyone could see Nick. Those that could, were thrilled at the sight and explained to the ones who couldn't what was happening. Their cheers louder now than they had been.

This was an entirely new light for me to see Nick in. The strong and usually sarcastic man that I could have never pictured laughing and smiling from ear to ear let alone dancing in front of a large group of people. It was truly astonishing. Ophelia laughed with joy as Nick led her around the circle for the final push of the song. They exchanged a few happy words as they danced, but I couldn't hear any of it. My spirit smiled at the sight of it. Seeing Nick like this somehow made me happier than I knew I could be.

The song came to a close with a bang as Nick dipped Ophelia in his arms. How she held herself in thin air like that I couldn't understand, but it was perfection. They headed back towards where Oseiden, Serena, and I had been waiting. We applauded their arrival. "Where did you learn to move like that?!" I asked Nick excitedly.

"My mother has taught dance since before I was born," he said looking at her with a massive smile. "It was never an option to not learn."

The music kicked up again. This really was a full out party and celebration. The energy in the air was electric. Ophelia turned to Oseiden now and said something to him in Valnorian. He took her hand, and they entered the circle. This song was a little slower, sexier even. They held each other close and moved their hips to the rhythm.

"May I have this dance?" Nick's voice said. I turned to look at him expecting him to be asking his sister. But he was looking at…me?

"Uh…" I started, unsure of what to say. A boy had never asked me to dance before. All sorts of fantasies about having a boy take me to the school dances started to rush back into my mind.

His hand was stretched out in front of me waiting to be taken. I stood there dumbfounded. "Can't dance?" he asked with a bit of serious concern in his tone.

"Definitely can't dance," I lied. I had rhythm. I could move. I always picked up choreography relatively easily. But it was the first thing that came to mind. *Why would I say that?* I asked myself.

"That's alright! Just follow my lead," Nick said as he grabbed my spirit's hand and pulled me into the circle, my body floating forward over the ground to keep up with him. Suddenly, parts of the crowd cheered in the same way they had when Nick pulled his mother onto the dance floor—the ones who could see us.

Nick pulled me in close with his right arm wrapped

around my waist and his left hand joined with mine. My brain was in overload with the different things that were happening. I could feel his spirit's groin against mine. But I blurted out, "Aren't you afraid people will see?"

He looked genuinely confused. "Some people *will* see," He said matter-of-factly. He continued to look into my eyes with a face I had never seen before. Concern? For me? He seemed to pick up on my reason for concern. "Sexuality is a societal construct that we Valnorians have evolved out of long ago. No one will care that two boys are dancing together. They will just see if they can at all, two people sharing happiness, and they will be happy for it."

He began to move his hips backward and then forward into mine, my mind still racing over all the things he just said. I had always wondered what Nick's sexuality was but assumed it was more of a nonissue being that he and I were not the same species. Whenever I would let my mind get carried away with thoughts of being held by him, kissing him, or worse, I would always come back to knowing that it simply wasn't an option. Who even knew what kind of equipment he was working with down there. As my mind fought a tiny war with itself, Nick continued to drag me around the circle. My spiritual body floated wherever he chose to take me.

"*Breathe. Be in this moment,*" Nick thought to me. I stared into his eyes. He was smiling even bigger than I had ever seen before. I closed my eyes, took a deep breath, and reopened them to be part of the moment I was in. I was finally dancing with a boy at a dance function. It was my high school dreams coming true. With the next pulse forward of his hips, I moved mine back in sync and danced with the man of my dreams.

I started to get the hang of the dance. Ophelia and Oseiden came fluttering by us as Nick twirled me around under his arm. They both smiled at us as I came back into Nick's arms. Halfway through the song, I had really come to understand the movement. I could tell that Nick was impressed. We bounced around the circle, sometimes flying through other Valnorian couples enjoying their time together. They paid no mind to us as our souls flew directly through their bodies. "So you can dance," Nick said before he dipped me over for the finale.

I whipped my head back up from the dip, looked him in the eyes, and said, "This was my first time with someone else. I always suspected but I couldn't be sure." He held me like that for a moment. Our eyes locked on each other, our smiles from ear to ear. I could feel the heartbeat of his spirit in his arm that supported my ethereal weight. The tension between us grew until I asked myself, *Are we going to kiss?* He pulled me up slowly towards him, his hands never leaving my body.

Suddenly, a loud voice boomed over the crowd speaking in Valnorian. The crowd cheered and the couples left the dance floor. Nick stood me upright completely. "Show's getting started," he said. He led me back to the area where his family was, his hand still wrapped around mine. My heart fluttering.

"Where did you learn to move like that?!" Ophelia yelled over the loud voice and cheers.

"Just learned I guess!" I told her. She and Oseiden were both smiling. Serena, who couldn't see us, was all smiles as well, playing with a light-up toy her parents had purchased for her in the crowd. We all turned to face the area where the voice was coming from.

A short, frail man with grey/purple wispy hair was speaking into the Valnorian version of a microphone. "That is our leader, Cerreon. He's the equivalent to your President on Earth," Ophelia told me.

"A little different than the President, Mother," Nick corrected her. "He is in charge of the entire planet. The President on Earth is only in charge of one specific landmass."

Ophelia and I both nodded our heads in understanding. Cerreon's voice continued to wash over the crowd of people as they cheered. "He is welcoming everyone and thanking them for their participation in this year's festival." Nick told me.

I listened on and watched the crowd's reactions. Everyone seemed so excited to be together. Except for the Iwanta, they sort of looked out of place and bored. Cerreon continued on until I heard a word that I recognized. He said Nick's father's name. Oseiden stepped into the circle and the crowd cheered in unison. "He just thanked my father for his efforts in setting up this evening's stage," Nick told me. I cheered from the crowd for Oseiden too. I had no idea he was responsible for setting all of this up. Surely he didn't do it alone.

Oseiden returned to the group with his family. Ophelia hugged him and I could almost feel the love radiating off the two of them. "He's about to introduce Asteros," Nick said. The crowd lessened their cheers and listened intently. The language may have been different for me to understand, but I could feel Cerreon pumping up Asteros with flattering words, exciting the crowd with each new description. This went on for only a moment before Cerreon screamed: "ASTEROS!"

The crowd went wilder than ever before. Valnorians jumped all over. Their bodies leaped high above the mass of the crowd. The Iwanta cheered too. Their screaming voices sounded like bird calls in the rainforest. I focused my attention back to the area where Cerreon had been on the microphone, and there he emerged. To put it mildly, Asteros was not what I was expecting. He looked like a human. A very old and wise human, with sharp features in his face. He almost resembled old depictions of Chinese rulers. Certainly, if we were back on Earth he would easily pass as having Asian heritage. But his brow bone was sharp on each side, jutting out a little further from his skull with harsh angles. His mustache and beard were strikingly Asian as well. A long handlebar mustache that blew effortlessly in the wind, and a thin long white beard that came only from his chin. His hair was long and tied up in a wonderful design with golden sticks poking out of it. He wore long white flowy robes as he approached the microphone to speak.

"Good evening," he said. The crowd went wild. "Many thanks to the great citizens of Valnor for hosting me on this wonderful holiday."

"He's speaking English?" I leaned over to ask Nick, never taking my eyes off Asteros.

"He's speaking whatever language the listener would prefer to hear," he said "My parents and I all hear him speaking in Valnorian. The Iwanta can likely hear him speaking their native language."

He must have been some powerful guy. A god even. I was reminded of how thoughts were a language with no need of interpretation. This guy was definitely powerful. I was marveled.

"Look there," Serena said, pointing to the sky. What I assumed was the asteroid we were here to celebrate was gleaming through the night sky.

"A little closer than usual…" Nick said as Asteros droned

on about his gratitude for being there and his pride in the Valnorians he had helped create.

"Too close," Ophelia said strongly.

"This is not my first visit to Valnor, though some of you believe it to be," Asteros continued. I was more focused on him than the mindful eyes of Nick's family behind me. "I was part of the original scout party that was sent here to decide which species to seed the planet with. I see we have some Iwantan here tonight as well." Asteros gestured towards the winged beings. "I visited Serena as well on that same trip. Both beautiful untouched planets, waiting for life to spring for—"

Asteros was interrupted by the bombastic sound of a sonic boom. I looked around the rest of the crowd as the Valnorians looked around for an answer to the sound. "It's coming here for him!" Nick shouted, pointing to the sky. I looked up and where the white light floating across the sky had once been, there was now a fireball in the atmosphere. The asteroid was heading right towards us.

Ophelia shouted over the crowd in Valnorian what I assumed was something like, "Everybody RUN!" because everyone scattered from the site as quickly as they could. I turned my attention to Asteros, who was slowly (but as quickly as he could) making his way off the stage, surrounded by Valnorians trying to help him.

"Cameron!" Nick yelled a few feet behind me. "Let's go!" My attention was again focused on the white-hot ball of flame plummeting from the sky. The asteroid was huge. I had seen it from space. And it was headed directly for us. No matter how fast the Valnorians ran, the asteroid would destroy everything in at least a hundred-mile radius. I couldn't just stand there and watch these people die. I watched as the golden light from my soul wrapped itself around my spiritual body. I knew that I had to do something. "Cameron!" Nick was now screaming at me, grabbing at my spirit. His family must have been already halfway down the cliff. "We have to GO!" He pulled on my arm, but I pulled it away hard and shot up directly into the sky.

Thoughts of Nick's family flashed through my mind as I flew upward. *This isn't how it ends for them*, I thought. Beautiful young Serena's lilac eyes loomed in my thoughts as I approached the giant asteroid. A golden light began to surround me. I saw Valnor's sky around me through a golden veil. The asteroid made unspeakable amounts of noise the closer I came to it. At this rate, it would reach the ground in a matter of seconds.

Pulling the golden light forward away from my body into two long strands leading my charge, they met the asteroid with enormous force. I could feel my biceps flexing the energy harder. Pressing firmly against the fiery front of the asteroid, it slowed ever so slightly. I knew that I needed more if I was going to do this. I drew the golden light to encompass the entirety of the massive rock and moved from pushing against it to going above and pulling it. I pulled as hard as I could and I could feel the veins in my neck bursting at the pressure. I grabbed onto the golden light with both hands firmly grasping, and pulled up as hard as I could. The asteroid, now only one hundred feet from impact, finally stopped in the air. It roared beneath me with frustration. A few Valnorians who had been too stunned to flee watched me as I slowly lowered the asteroid down onto the cliffside. The ground beneath it shuddered as I let its full weight collapse. I retracted the golden light back within myself as the asteroid sat flaming on the edge of the massive cliff.

Replaying what had just happened in my mind as I hovered just over the asteroid, I thought, *I did it*. I was shocked. As were all the faces of the Valnorians now making their way back up to see what I had done.

CHAPTER 17

"**A**STEROS HAS REQUESTED a meeting with the spirit responsible for stopping the asteroid," Ophelia said, entering the living room of her family's home. I had just fought my battle with the asteroid only a few hours ago. My spiritual body shook with the remaining adrenaline that couldn't seem to make its way out of my system.

"It's his fault it even came here in the first place!" Nick shouted. He had rushed to my side immediately after everything happened. I still remember the fear and shock of his spirit's eyes. Those beautiful eyes that reflected true terror as the asteroid came barreling towards Valnor. Nick was sure that the Hyamin had something to do with the asteroid's change in trajectory. Apparently, they had wanted Asteros dead for a long time. That's why no one ever knew where Asteros would be until just before he was there.

"That may be true," Ophelia said sternly. "All that matters now is that we are safe. Valnor is safe."

"We came here for the opportunity to speak to him," I reminded Nick. "We can't just blow it off."

"Yes, but he will want to speak to YOU!" He turned towards me and I could feel his anger. Nick was still worried about Asteros using me to get back in with the Hyamin.

"He will know right away that I wasn't the one who stopped the rock."

"I think it's pretty apparent that the Hyamin want him dead. Not back," I said.

"What the Hyamin want, is for the Daemon to go extinct so they can go back to living physical lives unchallenged. Amongst lesser souls who won't fight against their wrong-doings," he jabbed back. "You are the perfect bargaining chip to get him back in their favor. And we don't know what he really wants."

"Daharun," Ophelia said, approaching her son from behind. "I think Cameron has proven himself more than worthy of being able to handle an old man like Asteros. Even he couldn't stop the asteroid from crashing into Valnor." Nick thought about what she said. I could tell her argument was actually making some progress for him. "You came all the way here for this opportunity, and one way or another, the Universe has granted it."

Nick said nothing and stared off at the wall with frustration. "When do we go?" I asked his parents.

"Now," Ophelia said. "Oseiden will take you to him."

I reached over to Nick and touched his shoulder. His head did not turn to face me, though I knew he could feel it. "I can't do this alone," I said.

He sighed heavily. But took his weight off the counter he had been leaning on, and outstretched his arm in front of himself as if to say: "Well let's go then."

As we emerged from the dwelling onto the street, we were immediately met with roaring applause from what looked like hundreds of Valnorians waiting outside. "They've come to thank you," Ophelia whispered to me. My eyes looked out over the sea of purple-eyed humans. I could immediately tell that only a quarter of them could actually see me. The rest who could not see us looked around the area where I was, but never directly at me, taking their cue to applaud from those who were gifted with sight of the higher dimensions. I was overwhelmed with emotion at the sight of resounding support for what I had done. I lifted my spiritual right hand and waved to the people. The crowd roared in appreciation. I had never felt like this before. Never had I experienced this much attention. It was great, especially because immediately after I had stopped the asteroid from crashing into Valnor, I wondered if I had done the right thing. Was I supposed to take it back into space? I had no idea. But at this moment, I felt like I had done the right thing.

It took a while for Oseiden to make a way through the crowd onto a less busy street. "His ship is docked in the town center," Ophelia had told me. As we rounded the corner and his ship came into view, I thought it must be anything but a ship.

It stood as tall as the One World Trade Center in New York City, but that was where the resemblance stopped. It looked to be made of interwoven trees, or wood. Not so much trees in that there was no foliage to be seen, but the material had notches in it and resembled tree roots wrapped together, only much larger than any root I had seen on Earth. The base of the "ship" stood on four points. Each point made its way up and thickened immensely. The diameter of each at the thickest point must have been four school busses thick. The overall shape of the ship was mostly triangular, but not perfectly so. Much longer from the bottom to the top than your perfect triangle would be. There were gaps amongst the "wooden" windings. I wondered how he could travel through space, as the ship did not appear to be airtight. Two massive torches were lit at the triangular entrance to the ship, which our group now stood in front of.

"Wow," was all I could muster as I looked from the top of the ship all the way down. This was the first spaceship I had ever seen in person, eons beyond anything conceived on Earth. The ships NASA flew around back on Earth now looked like a joke in comparison.

"Wow is right," Ophelia said standing next to me, taking in the site for herself.

A small being emerged from the entrance to the ship. It looked remarkably like the aliens portrayed on Earth in film and comic books. The "Greys" I believe they are called. At about four feet tall, with deep black eyes that took up the upper half of its head, it was a sort of disturbing sight. He approached Nick and me rapidly where we stood in front of Ophelia and Oseiden. "Are you the one who stopped the asteroid?" he asked Nick. Clearly, this being had no issue seeing into higher dimensions.

"He is," Nick said flatly, pointing to me. He said it like he didn't want me to be there, but he was forced to bring me along. It bothered me a bit. I could understand his mood switching from the sweet guy who danced with me on a beautiful new world to a fear-based guy who thought his entire planet was going to be destroyed. But nothing happened and everyone was safe. Shouldn't he be thankful?

"Wonderful! Asteros awaits your company inside," the creature said. And with that, he moved back towards the ship. I looked at Nick and he looked at me. Then Nick stepped forward to follow, and I was right behind.

The first steps into the ship gave way to dark hallways lit by torches all around. The same wooden material that lined the outside of the ship seemed to line the walls of this hallway too. It was like something out of a Dungeons and Dragons fantasy. The hallway then gave way to a staircase that was made of black reflective stone. You could only see a few steps ahead of you as it appeared to curve up the length of the ship. The being in front of us began to ascend the stairs. Nick followed close behind.

"Who are you?" I blurted out, my curious mind getting the better of me.

"I do not have a name," the creature said. "Sometime's, the master calls me 47." He continued up the steps.

"*He is a computer essentially,*" Nick thought directly to me. "*A personal home assistant device grown inside a biological body.*"

So…an AI? I asked.

"*That would be giving him a little too much credit,*" Nick thought-replied. "*They are programmed by higher intelligence beings. Probably a gift to Asteros on his many travels. But he has no soul.*"

Interesting… I thought to myself. What was the difference between a living being that had a soul, and one that didn't?

We had been climbing now for what seemed like two minutes. More than once I considered just floating the rest of the way up but thought that might be rude. At some point, the staircase finally gave way to an opening on our left side. The stairs continued past the opening, but 47 turned into the room. We followed. The room was quite large and gave the impression of a medieval castle throne room, with Asteros sitting in his throne in front of a massive fireplace.

"Asteros, sir! These are the beings you wished to see," 47 notified him in his emotionless tone.

"Ahhh," Asteros' voice bellowed across the room. He

squinted as he looked at us. "Spirits on a sleepwalk? Quite interesting. You can't be the ones who stopped the asteroid. You have no holds in this dimension to affect physical change." That made sense to me. I had to consciously not fall directly through the floor of this room back out into the world. How I had actually grabbed onto the asteroid would require further explaining. "Come closer," he said.

I stepped forward before Nick. I could almost feel him willing me to stay behind him. But I was in the thick of it now, and I'd rather be an active participant than a passive victim.

"A human and a Valnorian. Interesting…You seek something from me," Asteros said. "What is it?"

"We have come here to ask for information or support in the battle for Earth," Nick said.

"Ah yes. The battle for Earth is gearing up to be quite the spectacle," Asteros teased. I couldn't tell if I liked this guy or not. "You there!" Asteros pointed to me. "Step forward, into the light."

I did as he asked, facing the old man who somehow seemed to be able to move as lightly as a feather. "Is that…" He squinted harder at me. "Ayan?" I could feel Nick's panic race up from behind me. I turned all my senses on full alert, ready to fight or fly at a moment's notice. "My goodness, they think you're dead!" He laughed.

"Who thinks I'm dead?" I asked fiercely.

"The ones whom I used to call my family. The war is all but won to them." Nick and I looked at each other. "No need to worry, boys, I won't be telling them anything. I've grown quite a strong hatred for my brothers. I believe the Universe would be a lot better off without them in it. You must know it was them who tried to destroy both myself and Valnor with the change in the trajectory of that asteroid?"

I breathed out a sigh of relief. Nick still stood on edge. "And you…" Asteros, now pointing at Nick, "you are the incarnate soul of Daia, are you not?"

"Daia? From the story?" I asked Nick directly. I recalled the History of Soul's story for a moment. It took some fact-checking in my mind to be certain, but yes. Daia was the lover of Ayan whom Ayan abandoned to save Earth. *Nick is Daia?* I wondered to myself *Nick is my soulmate?!* Nick was completely ignoring me as I looked at him.

"The outcome for the battle for Earth is still unknown. Even the greatest future tellers cannot see who will prevail," Asteros said. I turned my attention to him again. "There are many different options. Some of which it seems you are unaware of still…" Asteros trailed off as he stared directly at me. "Ayan, forgive me but…that vessel of yours. It's quite unique. I can't say that I've ever seen that genealogical signature before. There's something more than human here..." Asteros made his way towards me slowly, eyeing me up and down.

"What?" Nick asked with confusion.

"My mother," I started. "She told me that she was rescued from a planet that was being destroyed."

"She did?" Nick turned to ask. I had only told Kaylee about the contents of my meditation meeting with her. I don't think I had an opportunity to digest what I learned that day, let alone tell everyone else. Thinking back now, I'm realizing how significant it all was.

"How unfortunate…" Asteros was now right in front of my spirit, looking closely.

"She said she knew nothing about where she was from, but that she grew up orphaned with a bunch of other saved kids until she was sent to Earth as a teenager," I explained to them both.

"Well, that would be quite sad. But what is truly unfortunate is that your mother was lied to," Asteros said.

"What do you mean?" I asked, almost defensively.

"She was not rescued. She was kidnapped." Asteros made his way back to his chair. "Half of your genetic signature is Lyondran."

"Lyondran?!" Nick gasped. He then looked over to me, studying my spiritual body in a way he hadn't before, as if looking for clues.

"And not just any Lyondran genetic signature either. It appears to match identically with the Masadena line. I'm sure of it. I was just there recently and spoke with the king myself," Asteros said.

"Your mother was Princess Masadena…" Nick said with shock.

"Princess who? Who is Lyondran?" I asked. Having no context for this entire story.

"Lyondra is home to the most technologically advanced men in the known universe," Nick explained. "The Masadena family has ruled over the planet for thousands of years."

"A rule that was compromised some decades ago when the only living heir to the Masadena throne was kidnapped as a small child," Asteros added. "You chose this vessel for a reason. You must go to Lyondra and seek their help with the battle for Earth."

My brain was having a hard time keeping up with all this new information. First, Nick was my long lost soulmate. Now, I was the descendent of extraterrestrial royalty? "I don't understand…" I said.

"Your soul chose this specific vessel for many reasons," Asteros explained. "The Lyondran genetics help to keep that powerful soul of yours from ripping you apart at the seams for one. But your soul also must have known that King Masadena would do anything for his only descendent."

"The Lyondran forces would make the battle for Earth more fair…" Nick thought aloud.

"More fair, yes," Asteros replied. "But still not a sure thing. There will be other matters that need to be taken into consideration to tip the scales in your favor. You don't remember me, do you Ayan?" he asked.

"No, sir, I'm sorry I don't." I said.

"There's no need to adorn me with formalities, my friend. The things we forget when we take on these physical lives…" Asteros trailed off. "It makes you wonder why we chose them in the first place."

"Indeed," I agreed. It felt like the proper response.

"The Hyamin know that their dominion over the Universe is only put in question by the Daemon. Their power is only greater than yours because of their number of supporters in the spiritual world. Individually, you hold more power than they ever could. Which is why they seek to destroy the Daemon race entirely. Unlike my brothers, I see you as an equal. If not, a superior. It is I who should adorn you with formalities."

"That won't be necessary," I said. Nick looked concerned that I had somehow now taken over the conversation, and was handling it quite well. "Remind me of our last conversation?"

"It was on your way to Earth," Asteros started. "Your soul came here in this very same room, with a different soul whose name eludes me now." Nick seemed to get uncomfortable. "You had brought me something to keep safe, in case your journey was unsuccessful." Asteros got up from his chair. "I have it just here." He went around behind the chair to a wall of scrolls, fumbling around with them for a moment, he found the one he was looking for. "Here it is. Come and see for yourself."

It was a slow ten steps from where I stood to make it to the area behind the chair. Asteros rolled a scroll out across the wooden table that appeared to be made from the same material as the rest of the ship. It was covered in markings I didn't recognize.

"It's the scroll of the True History," Nick's spirit said behind me.

"Quite," Asteros confirmed.

"What is it?" I asked Nick.

"If it is true…" Nick started, "it is the story of the original soul. Born into the Universe by the Creators. This story contradicts the known knowledge of the Universe that the Hyamin were first and that the first soul to ever be created was in fact a Daemon. This scroll is the first written document in physical history, written by the first Andarian reptile race."

"It is true Daia," Asteros said. "My brothers stole this relic of history long ago, hiding it away on a long lost planet no one would ever think to look on. Until Ayan found it and brought it here."

"It also tells of the first physical inhabitation of a soul," Nick said, reading through the text. "That it was in fact the Daemon that seeded sentient beings first." I looked at Nick and he looked at me. His face was full of surprise.

"But what does that mean exactly?" I asked.

"Quite a stubborn physical existence you chose, Ayan. That body simply won't allow you to remember anything!" Asteros laughed at his joke. Somehow, I knew what he meant.

"It means that the Hyamin's claim to Universal supremacy is a lie. Over millions of years of these truths being lost, the Daemon were wrongfully placed in a subordinate category. It means that the Universe meant for all the lower dimensions to be ruled by the Daemon. Or at least for the Daemon to seed the first physical lives with their souls."

"It means this war isn't about fair treatment. It's our Universe-given right," Nick said. "All those stories we were taught as souls that the Hyamin chose which souls went where and gave them life… were a lie."

"Exactly," Asteros said. "And you, Ayan, are the direct descendent of this first soul. If I wasn't sure before you stopped an asteroid from crashing into a planet while soul walking, I certainly am now. I don't think that a Hyamin soul could even attempt such a feat."

I'm the descendant of the original soul. I let that thought turn around in my mind. It was the hardest one to digest yet, and I certainly didn't identify with it. Maybe there were just too many truths being shared with me in that moment.

"We have to get back to Earth," Nick said, taking one final look over the scroll.

"Before you go," Asteros started, "if I may offer one final piece of advice?"

"I would be entirely grateful," I said. His art of the English language rubbed off on me.

"You must find the soul that you came here with on your way to Earth. Wherever they are, they have surely spent their entire physical life preparing to aid you. This of course is not direct advice from me, but something that is being whispered into my ear from an even higher power."

I knew exactly what he meant by being whispered into his ear. Someone somewhere was giving me grand advice through Asteros. "I will," I said.

"OH!" he exclaimed. "The soul's name was Ashta!"

Ashta, I thought. Who was Ashta? Tilda? Kaylee? It certainly wasn't Nick. That much I now knew for sure.

I turned to Nick to see his arm outstretched in front of me, as if asking me to grab on for the ride. "Don't you want to say goodbye to your family?" I asked.

"There is no time," he said flatly. And with that, I grabbed his hand, and we ascended into the Valnorian sky..

CHAPTER 18

VALNOR AND SERENA slipped away from my view rapidly as the spirits of both Nick and I flew through space at a remarkable speed. I turned my focus to his hand placed on mine, guiding me through the abyss. That hand that led me was attached to a spirit, which was attached to a physical body, which was inhabited by the soul of my soul's long time lover. Nick was Daia, and as the Story of Souls had said, Daia and Ayan were soulmates. Such powerful soulmates that the entirety of the higher dimensions rang with songs of their love. Knowing this now made all the distance Nick tried to place between us, as well as all the awkward flirty moments suddenly make sense.

Nick had told me that because he was raised on Valnor, that he grew up knowing his soul and the purpose for his life. He had known this entire time that our souls had been together. He had kept that secret from me, and I wondered why. I also wondered if that meant he felt the same weird attraction to me that I had felt for him the moment I saw him on the subway. I studied his face as our spirits flew through space. He seemed focused only on the trip ahead, paying no attention to me now. Perhaps purposefully.

Then my attention turned to the conversation about my mother. Kidnapped from her home planet. Raised somewhere in a foreign solar system and dropped on Earth to live the rest of her life. She had no idea that the entire time that she was royalty for one of the most advanced civilizations in the known Universe. An advanced civilization that I still knew nothing about. These ideas were entirely believable for me though. My mother was an ethereal force among humans. She practically floated everywhere she went. Knowing that she was descended royalty fit perfectly with my vision of her. Knowing that I carried half of that genetic sequence within me was less believable. I wasn't nearly as graceful or beautiful as my mother.

"Where is Lyondra?" I blurted out to Nick. I was trying to keep quiet and just focus on the flight, not wanting to distract him with conversations about our history together. But I needed to know more about this place where I shared a heritage.

"Nearer to Earth than Valnor," he replied without looking at me.

"And you think they will help Earth in our fight?" I asked.

"Under normal circumstances, they wouldn't even consider it." He looked at me briefly while explaining. "But the story of the stolen princess from Lyondra is one that is known throughout the planets of The Collective. I've heard it since I was a child. It is said that King Masadena ripped apart half the Universe in search of his daughter. I think we stand a good chance of convincing him to help. But the way I see it, there are two possible outcomes."

"He helps us, or…?" I helped him along.

"Or he forces you to stay with him on Lyondra." Nick didn't like that response at all. "Family means everything to the Lyondrans. The Masadena reign will end with him if his descendants are not found."

"Well…that's not an option," I said flatly. I would never leave Earth behind to be destroyed.

"Unfortunately we don't have any other solutions available that will stand a chance against the Tahn. And your soul chose that body of yours for a reason. Ayan must have known the negotiating power your genetics would bring to the table. We have to try and ask for his help."

"So are we heading there now?" I asked.

"No," Nick said. He looked at me again briefly. His face showed a look of discomfort. "We will have to go in the flesh."

"How will we do that?" I couldn't conceive of a way to travel through space, let alone fast enough to return to Earth by the time the Tahn arrived.

"You just let me worry about that." He looked forward again as we continued to rush through the blackness of space.

I would because I had no other choice. "Who kidnapped her?"

"No one knows. It could have been a group of rebels from within Lyondra. It could have been someone from a warring planet. King Masadena has his own list of suspects I'm sure. But that part of the story never made it around to me at least," he said.

"Aren't you glad Asteros didn't try to kill me?" I joked, trying to lighten the mood of our interstellar travel.

"Thrilled," he said flatly.

That is not how you talk to your soulmate, I thought to myself. But then I wondered, because we were soulmates before our current physical lives, did that mean that we were bound to each other now too?

* * *

My body arose on the cave floor with a gasp for air. Sitting straight up, I could see the candlelight flickering all around. There was no one else down here with us. Kaylee and Tilda must have been upstairs or outside. Nick rose slowly next to me. Apparently he was much more prepared for the reentry into our physical bodies than I was. I tried to catch my breath.

"Hey," Nick said as our physical eyes met for the first time.

"Hey," I said.

A moment of silence hung between us. A thousand different phrases crossed my mind to begin a conversation, and I felt as though he was having the same struggle. We had avoided the conversation about our connection the entire trip home. But being back in our physical bodies again for the first time, it was inevitable that we needed to discuss it. This would be so much easier if he could still read my mind. I finally landed on what I thought was the most important thing to ask: "So…we're soulmates?" I Immediately regretted the choice of phrase that had left my mouth.

"It's not that simple," he began. His quickness to respond led me to believe he had been considering his answer for a while now. "Who I am, is Nick. Or, Daharun the Valnorian." Nick turned to sit cross-legged in front of me. "In this physical existence at least. Just like you are Cameron. This physical life brought baggage that has molded me into the person I am today standing in front of you. Daia is a part of me in the same way Ayan is a part of you."

"But you've known for a long time that your soul is the spirit of Daia," I said. Everything he said made perfect sense.

Just as I had thought, he was his own person in this life. His soul, an infinite being, would always be a part of him. But the man that stood before me had his own life with his own experiences. Cultivating him into his own man. Or…Valnorian, rather.

"My mother has told me since before I could remember. I communed with my soul for the first time at five years old. So, yes," he said. "The same pull that has pulled you here, pulled me to the destiny my soul had mapped before entering this body. But I honestly never identified with the whole 'soulmate' thing. I never had this personal pull to find you and be with you." That hurt to hear for some reason. "Until I saw you for the first time." Now butterflies began doing circles in my stomach. "That's why I've kept my distance from you as much as possible. I didn't want to tell you who I was, because I didn't understand why I felt the way that I felt about you."

"How did you feel about me?" I asked.

He laughed. "Inexplicably."

I knew what he meant. It was something far beyond a physical attraction. Even after all the times he was a total asshole to me, I would find myself wondering where he was and what he was doing when he wasn't around me. Thinking about him when my mind wasn't occupied with something else. Most of all, there was an underlying trust and comfort in him that no matter how hard I fought it, always prevailed.

He gestured for me to move next to him, so I scooted over. Our knees touched, and neither of us pulled away. The butterflies in my stomach were more than just fluttering now. I hadn't felt the sensation building inside me now since I was a teenager. Like our knees were on opposite magnets, and all the laws of the Universe pushed them to separate. But somehow, leaving them together created a force so strong, ending the connection would be a sin. I could feel him looking at me now, and I turned my head up to meet his.

"So I'm just supposed to believe that our souls were somehow…connected once?" I asked quietly.

"The Universe knows I sure didn't believe it. But if I'm being honest, I'm drawn to you. Constantly." His eyes bore into mine. Those damn purple eyes.

I didn't want to talk anymore. There was nothing left to say. No words to describe or define further what was happening or what had happened. All I wanted was to close the gap between our faces. "Would it be wrong of me to kiss you?" I blurted out. My mind raced with fears of alien contamination. Soulmates or not, I was sure there was some issue with us being different species.

Before he could answer, he leaned towards me, wrapped his hand around the back of my head, and kissed me. A wind seemed to rush through the cave around us. We kissed for a few seconds. Nothing crazy, very innocent. When our lips finally separated, we both pulled back only a few inches. Me, staring into his purple eyes, and him, staring into my blues. Only for a moment to catch our breath. Then, our animalistic sides took over. I grabbed him by his head with both my hands, kissing him hard. So hard that he fell back onto the cave floor with me on top of him.

We kissed each other with passion. If I would pull away, he would chase my head with his own, pulling me back in. His mouth tasted like any other human mouth. An experience I had thought about multiple times and feared some alien experience was totally normal. He pushed his tongue into my mouth first and I reciprocated, knowing we had crossed that threshold. I ran the fingers of my right hand through his hair. His short, rough hair. This moment felt significant, and I made a mental note to never forget it.

Our passion continued for minutes. His hand had slipped its way under my shirt, gripping the skin on my back. The roughness of each of his fingers against the smooth skin of my back felt incredible. It felt like I couldn't get deep enough into him with my kiss, always trying to go further. At some point I separated myself from him, gasping for air. When I did, I noticed a golden light between our faces. We both looked around and suddenly we were aware that we were floating a few feet above the ground, my body on top of his, supported by the golden light. I hadn't consciously made that happen at all. It was as if my soul, or his, had longed for this moment. We both smiled at each other, and I latched my mouth back onto his. Savoring this moment as much as I could.

In a moment, my shirt was being pulled up over my head. The cool cave air brushed across my skin. I reached to pull his shirt off to reveal a chest with an adequate amount of hair that bristled across my hand as it rose. We only broke our kiss to remove his shirt completely. The minute it was off, our lips met again with passion. It was like the energy between our faces was so strong, that our skin would pull and melt together.

Nick moved his lips from mine and began kissing down my neck, which gave me a moment to look around and realize that we were still hovering above the ground. We were quite literally kissing in the air. I made another mental note to remember this moment forever as his lips pressed against my collar bone, the stubble on his chin scratching in the perfect way.

His hands moved now down my back and onto my butt,

which answered the question of how this was going to all play out. A question that I had tossed around in my mind before this moment when in the brief times I would allow myself to fantasize about this experience. To level out the playing field, I reached and grabbed for his too. His response was to press his mouth harder against mine, seemingly letting me know that he was more than okay with that. And it was at this moment that I had a minor worry perk up in my mind. So far, everything about us was physically the same. Human to Valnorian I mean. Save, of course, the purple eyes. I had no idea if we were anatomically similar in every other way though. And this thought worried me. What would I find when his pants came off? Some sort of flower looking organ with teeth and eyes? It was all a possibility.

I think Nick picked up on the fact that I had gone out of my body and into my head for a moment, because his right hand made its way back up around my head again, gently running his fingers through my hair. Bringing me right back into the moment. But before I had a chance to find out what lied beneath, a huge crash sounded above us onto what would have been the kitchen floor.

In an instant, our bodies fell from the air and slammed into the cave floor, with me landing directly on top of Nick. "What was that?!" I whispered harshly. The sound wasn't one that would be expected of Kaylee or Tilda above us. Then, another crash sounded again. It sounded like someone was destroying the cottage above our heads.

"*Something's wrong,*" Nick thought directly to me.

We both rushed to stand up and put our shirts back on. The intensity of our physical connection quickly rushed away as our attention pulled to the chaos happening above our heads. After the first two crashes, there wasn't a single sound. It was dead quiet. We waited for a few minutes in the silence.

Should we go up? I thought to Nick.

"*I'll go*," he thought to me. Then he stood up and began to quietly climb the ladder that led back to the kitchen. He took his time making it to the top and as he progressed, there were still no sounds from above. I tried thinking direct thoughts to Tilda or Kaylee but I couldn't seem to find their minds to do so. The "direct thought" method of communication had been something so effortless for me to pick up on. But what I was realizing was that it required you to lock onto the person's mind with whom you wished to communicate. Tilda and Kaylee weren't close enough for me to connect with.

Nick pushed up on the cover to the cave which was a two square foot square cut out of the kitchen floor. It made a little noise as it slid across the floor above and we both cringed. He waited for a moment to listen for any sounds in reply until he climbed out. But there was nothing. He made his way quickly out of the hole and onto his feet. "*Stay there*," he thought to me.

I could hear Nick take a few steps around the whole to look around the corner of the kitchen and dining room which connected to a hallway. Then he stopped. I was just about to ask him if it was all clear when: "Stop right there." A man's voice sounded through the room above me.

My stomach sank and my heart began pounding.

"*He's pointing a gun at me*," Nick thought to me, more to convey what was happening rather than to convey fear.

"Who are you?" the man asked. His accent was heavy and clearly from the Middle East.

"Who are you?" Nick asked in a classic snarky Nick way.

"You're going to tell me who you are or I'm going to put a bullet in your head," the man replied, clearly not amused with Nick.

I moved slowly towards the ladder. *Is there anyone else up there?* I mentally asked Nick.

"*Not that I'm aware of,*" he answered.

As quietly and gently as I could, I began to ascend the ladder. It rose about ten feet from the ground, so I would need to climb up a few rungs to get a better look at what was going on. As I did so, I could only make out the arms of the man through the gap of the dining room table. Sure enough, his two arms held a gun. A big one.

Nick still hadn't answered the man, so he screamed, "WHERE IS HE?!" A hint of insanity seemed to drip through his voice.

"I have no idea who you're talking ab—" But before Nick could finish his sentence the man let out a loud cry as the gun in his arms was forced out of his arms and across the room by the golden light of my soul. In the same instant, I jumped from the ladder onto the floor next to Nick, my soul giving me the extra boost to make it all the way there. It almost felt like I was flying for a moment.

The man looked shocked at first, and then he looked angrily at Nick again. Before he could do another thing, I forced him back against the wall with a wave of golden light. His head slammed hard against it and he fell to the floor unconscious. Then suddenly, an insistent beeping came from the man's body that wouldn't stop.

Nick and I looked at each other. "What is that? A bomb?" I asked.

Nick ran over to the body checking his pockets for the source of the beep. Once he made it to the back pocket on the right side, he pulled out a small square device. I moved towards him as quickly as I could to see what it was.

"A Geiger counter?" I asked. The counter was slowly falling back down from the highest possible reading. The beeping lessening from every other second to every third, then fourth, until it wound all the way down.

"It's measuring radioactive material in the area." Nick looked up at me from the Geiger counter.

"What's radioactive around here? The cottage? Is it because it only exists in the higher dimension?" I asked him.

"Then it would still be going," he answered. "Lift him up into that chair."

"Ummm…Okay?" I began to move towards him. "You can't help?"

"No, not with your body…" He put his arm in front of me to stop me.

"Oh." I understood what he meant. Using the beautiful light of my soul's energy I picked the man up off the floor and moved him a few feet to the right into one of the dining chairs. He slouched down perfectly as I removed my support. The Geiger counter was going insane.

"It's measuring your power," Nick said. Our eyes locked. Mine filled with fear. His filled with confusion "Help me tie him up." He then went and ripped a long stretch of vine from the wall near Tilda's small library.

"Where are the girls?" I asked him as he wrapped the vine around the two wrists that I held together behind the chair.

"*Keep it in here*," Nick thought to me. "*We don't know if he's really unconscious. He could just be faking.*" He made a good point.

Sorry, I thought. *Where are the girls?*

"*Your guess is as good as mine. Let's wake him up and see what he knows.*" Nick finished tying the vines around his legs at the base of the chair. He was definitely secure. Nick pulled another chair in front of the man and sat in it. He took a deep breath and let it out. Then he said something to the man in a different language. It sounded Valnorian for sure.

The man looked up suddenly, eyes wide open. But the expression on his face was nothing like the expressions he had shown when conscious, even if I had only seen him for a few moments that way. His expression now smiled and seemed calm. I'd seen this expression now twice before and hadn't really noticed it. Both of the men that Nick "borrowed" cars from made that same face.

"Hello?" the man said softly.

"Hello," Nick replied. He was speaking directly to the man's soul. "I am Dahurun of the planet Valnor. I am going to ask you some questions. Your answers to those questions will help in a war against the human race. Will you help humanity in the war for Earth?"

"Yes," the man replied politely.

"What is your name?" Nick asked.

"Nabil."

"Why are you here?"

"To find the source of the signal." I felt as though the man had never spoken so kindly in his life. I couldn't picture it at least.

"What signal?" Nick asked.

"A radioactive signal."

"How did you find this place?" Nick was definitely playing good cop while I stood behind, still trying to get a grasp on what was happening.

"I came to the place where the signal was the strongest after the earthquake."

"How did you know where the signal was the strongest?"

"A satellite in space that is designed to watch for the signal," he continued nonchalantly.

A satellite that can monitor my powers? I thought to Nick. That seemed incredibly concerning.

"Whose satellite?" Nick asked.

"The Emirate Space Program."

"Who sent you?" I asked quickly.

Nabil looked up at me and did not reply. His face remained polite, but there was a hint of hatred in there. I could feel it.

"Who sent you here?" Nick repeated my question.

"Prince Amjad of Dubai."

My face turned to complete confusion. Kaylee was right. Someone was after me. And that someone was Prince Amjad. One of the richest and most powerful men in the world.

"Why does Prince Amjad want to find the source of the signal," Nick pressed on.

"I don't know. I was never told. Just sent to find. The only thing I was told was that it could be dangerous, and the source could kill us."

"There are others looking for the signal?" Nick asked.

"Many," Nabil replied.

Nick looked up to me. "Anything else? I can't hold him like this forever."

"Ask him where the girls are," I said.

"Was there anyone else here when you got to this house?"

"What house?" Nabil asked.

"This house that we are sitting in now."

"There is no house here. Only an old dilapidated foundation."

"He's not perceiving the house…" I said to Nick. The man hadn't taken the proper steps to see this place in all its glory.

"Did you see anyone else in the forest?" Nick asked.

"No," he said flatly. His politeness seemed to be wearing off.

"I can't hold him for much longer. His mind is pushing through too hard. We need to get out of here. The vines will give us a head start but they won't match his strength forever."

"Okay," I said.

* * *

On a bus. Once again. Heading back to Colorado the same way I left. Nick told me that we would need to find a ride to Lyondra. There were only a few places on Earth where you could charter a ship for interstellar travel, and apparently, Colorado was the only place in the United States. A place in the southern part of the state called the San Luis Valley. A place I had visited quite a few times in my childhood with my family. There's a national park with giant sand dunes pressed up against a mountain ridge that I rode down in a sled. Nick had also told me that was where he landed when he first came to Earth. It made me wonder if that's where my mother had been dropped off too.

Even though I knew they weren't there, I made another thorough sweep of the cottage before we left to be sure Kaylee and Tilda weren't there. There wasn't a sign of them anywhere. Nothing out of line throughout the house. No note left behind. Nothing. Nabil's soul said he hadn't seen them, and Nick confirmed that his soul wouldn't have lied to us. All the answers he gave us were the truth so far as he knew it to be. Nick said it was possible that they could have left before the man arrived. That Kaylee may have had a vision warning them to leave. I had resolved early on during our excursion through the forest to the bus stop that I would choose to believe just that. Kaylee and Tilda were somewhere safe working on their next portion of the plan while we continued on our own. That resolve just wouldn't stick as we rolled westward towards the place I was born. My fear for them grew with each passing mile.

Nick had "convinced" the bus driver to let us on without any tickets by communicating directly with his soul. He then proceeded to pass out in the first two hours of our drive. But I stayed awake watching the scenery flow by, all of it barely lit under the full moon above. That full moon which I had seen from such a different perspective just a few hours ago as my spirit returned to my body on Earth from a faraway planet. Time hadn't even gone by long enough for me to process that I was Ayan, let alone to process all the other revelations that had been thrust upon me recently. Just two months ago I was working two jobs in the busiest city in North America. Now I was a half-human, half Lyondran Prince filled with a Daemon soul whose heritage can be traced back to the original soul. Allegedly at least. Because I couldn't confirm any of this for myself.

The idea that I would soon wake up from this very immersive dream had slowly drifted away. My pressure to hold onto whatever I used to believe about myself and the world grinded too hard against what I had learned. Whether I liked it or not, this was my reality, and some part of it rang true to a deeper part of me. With that, I closed my eyes into meditation, trying to let go of more than I ever could to be released from the chains of physical life's bond that prevented me from realizing all the things I already knew. And the first thought to cross my mind was:

Who is Ashta?

The second book in the "Being Found" series will be released in Spring 2021. Please join our email list at **WWW.BEINGFOUNDBOOK.COM** to stay up to date.

Follow "Being Found" on social media **@beingfoundbook**.